TALES OF
STUDENT LIFE

Books by Hermann Hesse

PETER CAMENZIND

BENEATH THE WHEEL

GERTRUDE

ROSSHALDE

KNULP

DEMIAN

STRANGE NEWS FROM ANOTHER STAR

KLINGSOR'S LAST SUMMER

WANDERING

SIDDHARTHA

STEPPENWOLF

NARCISSUS AND GOLDMUND

THE JOURNEY TO THE EAST

THE GLASS BEAD GAME

IF THE WAR GOES ON . . .

POEMS

AUTOBIOGRAPHICAL WRITINGS

STORIES OF FIVE DECADES

MY BELIEF

REFLECTIONS

CRISIS

TALES OF STUDENT LIFE

Tales of
Student Life

HERMANN HESSE

Edited, and with an introduction, by
THEODORE ZIOLKOWSKI

Translated by
RALPH MANHEIM

Farrar, Straus and Giroux

NEW YORK

Published simultaneously in Canada
by McGraw-Hill Ryerson Ltd., Toronto

Printed in the United States of America

First edition, 1976

Library of Congress Cataloging in Publication Data
Hesse, Hermann.   Tales of student life.
Translation of Berthold, Freunde, and Der vierte Lebenslauf.
1. Students—Germany—Fiction.   I.   Title.
PZ3.H4525Tal3   [PT2617.E85]   833'.9'12   75-35871

Contents

The year of composition follows each title

INTRODUCTION BY THEODORE ZIOLKOWSKI   vii

Berthold (1907–8)   3

Friends (1907–8)   51

The Fourth Life (1934)

    First Version   125

    Second Version   195

Introduction

IN 1904 Hermann Hesse confided to his stepbrother Karl Isenberg that "schooling is the only modern cultural question that I take seriously and that occasionally gets me stirred up." At first glance, such solicitude may seem paradoxical and even hypocritical in a young man who only ten years earlier, at age sixteen, had implored his parents to take him out of school permanently. Hesse's brief stint of formal education amounted to a succession of tensions, problems, and misfortunes which were foreshadowed when the five-year-old future author had to be transferred from one nursery school to another because of headstrong and unruly behavior. The letters of his puzzled and despondent parents contain a dismaying account of the next ten years—a record not simply of ordinary schoolboy pranks but of suspected arson, incapacitating psychosomatic illnesses, and attempted suicide.

Yet everything seemed to suggest, on the surface at least, that a brilliant academic career could be expected of this talented youth, the scion on both sides of his family of well-educated Protestant missionaries. Hesse's performance in the grammar school of his Black Forest hometown, Calw, was so promising that he was sent away at age twelve to the Latin School in nearby Göppingen. Here he prepared himself for the state board examinations, which each year admitted a select group of students to the prestigious cloister schools of Württemberg, from which they normally proceeded to the University of Tübingen for training in an academic or clerical profession. As a result of his performance in the competition, Hesse was accepted at Maulbronn, a former Cistercian monastery, which he entered in September 1891. At first things seemed to go smoothly, to judge from the enthusiastic letters that the new seminarian wrote home to his parents. Only six months later, however, he ran away from school and had to be brought back by the local constabulary, and a few weeks after that, Hesse's parents withdrew him from Maulbronn. Still cherishing hopes for his education, the dispirited father and mother sent their recalcitrant son from one school to another for the next year and a half. Finally, in October of 1893, pleading a headache that had persisted for three weeks, Hesse persuaded his family to take him out of school for good. That marked the end of his formal education.

Hesse's interest in educational questions resulted directly from his own misadventures. "School ruined me in many respects," he continued in the letter to his step-brother, "and I know of few men of character who did not have a similar experience. All that I learned there was Latin and lying, because you couldn't get through Calw and the Gymnasium without lying." Up to a point, Hesse's concern reflected the spirit of the times in Germany shortly before World War I. For roughly a decade, so many plays and novels were written about school and its discontents that they produced a genre known simply as Schulliteratur: Emil Strauss's *Friend Death* (1902), Heinrich Mann's *The Blue Angel* (1905), and Robert Musil's *The Confusions of Young Törless* (1906) are among the most familiar examples. But Hesse's concern was more than a concession to a fashionable literary trend. For sixty years his writings—including letters, essays, and autobiographical reflections—return obsessively to his years in the schoolroom. From the beginning of his career to the end, many of his major works can properly be considered "pedagogical" in one sense or another: either they constitute an indictment of the existing school system, like the novel *Beneath the Wheel* (1906); or, like the "pedagogical province" that provides the background for *The Glass Bead Game* (1943), they represent an idealized educational system in which the individual is encouraged to develop his unique capacities to the fullest extent.

It is hardly surprising, therefore, to find in Hesse's fiction a number of stories that deal with schoolboys, students, and their problems. What distinguishes the three tales collected here—"Friends," "Berthold," and the so-called "Fourth Life"—is the liveliness with which they recreate student life at various moments in German history (the *fin de siècle,* the Thirty Years' War, and the early eighteenth century) and the close connection in which they stand to three of Hesse's major novels.

Like all of Hesse's fiction, these three stories are heavily autobiographical in substance. In his preface to *Gerbersau* (1949), a collection of works dealing with his Swabian hometown, Hesse remarked: "Whenever as a writer I speak of the forest or the river, of the meadow valley, of the shade of the chestnuts or the fragrance of the firs, it is always the forest around Calw, the river Nagold, the fir woods and the chestnut trees of Calw that are meant; and also the marketplace, the bridge and chapel, Bischofsstrasse and Ledergasse, the marsh and the meadow path to Hirsau can be recognized everywhere in my books—even in those that are not explicitly Swabian." It is clear that the heroes of all three tales grew up in Hesse's hometown. In "Friends," Hans Calwer's name hints at his origin, and even Erwin Mühletal's name (Mühletal = mill valley) suggests the narrow valley of the Nagold with its many mills. The attentive reader of

"Berthold" and "The Fourth Life" will soon note, moreover, that Berthold's unspecified hometown and Knecht's
Beutelsperg, or Beitelsperg an der Koller, are identical:
walled towns standing in a narrow valley above a rapid
mountain stream, with a splendid cobblestone square
flanked by timbered houses and adorned with a fountain,
and a Gothic church topped with a provisional wooden
tower. The monastery where Berthold becomes a skilled
Latinist is modeled after Maulbronn, and Berthold's life in
Cologne is based on Hesse's experiences in the pensions
where he lived while attending school following his deba-
cle at Maulbronn. Knecht's Denkendorf was in reality another of the famed cloister schools; and the pattern of life
there is precisely the same as that at Maulbronn.

Hesse never attended a university. In 1895 he wrote to
a friend still at Maulbronn that he had no intention of
going back to school. "In fact, there has never been a time
when the university was more dispensable than it is at
present—at least for people like me, who as a matter of
principle are not entering any kind of government service." Yet he became intimately familiar with the university in Tübingen, which is attended both by the students
in "Friends" and by Knecht in "The Fourth Life." The
University of Tübingen, especially in conjunction with
the famous Stift (the residence for theological students
which is mentioned in both stories), was long one of the
most influential institutions in German intellectual life.
During one glorious period at the end of the eighteenth
century, Hegel, Schelling, and Hölderlin were fellow students in the Stift. The poet Mörike, the theologian D. F.
Strauss, and the aesthetician F. T. Vischer are merely a
few of the distinguished Swabians who followed precisely
the same educational track through the cloister schools
to the Stift and the university in Tübingen. So Hesse was
familiar with Tübingen as an important institution both

from the history of his native Württemberg and from the biographies of some of his favorite writers.

Beyond that, he spent four years in Tübingen—from the autumn of 1895 through the summer of 1899—as an apprentice and then as a stock clerk in Heckenhauer's bookstore. To be sure, he did not lead the idle student's life described in "Friends": after working from 7:30 A.M. to 7:30 P.M. six days a week, he spent most of his evenings writing his first literary works (notably the poems of *Romantic Songs* and the *poèmes-en-prose* of *An Hour beyond Midnight*) and reading his way systematically through German literature of the Romantic period. However, through his association with former seminary friends now in Tübingen, Hesse was invited from time to time to participate in affairs at the Stift and the university, where he had frequent opportunity to observe the student fraternity life that he depicts with such irony in "Friends." As he subsequently wrote to a correspondent who mistakenly assumed that he had studied at the university: "Neither have I ever been a student, nor have I ever been sympathetic to student life. For the most part students—both the serious and the boisterous ones—are an abomination. I found the whole university business foolish and consider it a shame that such a large segment of the younger generation regards studying as the only respectable and proper career choice. In Tübingen, where I lived for four full years and spent a lot of time with students, I got my fill of the whole business." Yet these four years enabled Hesse to include in "Friends" a vivid and detailed portrayal of student life in Germany around the turn of the century.

The drama of friendship that is acted out against the background of university life in Tübingen is virtually archetypal for Hesse's fiction: a relationship, with pronounced homoerotic overtones, between two young men, one a leader with a strong craving for consciousness and independence, the other a talented but weaker follower, who is jolted out of his childlike innocence by his friend, but who longs to return to the security and approval of society. In a number of works Hesse has explored this relationship in its various configurations; but both archetypal figures represent aspects of his own character. "Friends" could be designated in one sense as a response to Hesse's immediately preceding novel. *Beneath the Wheel* ends when Hans Giebenrath, unable to endure the pressures of the academic system, drops out of school and commits suicide, while his stronger friend, Hermann Heilner (the first of many characters with Hesse's own initials) survives. In "Friends" the situation is balanced: Erwin Mühletal is awakened from innocence by Hans Calwer. Unable to follow his friend into an alienated independence, he at first sinks into profligacy, but then recovers and, with the approval of his fraternity brothers, becomes engaged and settles down to his medical studies, while Hans Calwer, forsaking his fruitless attempt to emulate the peasant philosopher Heinrich Wirth, moves on to another university to pursue his quest for knowledge.

This ambivalent resolution reflects Hesse's personal dilemma at the time he wrote the story. In 1907, at age thirty, Hesse underwent a profound emotional crisis following several months of illness. The success of his novel *Peter Camenzind* (1904) had enabled him to get married and to settle down in Gaienhofen, a remote village on the German shore of Lake Constance with—as Hesse wrote to Stefan Zweig—"no trains, no shops, no industry, and not even a pastor of its own." Since there were no craftsmen in the village, he had to manage all the repairs on his house; since there was no butcher, he had to row across the lake to the nearest Swiss town to purchase every sausage. For several years Hesse enjoyed the image of himself as a happy homeowner. But by 1907 he was already beginning to feel restricted and to believe that the very independence he sought was causing him to subside into precisely the kind of philistinism he had tried so desperately to avoid. This dilemma is reflected in the two leading figures of "Friends." Erwin Mühletal represents the concessions to wife, family, and career that Hesse had made when he moved to Gaienhofen; but Hans Calwer betrays Hesse's unsatisfied longing for freedom and, above all, for consciousness.

Hesse returned to this archetypal configuration when he wrote *Demian* (published in 1919), and the parallels between the early story and the novel are unmistakable. Like Erwin Mühletal, Emil Sinclair is led out of childhood into the realm of adult consciousness and responsibility by his bolder friend; and after their break he first longs to find his way back into the lost paradise of childhood innocence before he succumbs to the lure of profligacy. Hans Calwer, in turn, anticipates Demian's rather elitist contempt for the "herd people" as well as his religious quest for truth. And Calwer's friendship with Heinrich Wirth anticipates the crowd of religious seekers— vegetarians, Buddhists, utopians, Tolstoyans—who surround Demian. But the conclusion of the novel is wholly different. At the end, it is Max Demian who has perished, while Emil Sinclair remains behind to continue the work of the young man who had been his friend and leader. In other words, the archetypal relationship is identical with the one in "Friends" and *Beneath the Wheel*, but the balance is shifted experimentally in each work.

Hesse once remarked that he considered the religious impulse the "decisive characteristic" of his life and works. So it is hardly surprising that the common interest that brings Hans Calwer and Heinrich Wirth together should be their study of religion and that the central figures of "Berthold" and "The Fourth Life" are students of theology.

To be sure, the nature of this interest in the stories mirrors Hesse's mood at the time of composition. When he wrote "Friends" and "Berthold" (around 1907–8) the thirty-year-old writer was still in the throes of his rebellion against what he considered the narrow sterility of the pietism of his youth. As a result, we find the religious impulse manifesting itself as a fascination with other and specifically non-Protestant forms of religion. In "Friends" Hesse alludes to the spectrum of religious sects that sprang up in Europe toward the end of the nineteenth century, including notably an interest in Buddhism and other Oriental religions. Hesse had grown up in a home inspired with the spirit of India, for both his parents as well as his maternal grandfather had been missionaries there. "From the time I was a child," he later wrote, "I breathed in and absorbed the spiritual side of India just as deeply as Christianity." And this impulse led him, in 1911, to make the trip to India which resulted, years later, in the novel *Siddhartha* (1922). When Hans Calwer explores Buddhism and attends lectures on Oriental studies, he is acting out Hesse's own preoccupations.

The background of "Berthold," in contrast, is Catholic. In 1903, in one of the frequent letters that he wrote home in a calculated effort to shock his devout family, Hesse observed that no theology could be too radically modern for independent thinkers, but he knew of no more "brilliant model" of a people's religion than Catholicism. Hesse's genuine admiration for the ritual, symbolic, and aesthetic aspects of Catholicism lasted to the end of his life, manifesting itself in such works as his early biography of St. Francis of Assisi (1904) and the chapter in *The Glass Bead Game* that portrays the life of the Desert Fathers. In "Berthold," then, Hesse retraced his symbolic autobiography as it might have been had he grown up a Catholic during the time of the Thirty Years' War. Again we note many of the same fictional components that occur in "Friends," but here they appear in a different pattern. Here, too, the homoerotic friendship between student friends leads to the indoctrination into sex by a girl from the lower classes, the turmoil and confusions of youthful growth, and the loss of childhood innocence regarded as the fall from paradise into consciousness and guilt (an image that occurs as a leitmotiv in Hesse's fiction). For reasons that remain unclear, Hesse never completed this story of the renegade seminarian who kills his best friend and then vanishes into the excitement of the Thirty Years' War. Quite possibly Hesse decided that the pronounced sexuality of the theme was too explicit for the rather prudish tastes of Kaiser Wilhelm's Germany. However, the fragment (which was not published until 1945) contains most of the narrative elements that went into the novel *Narcissus and Goldmund* (1930), written some twenty years later.

In that novel the time has been shifted back from the seventeenth century into an unspecified but still monolithically Catholic era in the late Middle Ages. (It is not unlikely that Hesse wanted to focus on tensions within a unified Catholic world and not on the wholly different conflict between Catholicism and Protestantism which would have been inevitable during the Thirty Years' War.) Like Berthold, Goldmund grows up without a mother and is sent by his father into the monastery. Both Berthold and Goldmund are strong, handsome young men, inexperienced in the ways of the world but inordinately responsive to sensual pleasures; for both, the life of the senses begins when they are seduced by older and experienced girls. Berthold's closest friend at school is Johannes, the professional—albeit cynically Machiavellian—churchman who has the name that Narcissus adopts after his investiture as a priest. The most conspicuous physical characteristic of Johannes-Narcissus is a thin ascetic face with soulful eyes and long black eye-

lashes. It is Johannes—like Narcissus later—who first
awakens his younger friend to the realization that monas-
tic life is not his true calling, while he himself is happily
reconciled to the life of a prince of the church. In both
works a major crisis is precipitated by a girl named
Agnes. There are of course conspicuous differences: notably, the early fragment breaks off when Berthold kills
Johannes, while in the novel Narcissus becomes the abbot
of the monastery and finally rescues Goldmund from exe-
cution. "Berthold" ends when the protagonist flees
Cologne to enter the Thirty Years' War, just as Goldmund
leaves the monastery and becomes involved in the worldly
events of his age. Yet "Berthold," apart from its Catholic
and seventeenth-century variation of the student arche-
type in Hesse's fiction, is clearly the model that Hesse had
in mind for two decades until he finally reshaped it into
one of his most popular novels.

The so-called "Fourth Life" was undertaken many years
later under wholly different circumstances. When Hesse
began writing *The Glass Bead Game* in the early thirties,
its central idea was "reincarnation as a form of expression
for stability in the midst of flux, for the continuity of
tradition and of spiritual life in general." To this end and
as the structural principle of his *opus magnum,* he envi-
sioned "an individual but supratemporal life . . . a man
who experiences in a series of rebirths the grand epochs
in the history of mankind." As he told his sister in 1934,
"The book is going to contain several biographies of the
same man, who lived on earth at different times—or at
least thinks that he had such existences." By the time it
was published in 1943, however, the novel had gone
through a significant shift in plan: the originally en-
visaged "parallel lives" were reduced in their function to
"fictional autobiographies" written as school exercises by
the hero, Josef Knecht, and included in an appendix at
the end of the novel. The final version contains three of

these lives: a story of prehistoric times ("The Rain-maker"), an episode from the patristic era ("The Father Confessor"), and a tale of classical India ("The Indian Life").

"The Fourth Life," which is mentioned several times in the text of the novel, was to have centered around an eighteenth-century Swabian theologian who subsequently gave up his churchly duties for the sake of music. He was to have been "a pupil of Johann Albrecht Bengel, a friend of Oetinger, and a guest of the Zinzendorf community." To this end, the narrator of *The Glass Bead Game* continues, Knecht read and excerpted a number of often obscure works concerning ecclesiastical law and pietism, and studied the liturgy and Church music of the period. However, Knecht left his work unfinished: he had collected too many facts and had pursued too many tangents of investigation to be able to shape his material into a "Life" sufficiently integrated for the purposes of his Castalian education.

It was not until 1965 that two versions of this "Fourth Life" were posthumously published, revealing for the first time that Hesse had actually worked on the Swabian "life" described in his novel. And it was immediately apparent why Hesse had discarded the project: "The Fourth Life," undertaken according to the original plan of rather lengthy "parallel lives," was far too extensive to be reduced to the size of the much briefer fictional biographies actually included within the framework of *The Glass Bead Game*. As an exercise in symbolic autobiography, as a depiction of student life in the eighteenth century, and as a testimony to Hesse's obsession with pietism, however, this uncompleted "Fourth Life" is a fascinating document on its own merits.

Hesse was attracted to eighteenth-century Swabian pietism for a variety of reasons. It represented, first, a return to the spiritual and intellectual sources of his own youth, to which he was bound in an intense love-hate relationship. In this story Hesse is investigating fictionally the impact of his pietist home and education on his own development. Moreover, the scenes and locales of his early life have a prominent place in the history of Swabian pietism. From the seventeenth century on, Calw was a focal point for pietism. Göppingen, where Hesse attended Latin School, was the birthplace of the noted theologian Friedrich Christoph Oetinger and the fiery preacher Johann Friedrich Rock. Maulbronn and the other cloister schools had been centers of pietism, and their pedagogical methods were shaped in no small measure by the biblical scholar Bengel, who was a preceptor for thirty years at Denkendorf. In fact, the works of Bengel and Oetinger still belonged to the standard curriculum at Maulbronn while Hesse was a student there. Tübingen, finally, was the intellectual center of pietism during the early eighteenth century. It was there that Oetinger, Bilfinger, and others formulated the doctrines of pietism; that Rock fought ideological battles for his congregation of "Inspired"; that Zinzendorf sought official recognition for his teachings and for his Moravian community at Herrnhut. In turning back to pietism, Hesse was recapturing many memories of his own childhood and youth, and he was returning to the period of cultural and intellectual history in which, as he often proclaimed, he felt most at home.

We can ascertain with fair accuracy what Hesse read in preparation for his undertaking. In 1934 he wrote to his sister Adele that he had borrowed all the volumes of Spangenberg's biography of Zinzendorf from the Zurich library. The narrator of the first fragment reports that in the nineteenth century two books about Bengel appeared, "which, to be sure, tell little about his life, but impart many sayings, sermons, and letters by him"—a description that enables us to identify the biographies by J. C. F.

Burk and Oscar Wächter. And in the text itself Hesse
recounts certain episodes from Oetinger's life that he
could have found only in Oetinger's autobiography. Of
course, Hesse had read a great deal more: he was generally familiar with the history and culture of Württemberg in the later seventeenth and eighteenth centuries.
But by far most of his material came from the cited biographies of Bengel, Zinzendorf, and Oetinger.

Josef Knecht, to be sure, is a fictitious figure in "The
Fourth Life." But he moves through a framework of historical reality that reveals Hesse's careful study of his
sources. Many of the figures in the story—Bengel,
Oetinger, Rock, Zinzendorf—are historical personages.
Knecht's birth (around 1709) is dated by reference to a
historical event—the treaty of Rijswijk, which in 1697
settled the War of the Palatinate Succession. And even
though Hesse does not mention the ruling monarch by
name, the characterization of the man and his reign in
the opening paragraphs is so clear that we have no difficulty in recognizing Eberhard Ludwig, the profligate but
popular Duke of Württemberg from 1693 to 1733, who
was courageous enough to shelter French émigrés from
the religious persecutions of Louis XIV.

The historical background is conjured up by a variety
of means. In every case, for instance, Hesse borrowed the
names of his non-historical figures from contemporary
sources. In the first version Knecht's sister is called
Benigna, a name that Hesse knew from Oetinger's autobiography as the name of Oetinger's daughter. Knecht's
first teacher, Preceptor Roos, bears the names of a well-
known pietist, Magnus Friedrich Roos (1727–1803).
Another key figure of Knecht's youth, Spezial Bilfinger, is
a nominal cousin of Georg Bernhard Bilfinger (1693–
1750), Professor of Theology and superintendent of the
Tübingen Stift, who was a protégé of Bengel and a colleague of Oetinger.

While the general background is suffused with details of eighteenth-century history, in his treatment of Bengel, Oetinger, and Zinzendorf Hesse stayed conspicuously close to his sources. Bengel, for instance, does not say a word that is not in strict keeping with the image of the man that emerges from his letters and recorded conversations. Moreover, many of Bengel's utterances in the story are adapted from his own writings. The characterization of Oetinger is more indirect, representing frequently a fictional distillation of passages from his autobiography (e.g., the account of his meeting with the Cabalist Kappel Hecht). And the description of Zinzendorf's visit to Tübingen is simply a creative expansion of a passage in Spangenberg's biography.

Hesse's use of his various sources amounts to far more than mechanical copying. To cite just two examples: a passage in a letter by Bengel in which Bengel ruminates on the profession of fountain master prompted Hesse to make Knecht's father one so that he could incorporate that passage into his text. But that means, in turn, that all the passages concerning fountains and the profession of fountain master were stimulated indirectly at least by this external source. Second, it turns out that many of the details of Oetinger's life—indeed, the whole outline of his biography—contributed significantly to the portrayal of Knecht's life (e.g., the encounter with the miller who urges the students to read Jakob Böhme). To study Hesse's use of his sources is a fruitful exercise in the techniques of literary montage.

When he had reached the point at which Knecht leaves Tübingen, Hesse attempted to recast his story. In the first version the masses of eclectic material that he had appropriated for his narrative were not satisfactorily assimilated into the body of the story. Hesse seems to have worked rather rapidly, retaining the essential outline of the first version—indeed, following it so closely that many passages are simply copied word for word into the second version—but trying to integrate his material more effectively. This striving for integration is the principle that explains almost all of the stylistic changes between the two versions. As Hesse worked and as the conception of the novel itself changed, however, it became evident that the material from this richly documented period of German cultural history was too overwhelming to allow itself to be reduced to a brief chapter in *The Glass Bead Game* on the scale of the other three "lives." So Hesse discontinued his work on one of his most fascinating and revealing literary endeavors.

These three stories, then, afford us an unusual glimpse into the writer's workshop, representing as they do the archetypal structure of *Demian,* the preliminary plot of *Narcissus and Goldmund,* and a discarded section of *The Glass Bead Game.* And like all of Hesse's works, they amount to exercises in symbolic autobiography that provide us with illuminating insights into the life and mind of the author. Specifically, they reflect Hesse's profound concern with questions of religion and education, and they reveal his growing interest in the cultural past of Germany. Above all, however, they are good stories that provide the ultimate justification for Hesse's strong-willed decision, at such an early age, to reject the institutions of formal education which had exerted such a stifling effect upon a generation of German creativity in order to devote himself to the exploration of his own consciousness and to the writing that expresses it.

BERTHOLD

Berthold

Fragment of a Novel

I

BERTHOLD had no memory of his first years. When in later life he thought of his early childhood, he saw no more than a blurred and formless dream image hovering in a golden mist, remote and unfathomable to his waking mind. When, as he sometimes did, he reached out for it in homesick yearning, a soft, nostalgic breeze brought him tatters of shapes and names from the lost land, but none took on life in his mind. Even the face of his mother, who had died young, lay shadowy and irretrievable in deep twilight.

Berthold's memories began with the sixth or seventh year of his life.

There in the green valley lay the walled town, a small German town whose very name was unknown to the outside world, a forsaken, impoverished hole, which nevertheless was a universe to its burghers and children, providing generation after generation with room to live in and room to be buried in. The body of the church had been built in an earlier, more prosperous day, and later completed incongruously with a makeshift roof and a paltry wooden steeple. Neglected and unnecessarily large, the church stood like a ruin amid a jumble of small houses, grieving with its tall, finely carved portals and proclaiming a message of transience. In front of it, on the large, well-paved marketplace, the burghers' modest wooden or half-timbered houses with their pointed gables were mirrored in the great stone basin of a fountain. The southern town gate was low and insignificant, but the north gate was tall and imposing, and there, for lack of a church tower, lived the watchman and fire warden. He could be seen now and then, a tired, taciturn man, silently pacing his lofty gallery and then disappearing into his dwelling. Berthold's first childhood dream was that he might one day take this man's place and become a watchman with a horn at his belt.

A swift little river passed through the middle of the town. Its upper valley was narrow, squeezed between two chains of wooded mountains, leaving barely enough room for a few fields, an ancient, little-used road, and, on its rising slopes, an occasional steep, stony meadow. Upstream there were only a few wooden cottages and, close to the water, the tumbledown pesthouse, built long ago at the time of a great plague and now carefully avoided by the awed townspeople.

Downstream, however, a well-kept road now skirted the riverbank, now passed through grain fields and meadows. The mountains soon receded on both sides, the valley spread out, and the soil grew richer. At length one came to a lovely, sunny plain, sheltered from the north wind by a bend in the range. Above the town, and hardly an hour's walk below it, the valley was poor and inhospitable, the sole wealth of the countryside consisting in the mountain forests. But here, in quiet seclusion, ringed around by green mountains, lay a fruitful little garden of Eden. In the middle of it there was a large, opulent monastery with its own dairy and mill. To the tired wayfarer, passing on the valley road and looking in at the white-clad monks as they strolled beneath the shade trees in their garden, this peaceful spot must have seemed a blessed refuge.

Throughout his boyhood, Berthold took the path across the meadows from the town to the monastery almost every day. He went to school at the monastery. His father had decided that he should become a priest, for after his wife's early death he had allowed his older son, a wild boy tempted by travels, to leave home too soon, and instead of taking up a trade, the young man had become involved in shady dealings and gone to the dogs. Whereupon the father, remembering the failings of his own wayward youth, had vowed to keep a closer watch on his second son and if possible make a priest of him.

One late-summer day, Berthold, still a small schoolboy, was on his way back to town from the monastery. As he walked along, he was trying to think up an excuse for being late, for he had stopped in the fields and spent a good hour watching the wild ducks. The sun had already set behind the mountain and the sky was red. But even as he cast about for an excuse, his young mind was busy with other things. That day his teacher, an eccentric old scholar, had spoken to him of God's justice and tried to explain it. It seemed a strange and complicated business to Berthold, whom the padre's examples and explanations did not satisfy. For one thing, God seemed to concern himself very little with animals. Why, for instance, should the marten eat young birds, which were also God's creatures and much more innocent than the marten?

And why were murderers hanged or beheaded, since sin was its own punishment? And if everything that happened had its root and sanction in God's justice, why wasn't it all the same what one did or did not do?

But these childlike doubts and attempts at thought vanished like the reflections in a wind-ruffled pond when Berthold reached the town gate and his suddenly alerted senses told him that something unusual had happened in the town.

So far he knew nothing; he merely saw the familiar street in the warm glow of the evening sky; but so strong is the power of habit and routine that even a child detects the slightest disturbance in the familiar order of things long before he has seen or heard its cause. Thus, Berthold knew instantly that something unusual was afoot, though all he had actually noticed was the absence of the women and children who on other evenings filled the street with their chatter and play.

A few minutes later he heard the distant rise and fall of many voices, indistinct cries, the drumlike beat of horses' hoofs, and the unknown, rousing sound of a trumpet. Forgetting that he was late, forgetting that he was supposed to go home, he trotted up to the marketplace through a narrow, steep, and already darkening side street. With burning forehead and wildly pounding heart, he emerged from between the tall houses and entered the square, where it was still broad daylight. That was where all the different noises had been coming from! A welter of amazing sights met his eager eyes, and it seemed to him that from realms of legend all the diversity and adventure in the world had suddenly, by magic, invaded the scene of his everyday life.

The marketplace, where ordinarily there was nothing to be seen at this evening hour but boys at play, servant girls carrying water, and burghers resting on the stone benches in front of their houses, was teeming with chaotic, colorful activity. A troop of foreign soldiers had arrived, lansquenets and mounted officers, wagoners, sutlers, and gaudy women. They lurched about, demanding lodgings, bread, stables for their horses, beds, and wine; cursing, shouting, talking in strange dialects and foreign languages. Some who had already found lodgings leaned out the windows of well-to-do burghers' houses and laughed as they watched the confusion. Officers barked commands, sergeants cursed; burghers spoke words of appeasement; the burgomaster ran back and forth in a frenzy of fear and excitement; horses were led away.

Berthold looked on with feverish curiosity, overjoyed and at the same time frightened by the tumult, the violence, the terror, the laughter. In a flash the narrow sphere of his little boy's experience was breached and the great world appeared before his eyes. Of course he had heard tell of foreign lands, of soldiers, wars, and battles, and had conjured up bold, colorful pictures of them; but as far as he was concerned, these things might just as well have happened in fairy tales; he couldn't have said whether they really existed or were only pleasant imaginings. But now with his own eyes he saw soldiers, horses, weapons, pikes, swords, insignia, horses in beautiful trappings, and terrifying firearms. He saw men with brown, bearded, foreign-looking faces and coarse, outlandish-looking women; he heard raucous voices speaking unfamiliar languages, and avidly his naïve, defenseless mind soaked up the pungent savor of wild, exotic novelty.

Cautiously he went about among the unruly soldiery, intent on seeing everything, undismayed by curses and an occasional thrust in the ribs, without a thought of going home until his curiosity was satisfied. He gaped at the harquebuses and pennants, felt a pike, admired high cavalry boots with sharp spurs, and delighted in the free, warlike ways of the soldiers, their rough, bold, boastful words and gestures. There before him were glory, courage, pride, and savagery, flaming colors, waving plumes, the magic of war and heroism.

It was very late when Berthold arrived home, dazed and overheated. His father had begun to worry and scolded him lovingly. But in his excitement the boy heard nothing; he hardly touched his supper, and the questions bubbled out of him: Who were these soldiers? Where did

they come from? Who was their captain? Was there
going to be a battle? He heard a good deal that he did not
understand, about French or imperial troops passing
through, about billeting and looting; actually his father
didn't know very much about it. But when Berthold heard
that three soldiers were quartered in the house, he jumped
up and insisted on seeing them. His father raised his voice
and tried to stop him, but in vain; Berthold stormed up
the stairs to the soldiers' room. At the door he stopped,
held his breath, and listened. Hearing steps and voices but
nothing frightening, he plucked up his courage, cautiously opened the door, and tiptoed in. He almost
bumped into one of the soldiers, a tall, gaunt, raggedly
dressed man with an ungainly plaster on his cheek. The
soldier turned around, gave the boy a ferocious look, and
with a threatening gesture told him to go away. But before Berthold could comply, one of the others laughingly
interceded for him and motioned the frightened boy over
to him.

"Never seen a lansquenet before?" he asked in a friendly
tone. When Berthold shook his head, the soldier laughed
and asked him his name. Shyly Berthold told him. The
gaunt soldier muttered "Berthold? That's my name, too,"
and examined him intently, as though looking for a picture of his own childhood in Berthold's pretty face. The
third soldier made a joke that Berthold did not understand, and after that they paid no attention to him. Two
of them picked up a deck of filthy old cards and began to
play; the third poured himself a glass of wine, made himself comfortable, and set about mending a seam in his
leather breeches with waxed thread. A few minutes later,
Berthold's father called from down below, and he left the
room regretfully, his curiosity far from satisfied. The next
morning he was only too glad to help the servant polish
the soldiers' heavy boots.

Then very much against his will he had to go off to

school, and when he came running back in the late afternoon, he was bitterly disappointed to find the lansquenets
and officers, horses and banners gone. He couldn't forget
them, and they were long to be remembered in the town,
for in the course of that one night there had been a murder, numerous robberies, and other acts of violence, and
several persons had been wounded. In the weeks and
months that followed, there were rumors of troops passing through other parts of the region, but the town was
long spared, an island of peace amid the alarms of war
that soon filled half the empire.

After that visitation the boys could think of nothing but
playing soldiers. To his father's dismay, Berthold ceased
to be the quiet, dreamy child he had been, and became the
most warlike of them all, a ringleader. His physical
strength, of which he now became aware as though waking from sleep, made him famous and feared among his
comrades; his exercises in warfare and tests of bravery
were soon followed by less noble exploits, which angered
and worried the old man. For young Berthold excelled not
only in war games but also in brawling and such mischief
as apple stealing.

Yet while scandalizing the townspeople, his father, and
his good teacher with his wildness, Berthold himself was
not entirely happy, for his conscience often plagued him,
and sometimes in the midst of the merriest brawl he felt
as if he were under a spell and no longer responding to
his own will. His own will, it seemed to him, lay captive
and dazed, and when in anguished moments it stirred and
remonstrated, he suffered keenly.

True, this happened only now and then. Most of the
time he followed his impulses with a light heart and made
mischief like any other boy. Actually, the loser in all this
was not so much his will as his thoughtful, contemplative
side, which had been stunned by the eruption within him
of other, cruder forces and reduced for the time being to a

sleep from which it stirred only fitfully. This his astute teacher soon understood, and was greatly relieved, for at first he had been horrified by the change in the boy.

"The child was thinking too much," he said to Berthold's father. "Now original sin is demanding its rights, and so is his healthy body. It's much better for them to work themselves out now than to turn up later, at a more dangerous age. Repression won't help; my advice is to let the goat buck."

And so original sin was given free rein, and the goat bucked till someone was hurt. That happened one winter afternoon in the course of a pitched battle in the snow. Two armies of boys, one led by Berthold, bombarded each other with snowballs. Both armies advanced, and the fiercest fighters of all were the two captains. Well supplied with projectiles, the rival captain approached Berthold, and at point-blank range hurled one snowball and then another in his face. With mounting anger, Berthold plotted revenge. Then came a snowball with a stone in it; he could feel the bump rising on his forehead. In a blind fury, he leaped at the foe and forced him to wrestle. Both armies stopped fighting and formed a circle around the contestants.

Soon Berthold's enemy was in trouble. Unable to hold his own by the strength of his arms, he bit Berthold on the ear. That was too much for Berthold. Enraged by the pain, he flung the biter away from him with all his might, without looking to see where he would land. His adversary's head hit a curbstone, and he lay motionless. His face grew white and thin; a trickle of red blood emerged from his hair, flowed over his forehead, over a closed, unquivering eyelid, and, drying, stopped on his cheek.

The onlookers, who a moment before had applauded every maneuver of the wrestlers and cheered Berthold's final act of prowess, fell silent. Only a very small boy who should have been at home with his mother cried out in a shrill, horror-stricken voice, "He's killed him!" For a minute or two, all stared goggle-eyed at the motionless, broken body. Then, seized with dread, most of the boys crept silently away, some to find safety and forget the horror, some to report the incident. Even those who remained behind moved uneasily away from Berthold and left him standing alone.

His violent gesture had exhausted his rage. For a short moment he stood there calmly relishing his triumph, prepared to forgive the treacherous stone in the snowball and the bite on the ear. The hard fall and the bit of blood had not frightened him, for, as he saw it, he had done no wrong. But when his fallen adversary failed to get up, when his face went white and stony, the victor's blood ran cold; he stared aghast at the trickle of blood, and when the little boy's cry rang out, he began to tremble. Despite his confusion, he saw it all with uncanny clarity; not only the deathly rigidity of his victim, the blue shadows under his eyes, and the trail of blood on his cheek, but also the horror and cowardly desertion of his comrades, who had been applauding him only a moment before. He saw himself as a murderer, an object of horror, abandoned by his friends, not one of whom, he was certain, would stand up for him. For the first time in his life, he felt hopelessly alone, his warm heart in the icy clutches of despair and death.

For a moment or two, he stared at his fallen comrade. Then the thought of punishment assailed him with hideous visions; he saw himself standing before the judge, threatened with disgrace and death. That drove everything else from his mind; in the face of unknown perils, his one instinct was to save his life.

Just as a frightened horse, once the first brief paralysis of fear has passed, breaks into a wild gallop, driven by an unreasoning urge to seek safety in flight, so Berthold shook himself out of his daze and ran away as though

pursued by devils; he ran through the town gate and up
the hill to the woods—for where else would a fugitive
hide? In his imagination he saw constables pursuing him,
arms reaching out to seize him, fists clenched to strike
him. Feverish and trembling, he avoided the paths and
ran aimlessly, sinking into snowdrifts and tearing his skin
and clothes in the winter underbrush.

The day was drawing to an end; the snow shone pale in
the dusk. He was dead tired and half frozen; he thought
he would perish in the snow or be devoured by wolves.
Resolved to get out of the forest, he fought his way
through the thickets with his last strength. The rising
moon was some help and comfort to him. At length, reel-
ing with exhaustion, he found himself at the edge of the
woods. Looking down over the silent slopes in the snowy
moonlight, he saw not the inhospitable wilderness he expected but the beautiful valley he knew so well and, in the
background, snow-covered and peaceful, the monastery.

The sight filled him with grief and shame, but at the
same time it brought a comforting glimmer of hope. He
climbed down the steep slope. His frozen feet could barely
carry him and he kept falling, but he managed to drag
himself to the road, the bridge, and finally to the monastery gate. With his last strength, he lifted the heavy
knocker and let it fall back on the iron plate. Then while
the gatekeeper, surprised in his warm lodge, was coming
out to open up, Berthold collapsed in the snow. The monk
picked him up, found him in a state between sleep and
fainting, saw that his fingers and ears were frozen blue,
and carried him in, for he had recognized the schoolboy.

Berthold did not wake until late the next day. He was
lying in bed in an unfamiliar room. Before he had recovered his memory, his teacher came in, followed by his
father. They looked him over, and when they found there
was nothing wrong with him, there were questions,
lamentations, and scolding. But all that he really took in

was the information that the injured boy was not dead, but had recovered consciousness in the course of the night.

Timidly Berthold's darkened soul opened its eyes, saw that its wings, though damaged, were unbroken, and that the sky was clear again. Tears brought release, carrying away the despair and deadly fear that had followed him into his dreams.

But at the same time his wildness and bravado, the soldier and bandit in him, fell away like a mask, and to his father's joy the face of the old solitary, contemplative Berthold reappeared. For a week or two, his father—who day after day with a sigh paid out money to appease the mother of the injured boy, who lay sick for quite some time—distrusted his quietness, expecting the demon to erupt at any moment. But Berthold seemed to be thoroughly reformed; he abandoned all dealings with boys of his age, kept away from the streets and playgrounds, worked hard at his Latin, and devoted himself more than ever to meditating about God and life. The sorry outcome of his last battle had taught him that earthly glory is transient, and he found further confirmation of this truth in the fact that his former comrades did not seem to miss him. They followed new captains. At first they spared Berthold's feelings by keeping out of his way, then they teased him for a while, and then they forgot him. No one spoke of his heroic deeds any longer, and because he was studying Latin and destined for the priesthood, the town boys, partly in envy and partly in contempt, resumed their old habit of calling him St. Berthold. The one thing that was not forgotten was his ill luck in almost causing the death of a comrade. Like his father, he thought he was changed and reformed; the truth of the matter was that his natural impatience and his unsatisfied lust for life were merely expressing themselves in a different way.

Berthold's teacher saw with concern what he and his

father failed to see. The high-spirited child had indeed become quiet and well behaved, but to Father Paul his new zeal for repentance, piety, and study seemed no less exaggerated than his previous misconduct. The padre saw that in the still-dawning life of this young soul an intimation of all that is doubtful and inadequate in human life was growing like a premature evening shadow, and he knew that for this illness there could be no remedy. He knew it well, because he himself belonged to the silent community of the dissatisfied who never know whether what troubles them is their own shortcomings or the condition of the world. That made him love the handsome, restless boy and fear for him.

"But if God is just," said Berthold, "and if everything that happens in the world is determined by His law and His will, why should there be wars and battles; why should there be soldiers, whose trade it is to kill people? What's more, they are honored for it, and great captains are said to be heroes."

Father Paul replied: "They are instruments of God. We must indeed hold the life of every man sacred, but no life is perfect, and God Himself causes every man to die, one young, another old; one of sickness, another by the sword or other violence. So we see that physical life in itself is of little worth, that it's only a metaphor or image. And this should teach us to harness this frail life of ours to the service of God."

"Yes, but you've said that soldiers and murderers are also in the service of God, and they are evil."

"A blacksmith can't very well shoe a horse by himself, can he?"

"No."

"Exactly. He needs a helper, but he also needs a hammer."

"Yes."

"Well, the helper is more than a hammer; he is a living man, endowed not only with strength but also with reason. In the same way, there is a difference between God's servants and His instruments. Every man, even a murderer, is an instrument; he must help to carry out God's will, whether he wants to or not; there's no merit in it. To be God's servant is a very different matter; it means to submit to God even when it hurts, even when it goes counter to one's own desires. Once a man has recognized that, he can't content himself with being an instrument; he must aspire at all times to be a servant. If he forgets this and pursues his earthly drives and desires, he is a greater sinner than any thief or murderer. You say all soldiers are evil. How do you know what is evil? Perhaps the man who does a wicked deed in folly and ignorance is not so great a sinner as the man who knows what is good and fails to act on his knowledge."

"But why does God leave so many in ignorance?"

"That we shall never know. Why does He make some flowers red and others yellow or blue? And something else that I don't know is whether in His eyes there is so great a difference between the knowing and the unknowing or between the good and the wicked. But rest assured that the man to whom God has given knowledge has greater duties and greater responsibilities than other men."

There were many talks of this kind between the wise, patient priest and his inquiring pupil. Berthold learned a good deal and grew in knowledge, but he grew no less in secret pride. He came to look down on his former comrades and even on his father, and the better he learned to speak and debate about God and things divine, the more his dissatisfied soul lost its piety and modesty. In his thoughts he began to doubt everything, to submit everything to his own judgment. His teacher felt strangely torn. He saw that he was training the boy's mind and not his heart, but he had lost control of the reins. And though he reproached himself for this, he was glad to have so bright a pupil, with whom he could engage in loftier disputations than with any of the monks.

In his pride, Berthold failed to see that he was living the years of his childhood in an utterly unchildlike manner, depriving himself of something irretrievable. Once he had become interested in reading and Father Paul took to providing him with books, he led a quiet but intense shadow life in the pale land of written characters, and forgot the world that he belonged to and that should have been his. He did not miss the companionship of his contemporaries, whom he more or less despised, and when his father or uncle occasionally told him that he looked pale and had been studying too much, he took it as a compliment. Sometimes, to be sure, he was seized with the old hunger for a rich, full, active life such as he had once sought in war games, but now his yearning was directed toward a future in which he hoped to attain honor and power, and toward the world of thought, which for the precocious child had become a challenging game with the unknowable. He considered himself noble and distinguished, because he strove for intellectual riches, and no one told him that his striving for knowledge was merely an unwholesome hunger that no amount of knowledge could satisfy, because in it he was seeking nothing but himself.

When Father Paul said the time had come to send the boy away to study, Berthold's father, in the belief that his hope of seeing his son ordained was nearing fulfillment, gladly gave his consent. Berthold himself was even more delighted, for he was now fifteen and longed to see the wide world.

Through the padre, who came from the Rhineland and still had friends there, lodgings were found for the young student in the great city of Cologne, which swarmed with

clerics young and old. He was to live at the house of a
canon and attend the seminary in good company. Ar-
rangements were soon made, and one cool autumn morning, speeded on his way with blessings and good wishes
and amply provided with travel money and provisions,
Berthold left home in a conveyance for which he had
been impatiently waiting for two weeks. Great flocks of
birds traversed the bright blue sky; the horses trotted
gaily down the valley. Soon the country was strange and
new to him, and after a few hours the river valley opened
into a wide, unknown plain, radiant with autumn colors.

2

B ERTHOLD had a good year in Cologne. True, there
were difficulties at first. There were two other students staying at the canon's house, Adam and Johannes,
who for the first few days tormented Berthold with their
supercilious mockery. The small-town boy, unaccustomed
to polite society and Rhenish refinement, was mercilessly
teased and treated with benevolent condescension. This
made him so unhappy that, though the merry, easygoing
canon comforted him and came to his defense, he cried in
his bed at night.

This went on for six or eight days; then Berthold finally
had enough. One morning, when his enemies resumed
their malicious questions, he remembered his heroism of
former days and thrashed them both so thoroughly that
they begged for mercy. From then on they treated him
with respect. When it turned out that he was also one of

the best Latin scholars in the seminary, his standing rose quickly and he did not lack for friends.

Latin played a far more important part in the school curriculum than the actual study of religion. Church ritual was indeed taught and practiced; the Bible and some of the Church Fathers were studied, and considerable time was spent in refuting the heresies of all ages, especially the modern doctrines of Luther and others. But on the whole the life and course of study were pleasantly worldly, and no special importance was attached to piety. It was a long while before Berthold heard of the relics of the eleven thousand virgins preserved in Cologne, and the comrade who finally took him to see them made no undue fuss about them.

Among his friends, it was of Johannes that he soon grew fondest, and it was also from him that he learned the most. Johannes was a fine, handsome boy, descended from a lowly family in Luxembourg but equal to any scion of the nobility in stature and refinement. He knew French and a little Italian, played the zither, and was well informed on the subjects of wine, women's dress, jewels, and painting. But his greatest gift was storytelling. He knew a thousand stories, and they always occurred to him at the right time. In the evening, as the three students sat in their room or in the garden, Johannes would often tell stories, which flowed along as effortlessly and melodiously as the Rhine beneath the city's bridges.

He told of the troll who one summer evening came in fine clothes to dance under the lime tree. He was the best dancer there, but his hands were as cold as ice. He chose the most beautiful of the girls and with her danced away from the lime tree; on he went, leading her in graceful figures, until they came to the bridge, where he picked her up in his arms and jumped into the river with her. Then Johannes told the story of the fisherman in Speyer. One night some little men called him and asked to be ferried across the Rhine. And then came more and more little men, and all night he was busy rowing one boatload after another. And in the morning he found his hat, which he had left on the bank, full of little gold pieces.

He told them how, long ago, two seminarians had taken a third up on a high church steeple to rob crows' nests. The two put a board out through the sound hole and held it fast while the third climbed out and robbed a nest in a niche in the wall. When all his pockets were full of eggs, the others wanted some, too, but he told them they could climb out there themselves if they weren't afraid. They threatened to let go of the board unless he gave them some eggs. He thought they wouldn't dare, and gave them nothing. Whereupon they let go of the board, and he fell into space. But, lo and behold, the air caught under his long buttoned coat and blew it up like a bell, and to everyone's amazement he floated down to the marketplace as slowly and gently as a big black bird.

He also had a whole sackful of stories about the devil. For instance, the one about the three journeymen who played cards in church during services. The devil sat down and played with them. One of the journeymen recognized him and went away, and so did the second; but in the excitement of the game the third noticed nothing and went on playing with the devil. Suddenly a fearful cry of distress was heard; the congregation ran away in horror. Later on, a great spot of blood was found in the place where the player had been, and rub and scrape as they might, the spot could never be removed.

Johannes also told stories about the finding of treasure; about the unredeemed souls of murdered men, dwarflike figures in red shirts who stood outside their houses at night lamenting; about friendly, good-natured ghosts, goblins, and snake kings.

He knew still other stories that Berthold was not allowed to hear and that he told only to his comrade Adam.

To Berthold's dismay, Johannes was always sharing secrets with Adam; they had even invented a language, and in answer to Berthold's persistent questions they would only say it was a magician's language.

Apart from this bit of jealousy, Berthold's days were pleasant. He shone as a Latinist, was feared and respected for his prowess in wrestling, and once he plucked up his courage and tried his hand at the little social graces, he was a great success. He frequently saw distinguished clergymen and laymen in the house, and sometimes had to help wait on them at table. When it became clear to him that diffidence accomplishes nothing, he quickly and radically overcame his bashful blushing. The great, beautiful city was very much to his liking; he came to know its streets and squares, and admired its fine houses and palaces, its carriages and riders, its uniforms and richly dressed burghers, its mountebanks and musicians. He took to using certain local words and turns of phrase, and sometimes when he thought of home, he had dreams of being received there as an urbane, well-traveled guest and then soon returning to the glittering world.

He did not lose his taste for disputation. But he was no longer interested in seeking explanations for disquieting enigmas; what appealed to him now was to fence playfully and elegantly with the rapier of dialectics, which fascinated him with its magical glitter. He learned to thrust about him with logic, with syllogisms and Bible quotations, and soon he was able to confute any truth or to prove any notion that entered his head, unless his adversary happened to be a still abler dialectician. He often practiced his skill on Johannes.

Every three months, in excellent Latin, he wrote a letter home, which his father was obliged to take to the monastery for Father Paul to translate. His third or fourth letter remained unanswered. Then after quite some time a wagoner arrived from his native town bearing the news that Berthold's father had died. From Berthold's uncle, who was to administer the young man's inheritance, the messenger brought a small sack of money and two fat geese for the canon. When Berthold asked for news from the town, the wagoner told him that the burgomaster had died three months before and a few weeks later the watchman, and that the old pesthouse outside the town had burned down—some boys had set fire to it. After being fortified with wine in the kitchen, the wagoner went his way. Berthold was amazed at how much had happened at home since his departure, and tried to visualize his dead father. The canon tapped him on the shoulder, said a comforting word or two, and promised to say Masses for the departed. Then Berthold told his friends of his father's death. They made grave faces, Johannes shook his hand solemnly, and Adam asked how old his father had been. Berthold, who didn't know and was ashamed of not knowing, lied and said, "Sixty."

Sometime later, when he had utterly forgotten the messenger, his home, and his father, a letter came from Father Paul. Though Berthold admired the padre's Latin, he found his admonitions and questions importunate and did not reply. He was concerned with very different matters at the time.

It was not his fault that he had had no true childhood, that his home and early years were so easily and quickly lost and forgotten. He had hardly known his older brother and had grown up alone with his father. A boy who grows up without a mother and without brothers and sisters is deprived of half his childhood, and more than half if there are no other women in his life. Whatever may be our estimation of women in other respects, they have a sacred mission as guardians and protectors of childhood, and in this no man can replace them.

Berthold had been deprived of this protection and its

manifold tender influences. The only women he had known were a severe, unkind aunt and his father's coarse or indifferent maidservants; indeed, he knew less of womankind than he did of the moon. Worldly and independent as he had become in other ways, he was still shy and on the defensive with women. Apart from the maids in the canon's house, the only women he had seen in Cologne were those who passed him on the street. Of course he had heard that these strange beings could be a source of great pleasure to a young man, but this garden was closed to him, and with all his Latin he could find no key to it.

He had recently discovered, however, that Johannes and Adam spoke of these very matters in their secret colloquies. And from the lips of unguarded persons, he had heard rumors of amours and private entertainments among the higher and lower clergy. At first he took these reports for malicious gossip, but as he increased in wisdom he decided that they might be true, for the longer he thought about such matters, the more he doubted whether he or anyone else had virtue enough to resist a temptation of this kind.

For to tell the truth, he had become increasingly dissatisfied with his customary train of thought. It now seemed to him that not honor and glory, or learning and the high offices it might confer, but to a far greater degree the favor and kisses of a beautiful girl were the things most to be desired in this imperfect world—though as yet he had no particular girl in mind.

One dark evening shortly before Christmas, he was sitting in the faint candlelight with his two roommates. Adam was sleepily reading the *Graduale Romanum,* and Berthold was listening to Johannes. They had been talking about Rome and the papal household. But rich as this subject matter was, Johannes, what with the howling of the snowy wind in the rafters and the flickering candlelight in the large room, had gradually shifted to horror stories and had begun to tell them one after another. He told Berthold how in building large structures, especially fortresses and bridges, architects had discovered that the only way to make the foundations absolutely secure was to immure a live human being, preferably a child or a virgin, in them. Once in Thuringia a fortress was being built, and to make it as strong as possible the builders bought a child from its mother for a large sum of money. They placed the child in a niche and, with the mother looking on, began to wall it in. After a while the child cried out, "Mother, I can still see you just a little." And then after another while, "Mother, I can't see you any more."

And when another fortress was being built, a mason not only took money to let his little son be immured but undertook to do it himself and started right in. He built walls around the child and made them higher and higher, till in the end he needed a ladder. The little boy had no idea what was being done to him and sat there patiently. But as the walls grew higher and higher he cried out, "Father, Father, it's getting so dark!" That touched the cruel mason's heart. In horror, he let go of the ladder and fell to the ground, where he lay dead.

"Served him right!" Berthold cried aloud, not so much to applaud the triumph of justice as to dispel the grisly feeling that had gradually come over him while listening to these stories.

Johannes looked at him, and his intelligent, girlish eyes twinkled as he went on: "Back home in Luxembourg, there was once an architect . . ." But Berthold interrupted him and pleaded, "For goodness' sake, tell me a story about something else."

"What?" asked Johannes.

Berthold hesitated in embarrassment. Then he took courage and said, "Tell me what it's like when you go to see girls. —No, don't deny it, I know what I know."

When he saw that Johannes distrusted him and sensed

danger, he affected indifference and said, "Very well. I can talk it over with the old man."

Adam, who had been listening, jumped up and shouted, "If you do that, you're a dog. We'll kill you."

Berthold laughed. "That's something I'd like to see," he said and, seizing Adam's hand, squeezed it in his fist. Adam screamed. "All right," he said in a frightened voice. "What do you want?"

Berthold looked him straight in the eye. "I want to go with you the next time you stay away from Mass. I want to have a sweetheart, too."

Johannes gave him a sly look and laughed softly. Then he said ingratiatingly, "Why, my dear Berthold. Are you in love? With whom? If I knew, maybe I could help you."

Berthold eyed him with suspicion. Then he blurted out, "I'm not in love. I don't know anything about these things. But I'd like to meet a girl and give her a kiss, and if you won't help me and keep laughing at me, I'll make you laugh on the other side of your face."

He looked so dangerous that Johannes stopped laughing. He thought for a moment and then said calmly, "You're a funny one, asking me who you should fall in love with. I can't tell you that. But if you're really dying for a kiss, you could try the maid at the silk merchant's across the street. I think she might help you."

"The skinny one with the black hair?" Berthold asked.

"That's right. Give it a try."

"But how do I go about it?"

"Son, that's your affair. If you need a nursemaid, you're not ready to take up with girls."

"But what should I do? What should I say to her?"

"Just say, 'I want a kiss, but I have no nerve.' Seriously —you don't need to say anything. Just look at her in a way that shows you like her. The rest will take care of itself, don't worry."

Berthold asked no further questions, because Adam

was grunting and Johannes's pretty girlish eyes were sparkling with amusement. He decided to follow Johannes's advice and, if it should prove to be bad advice, to make Johannes pay for it. Calmly he said, "All right, now tell me another story."

Johannes smiled, passed his tongue over his bright-red lips, fluttered his long brown lashes for a moment, and began: "There were once three brothers who loved each other dearly and faithfully. It so happened that a man was murdered in their town and one of them was unjustly suspected and thrown into prison. Even under torture, he protested his innocence, but it did him no good and the judge condemned him to death. When his brothers heard the news, they both ran to the judge, and each declared that he had committed the murder. But when the prisoner heard about it, he cried out that he was the murderer and was now prepared to confess. For the brothers loved each other so dearly that each one preferred to die rather than let one of the others die. The judge was perplexed, for now he had three murderers, each of whom claimed to be the right one. Finally, he bade each of them to plant a lime sapling, but with the crown in the earth and the roots in the air. Those whose trees grew nevertheless would be declared innocent and set free. Then each of the brothers planted his sapling. It was springtime. In a few weeks, all three lime trees sprang merrily into leaf and throve so well that they are standing there to this day. Then the judge knew that all three were innocent."

Before they went to sleep, Johannes, to please Berthold, told an amorous story, the story of the pagan god Vulcan, whose wife was having an affair with the god Mars, and how Vulcan got wind of it, and how when the two of them were embracing he caught them in a net of the finest wire and exhibited them to the gods in their disgrace, so that the gods nearly died of laughter and they of shame.

This anecdote was so different from Johannes's other stories that Berthold turned it over in his mind for an hour or more before he was able to fall asleep, and it followed him into his dreams. An intimation of the joys of love caught the hardhearted boy in its oppressive, magic snares, and the garden of Venus showed the timid novice only its smiling side, where the roses are without thorns and the paths free from snakes. In blissfully hovering dreams, his oppression was transformed into smiling, winged happiness, which drove all the hardness and dissatisfaction from his arrogant soul and turned him into a child playing in the grass, a bird rejoicing in the sky.

In the cold morning, Berthold awoke shivering, feeling sad and cheated by his sweet dreams. In a dream he had drunk sweet wine with a tall, beautiful girl; she had said sweet things to him, and he had answered without bashfulness and kissed her on her warm, fresh lips. But now it was cold; in half an hour he would have to go to the dark church for early Mass, and then to school, and if on the way he were to meet seven of the most beautiful princesses on earth, he would hardly dare to raise his eyes, and his heart would pound so that he would be glad when they had passed.

Sad and silent, he got out of bed, washed the sweet sleep from his eyes with cold water, slipped into his cold black clothes, and started his accustomed day. On the way to Mass, he did not fail to look up at the silk merchant's house, to see whether the black-haired maid was there, but at that early hour she was not to be seen, and morosely he went his way.

When they returned home toward noon and when, outside the silk merchant's house, Berthold looked up again after a moment's anxious hesitation, Adam poked Johannes in the ribs and grinned. It so happened that Berthold noticed; he said nothing, but he gave the scoffer such a look that Adam took fright and hurried on. In this moment, Berthold decided to go through with the adventure if it killed him, and to choke the next person who made fun of him.

And so, on that day and the next, he glanced eagerly at the house across the street. Twice he saw the slender girl, but try as he would, he could not look at her boldly, but blushed in his confusion and quickly averted his gaze. For all his resolutions, he would not have advanced one step unaided. But the girl had a keen eye and soon saw what was what. She was so touched by the boy's unspoiled innocence, and so attracted by his strong, broad-shouldered frame, that she was quite willing to help him out of his distress. How to do it was no problem for her, for she had always been well disposed toward the young seminarians.

But this new one really made things hard for her. As he was passing by the next day, looking like a man condemned to the gallows, she stepped through the gate. When he raised his eyes half in terror and looked into her face for a second, she illumined her pleasant countenance with a blissful smile in his honor. He saw it, blushed deeply, lowered his eyes, and ran down the street like a thief, in such haste that his long cloak flapped around his calves and the well-disposed girl could not help turning her smile into a laugh. But even in his confusion the fugitive carried a warm glimmer of love away with him; for all his blushes, his head was full of sweet dreams, and his hardness melted like snow in the springtime, giving way to a strange surge of gentle feeling.

Maid Barbara hoped that after this beginning her scholar would make rapid progress, but in vain. Every day she hung out her enticing sign, and the lover never failed to blush and beam, but as for stopping, saying a word, making a gesture, or boldly entering the house, nothing of the kind ever happened. After three or four weeks had been squandered in this way, she began to regret her futile pains, and the next time Berthold came by, anxiously blushing in advance, she gave him a cold, angry look that filled his beautiful blue sky with clouds. The next day, when she looked for the effect, she saw deep misery in his face. There was such passion, such anxious supplication in his tearful eyes, that she saw she would never get rid of this captive bird.

And so she changed her plan and resolved to do what he should properly have done. She waited until he passed the house alone and there was no one in the street; then she stepped out quickly, came close to him, and without looking at him said softly, "Wouldn't you like to come and see me? This evening at eight."

Her words struck the bashful scholar like a thunderbolt. He saw the gates of paradise opening, and he also saw that he had been an ass with all his fears and torment. For weeks he had waited day after day for a glance from her, fearing to make her angry, afraid to trust her friendliness, always thinking he had made a mistake, and piling worry on worry. He had worn himself out wondering how he might write her a letter or send her a present, but everything he could think of had seemed too bold, too forward, too dangerous. And now it was all so easy and simple!

Only one thing was not easy: to get through the long day with his great secret in his heart, to let the hours go by as usual while wondering the whole time how it would be, what would happen that evening. Berthold ran this way and that like a man on the point of setting out for China, and Johannes, the shrewd observer, who had been watching him for weeks with silent amusement, saw that something was afoot. He was not surprised when that afternoon Berthold drew him aside with a grave, mysterious air, informed him that he would be obliged to go out that evening on very important business, and said he was counting on him to keep the secret and to stand by him if necessary. Solemnly Johannes gave him his promise and hastened to communicate the news to Adam, who was no less pleased.

"Good old Bärbel," he said with a laugh. "Now she's got that clod to initiate!"

Endless as the short winter day seemed, evening came at last and the beginner was in luck. He found the gate still unlocked at eight o'clock, slipped out without a sound, and irresolutely approached the silk merchant's house. His heart pounded as never before, and his knees trembled. Then a shadow glided past in the darkness, and a voice whispered softly, "Keep right behind me, I'll go ahead." She vanished in the shadow of the tall houses and slipped around the corner so quickly that he could hardly follow her. They went down a narrow side street, across a tangled back yard, through a tiny bare garden, which lay in deep snow and half of which glistened in the moonlight, through a shed full of old wine barrels, one of which Berthold overturned in his haste, so that it rang hollow in the night silence. Then the girl opened a little door and quietly closed it again behind her companion, and led him down a stone corridor and up a dark, narrow stairway. At the top, they entered a half-empty little room that smelled of hay and leather.

Giggling, she asked him, "Were you afraid?"

"I'm never afraid," he said solemnly. "Where are we?"

"In our back building. This is the harness room. Nobody ever comes here in the winter. Your name's Berthold, isn't it? Oh yes, I knew. Don't you want to give me a kiss?"

He very much wanted to. He was amazed at how few words and how little reflection were required. His great worry had been what to say to the girl, but now as he sat beside her on a little bench, over which she laid a woolen horse blanket, a simple, natural conversation sprang up of its own accord. She asked him where he was from, and was full of admiration when she heard that he came from so far away. She asked him about the servants in the canon's house, and then they spoke of food, drink, and other familiar things. Meanwhile, she pressed her cheek to his. Though this and the kissing were strange and new to him, though they gave him such tremulous pleasure that it almost hurt, he kept up his courage and came through the test with flying colors. Now it was Barbara's turn to be amazed, for she had never thought this timid, shamefaced boy would turn out to be so resolute a man. In the course of their quiet conversation, she had shown his uncertain hands a few discreet paths, but then, with very little fumbling or hesitation, he found his way by himself. And when he had left her and negotiated the whole complicated return journey—stairway, shed, garden, and alley—alone, the amazed Barbara knew she had nothing more to teach the strange young man.

It was not good for Berthold, and it is not good for anyone, to make his first acquaintance with the miracle of love in this contrived way. But at first, and outwardly, the effect of that evening on Berthold was a sudden flowering. The morose reserve that his comrades and teachers had observed of late vanished like a brief illness; his look recovered all its old openness and radiance, once more he took pleasure in gymnastics of the mind and body, and he seemed to have grown at once younger and more mature.

Johannes and Adam saw that he was no longer a child, and honored him in their own way by initiating him into the manly pleasure of wine drinking. At first Berthold enjoyed the wine only because it was forbidden. How glorious it seemed to creep silently down into the dark cellar, to grope until they found the right keg, and to fill their stupid old water pitcher at the sighing tap with clear, gently flowing wine. The danger meant nothing to him, and indeed it was not very great, for a good deal of wine was consumed at the canon's table in the course of the year and a shortage was not likely to be noticed as long as the little keg with the canon's favorite wine was

spared. And this one they bled only sparingly and on festive occasions, mostly for the sake of Johannes, who despite his tender years was already a connoisseur and
occasionally claimed that he needed a choice dram.

If anyone had told Berthold before he went to Cologne
that he would there learn to steal, lie, drink, and indulge
his lust, he would have crossed himself. Now he did all
these things with an easy mind and could not have been
happier. Without exactly neglecting his studies, he gave
himself up to the pleasures of the flesh and found a contentment he had never before experienced. Sturdy enough
to begin with, he grew in height and breadth, and blos-
somed out into a strapping young man whom one would
have been glad to see engaged in some worthwhile
pursuit.

Twice a week, on Monday and Thursday evenings, he
had his meetings with Barbara. Trusting in his strength
and cunning, he went to her own room, something none
of her other young lovers had dared to do. She rewarded
him not only with caresses but also with helpings of roast
and cake and other tidbits from her kitchen, while he
brought a bottle filled with wine; he often stayed the
whole night, or most of it.

It occurred to him after a while that she had been
astonishingly willing to grant him her favors. And when,
as happened now and then, he asked leave to come on
other nights than those she had set aside for him, her
agitation and the firmness of her opposition did not
escape him. Then he began to wonder why his friend
Johannes had referred him especially to Barbara, and the
question tormented him. He plied Johannes with questions, and after trying to put him off with evasive an-
swers, Johannes finally told him in his free-and-easy way
what he knew of the girl. As he saw it, she was a good
soul, but with a great weakness for young boys, especially
seminarians. She had been only too glad to teach Johannes, Adam, Berthold, and an unknown number of

predecessors the ways of love—a kindly and selfless teacher. True, she had learned by bitter experience that gratitude and fidelity are rare virtues, and lived in perpetual fear of losing her present favorite, assuming there was only one.

In the same breath, the skillful storyteller defended Barbara and exposed her; in the end he advised the glowering Berthold to think mildly of her and not to let his disillusionment detract from the gratitude he owed her. Berthold made no answer. He had never thought he was Barbara's first lover. But it wounded him deeply to learn that she made a habit of luring boys of his age, and that in all likelihood she was entertaining other lovers at that very time.

He decided to investigate. He spent several evenings circling around the silk merchant's house. He watched the alleys, the yard, and the little garden, and twice he saw his sweetheart going into the back building with a student he knew. Though trembling with rage, he held himself in check. After a sleepless night he decided to say nothing and to keep his contempt to himself. But he could not control himself entirely. The next time they met in the deserted street, she gave him a look of friendly reproach —for he had twice been absent from their rendezvous— whereupon he made a face and stuck his tongue out at her. That was his parting from his first love.

Once again he became morose and refractory. He was seen drunk on several occasions, and neither remonstrance nor punishment could bring him to mend his ways. At the suggestion of a well-disposed teacher, it was decided that he should be sent home for a short visit. This was not at all to his liking, for that spring he had fallen in love for the first time. But he was obliged to obey, and one fine blue day at the end of April he left Cologne on a ship that was sailing up the Rhine.

At home he felt alien and ill at ease. His uncle received

him with kindness and even with a certain respect, and everyone greeted him with friendly esteem as an almost-hatched priest. But the narrow, humdrum life struck him as shallow and joyless; his girl cousins were shy and boring, and he longed for the blond hair of a merchant's daughter in Cologne whom he had seen a number of times in the cathedral and worshipped without hope. For he was well aware that this girl, even if she loved him, would never call him in from the street to the back door of her father's house.

Nothing in his native town aroused tender thoughts of the old days. Of course, he remembered his boyhood, the pitched battles, the boy he thought he had killed, his flight into the woods, but all that was far away, irrelevant, relegated to the vast territory of the past, which means so little to young people. His memories told him only that he had become a stranger to this life and these scenes, and that his place was no longer there.

After he had wandered about for a few days, immersed in cheerless thoughts, a vague feeling drew him down the valley to the monastery, and at the sight of it, stronger, warmer memories of his childhood were kindled. Not without emotion, he went in and asked for his old teacher. He was brought to Father Paul, who was writing in his cell. Father Paul recognized him at once and greeted him in Latin with his old cheerfulness. But he had aged greatly and his face was yellow.

As soon as the first curiosity on both sides was satisfied, the old philosophical questions came up.

"Well, my son, how do you look at life now? Are you still plagued by the same old riddles, or have you exchanged them for new ones?"

"I don't know," said Berthold. "I haven't thought about those things very much. I'm really not a philosopher. After all, I'm not responsible for the world. But I can't bring myself to believe that it's perfect."

"Is that because of experiences you've had in Cologne?"

"Not really. But I've seen that learning doesn't make for happiness, and that a scoundrel can become a priest, an abbot, a capitulary, or anything else you can think of."

"What can I say? Is the cloth to blame if a scoundrel puts it on? And besides, it's hard to judge. God needs us all, even the wicked, for His purposes. Unworthy men have done great good, and saints have brought great misery into the world. Think of Father Girolamo in Florence, whom I used to tell you about."

"Yes, I suppose you're right. I didn't mean anything in particular, and it's not for me to judge. Probably the whole world is just as it should be and the trouble is all with me."

"Still so bitter? Can't you tell me what the trouble is? I might be able to advise you."

"Thank you. You're very kind, but I have nothing to say. All I know is that there must be something better in human life than what I know of it; otherwise, it wouldn't be worth living or talking about."

"Perhaps you weren't cut out to be a priest."

"Perhaps . . ."

A feeling of distrust came over him. He had no intention of asking the old man for advice, still less of confessing to him. But in the course of the conversation a yearning, a wild lust for life, more passionate and hopeless than ever, arose in him. He thought of his pleasures in Cologne, the stolen wine and counterfeit love that had gone down so sweetly, and saw the dismal emptiness of his follies and dissipations. His whole life, past and present, became a bad taste in his mouth. Here he was, seventeen years old, big and strong, healthy and by no means stupid, and yet he had nothing better to do than read Latin and learn scholastic philosophy with a lot of pale schoolboys and to join in their silly exploits. And to what end? At best he would become an unneeded priest, saying his Masses, keeping a good table, and picking up the crumbs of love that others have left over, or else content-

ing himself with the unsavory glory of involuntary sainthood. He forgot that this is by no means the lot of every
priest; he exaggerated because in his dejection he wanted
to suffer, and took bitter pleasure in denigrating and
ridiculing himself, his life, his calling, and everything
connected with him.

He bade the padre a polite but cool goodbye and did not
keep his promise to come and see him soon again. After
fretful deliberations, he decided to go away and leave his
whole past behind him. And then he thought of the beautiful blond girl in Cologne and resolved that he must see
her again, even if there was no hope.

3

BERTHOLD returned to Cologne on St. Urban's Day. It
soon became clear to all who knew him that his trip
home had done him no good. Nothing could have made
him go back to the dark-haired Barbara, and as time went
on the absence of his accustomed pleasure became more
and more of a torment. And since his thoughts were taken
up with the blond young lady from the cathedral, who
tormented him with all the cruel charms of the unattainable, he neglected his studies. Remonstrances, whether
gentle or severe, left him indifferent. He soon forfeited his
reputation as a Latinist and came to be regarded as a
mediocre or even poor scholar. His fallow energies op-
pressed him, and oblivious of his silent passion, the pretty
burgher's daughter, dressed in her Sunday best, passed
by without so much as seeing him. His easy victory over
the serving maid, he now saw, had been no victory at all.

In those days, he came closer to the elegant Johannes, whose polite, noncommittal friendship was always available. One day they had a philosophical discussion, more to pass the time than because they had any need of it. In the end, Berthold said: "Why all this talk? There's no point in it, and you don't take it seriously any more than I do. Cicero or Thomas Aquinas, it's all nonsense. Tell me instead what you really think about life. You're so contented. Why? What do you expect from life?"

Johannes's fine, cool eyes lit up under their long lashes. "I expect a good deal from life, or very little, depending on how you look at it. I'm poor, a child *sine patre*, and I intend to become rich and powerful. Most of all, powerful. I have no intention of becoming a village priest; no, I'm going to serve at court, where they need educated men who know how to hold their tongue, and there I'll acquire power. I'll bow to others until they have to bow to me. Then I'll be rich; I'll have houses, fine clothes, women, paintings, horses, hounds, and servants. But that's secondary. The main thing is power. Those who love me will get presents; those who hate me will die. That's what I want and what I'll get; I don't know if it's much or little."

"It's little," said Berthold. "You're dividing your life into two halves: a period of serving and a period of commanding. The first will be long, the second will be short, and in the meantime you'll have lost your youth."

"No one can stay young. And besides, I'm not young. I have had no parents, no home, no freedom; I've always been obliged to serve others, and that's not youth. Ever since I was ten years old, I've had no other thought than to become powerful and stop having to oblige others. I'm a good student, a good comrade; I do what I can to please my teachers, to please the canon, to please Adam, to please you."

"But you've also been down in the cellar with us."

"I've also been down in the cellar with you. And I've

also slept with the rich prelate Arnulf's mistress, which could have cost me my neck, not because I wanted it, but because she wanted it."

"And you tell *me* this?"

"Yes. You won't repeat it. I know you. You're not good. Maybe you're even worse than I am, but you won't tell anyone. I'm closer to Adam than to you, but I'd never tell him such a thing."

"Then it's true!" Berthold cried out in consternation. He was amazed and almost aghast to learn the true nature of this friend with whom he had lived for two years, and who had always struck him as intelligent but easygoing and undemanding.

"Johannes!" he cried out. "I didn't know you. I always thought I was the only one, that everyone else was satisfied with life. It was very hard for me. How have you been able to bear it all by yourself?"

Johannes looked at him smilingly, with the expression of faint mockery that never left him. "Talking won't change anything. And I have nothing to complain of. Some people are worse off. You're a child, Berthold. What's more, you're in love. Let's talk about that."

"What for? You can't help me."

"Who knows? Maybe you need a messenger or a spy. You know how glad I am to oblige."

"Why should you, when it's no use to you? You can't expect to get anything out of it."

"You never can tell. You're very strong, for instance, that's something. But seriously, tell me about it."

Berthold was willing enough. He told Johannes about his blond beauty and indicated the part of the church where he had seen her. He knew her last name but not her first.

"I don't know her," Johannes said. "You'll have to point her out to me. I'm afraid there's not much we can do. Burghers' daughters don't usually bother with the likes of us; they want to get married. Once that's over with, they're not so difficult."

"Don't talk like that!" Berthold pleaded. "I don't want to be loved by another man's wife; that would be hardly better than Barbara. Why shouldn't I have a nice sweet girl to myself like other young men?"

"How can you expect a beautiful young girl of good family to throw herself into your arms when you can't marry her and can't even give her presents? She'd have to be mad. You're asking too much. Besides, it's enjoyable to make lovers or husbands jealous, maybe as enjoyable as love itself. There's a big difference between us and other young men. You're asking for trouble if you close your eyes to the facts. These black coats of ours give us so many advantages that we can put up with some slight drawbacks."

"You call going without love a slight drawback?"

"What kind of love have laymen got? They have the privilege, or obligation, to marry the girl they love. And then they're stuck with her as long as they live, children and all. That's the only advantage they have over us. If your blond beauty doesn't care for you, it makes no difference whether you're a priest or a layman. And if it's marriage you want, you'd need a pile of money. A poor man has no choice but to take a woman no one else wants, or to stay single."

"But it is possible for two people to love each other without thinking of money and all that."

"Oh yes. Most people who fall in love are like that. But fathers and mothers, uncles and aunts, guardians and cousins do their thinking for them. You're under the misapprehension that other people are better off than you are, and you blame your calling for your lack of ingenuity or luck. That won't get you very far. And speaking of true love, there's good reason to believe that only an unmarriageable man can experience it. When a woman loves a man from whom she can expect neither money, marriage, support, nor a good name for herself and her children, it means she really loves him. A man who offers her all that can never know whether she loves him for himself or for the sake of all those advantages."

This analysis did not appeal to Berthold. It did not comfort him, and it went counter to his own innermost conception of love. He changed the subject.

"Johannes," he said thoughtfully. "You've said you were not good and that maybe I was even worse. What did you mean by that? Are there people who can really be said to be good?"

"Yes, indeed, and I know a few. Our teacher Eulogius may be ridiculous, but he's good through and through, and among the students there's Konrad from Treves. Hasn't that ever occurred to you?"

"You're right. Do you think they're happier than we are?"

"Can't you see that for yourself? Of course they're happier, though there's hardly a pleasure they don't deny themselves. It's their nature. There's no merit in it, it's all a matter of predestination."

"Do you really believe in predestination? It has always struck me as a preposterous idea."

"So it would be if the world were governed by logic. But logic, justice, and all these seemingly rational and flawless notions are inventions of man; they are not found in nature. Whereas predestination, or call it chance, is the real law of the world. Why is a simpleton born rich and noble? Why is a man with a good, keen mind born into poverty? Why am I so constituted that I can't live without women, when the only profession in which I can make use of my gifts is the priesthood? Why are so many vicious girls as beautiful as angels? Can the ugly ones, whom no one loves, help it if they're ugly? Why are you, with a body like Hercules, mentally unstable and melancholy? Is there any sense in all that? Isn't it all stupid chance, in other words, predestination?"

Berthold was horrified. "Then what becomes of God?"

Johannes smiled and shrugged his shoulders. "That's a question you mustn't ask, something to take up at school, in theology class."

"Johannes! Do you mean you deny the existence of God?"

"Deny? No, my boy. I never deny an authority, not even the most dubious saint. What has God got to do with philosophy? When I philosophize about life, I'm not questioning dogma, I'm only exercising my mind for the fun of it."

"But there can't be more than one truth."

"Logically, you mean? You're a good, faithful logician. But why shouldn't there be three truths, or ten, as well as one?"

"That's nonsense. If what's true can also be false, then it simply ceases to be true."

"Yes, there's no way out. Then there isn't one truth or two, but none at all. That's what it amounts to."

After that they had many such conversations. Johannes was always willing to expatiate on Berthold's questions, but when Berthold tried to pin him down, to make him profess some firm belief, he explained that his whole discourse had been nothing more than a dialectical exercise and that he did not care in the least whether he was right or wrong, or whether anyone took him seriously. The skepticism of this talkative Lothario, this inspired storyteller and excellent comrade, never ceased to amaze Berthold; his view of the world and its inhabitants was as cold and passionless as a textbook in mathematics. He took all men, good and bad, intelligent and stupid, as he found them, and judged them only insofar as they might prove to be a help or a hindrance to himself and his plans.

He defended the clergy, but as to whether there was a God outside the imagination of a few theologians, he left the question open. Sometimes Berthold admired his unruffled coolness, and sometimes it exasperated him. Though in his heart he felt more and more strongly that such an outlook was foreign and hateful to his nature, he came to love these talks and to look upon Johannes as his favorite, indeed as his only friend.

Johannes tried to talk him out of his lovesickness. He laughed at Berthold, took him on amusing expeditions, recommended girls of easy virtue. But Berthold was not to be consoled. The blond maiden, whose name, he finally discovered, was Agnes, seemed to him more desirable than all the pleasures on earth. He followed her to church and back with silent passion, dreamed of her, and prayed to her. For her sake, he would have cast off his black coat without a tremor and performed any deed, however noble or infamous. He renounced the fleeting pleasure he might have had with others and rejoiced in his sacrifice. He fasted when not required to, merely to give his love an expression. Once he said to Johannes, "You don't know what it is to love. You know, I wouldn't be surprised if some priests stayed chaste all their lives because they were in love with a woman they couldn't honorably have."

"That may be," said Johannes. "There are all kinds of saints. Some of them are very strange. I've heard of a man sacrificing everything under the sun for the sake of a woman who gains nothing by his sacrifice and isn't even aware of it. She gets married, she has children, she has lovers, while he languishes and eats his heart out for no good reason. Such things happen, I'm sure they do, but that doesn't make them any less ridiculous. It's a kind of madonna cult. There are priests who really and truly worship the madonna as an unattainable beloved. Some people claim in all seriousness that women are better, holier beings than men. But it's not true. If you refuse to believe me or trust your own experience, just take a look at the doctrines of our Holy Church. Some of the older Church Fathers went so far as to say that women had no souls, and all the Fathers agree that woman is an inferior being, if not an instrument of the devil. That strikes me as cruel and you know I don't despise women, but all the same it's rather silly to make angels of them and hold them sacred."

Berthold had no answer to these arguments, but they pained him and he thought them false and unjust. He stopped talking to Johannes of his love, and listened sadly, but without envy, to his accounts of his numerous and dazzling amorous adventures, which he initiated and carried through with infinite guile. Berthold bore his love like a martyrdom that set him apart from other men, and in the saints and angels of the old Cologne masters he saw the sisters and likenesses of the winsome Agnes, whose blond hair and small, finely carved mouth illumined all his thoughts. He often watched outside the house of her father, who was a small merchant, an unassuming man with the good, congenial face of a lover of fine wines. He crept through the streets nearby, peered into the little vegetable garden, saw Agnes's girl friends going in and out. If instead of a seminarian he had only been a young merchant, a clerk, an architect, a silversmith, or even a journeyman cooper, he thought, he could have found an honorable way of making her acquaintance. As it was, he could not hope to approach her, because in view of his calling she would have taken any overture as an insult. In his misery he even tried to write poetry. He began a poem:

> *I know a maiden fair*
> *And Agnes is her name . . .*

But he got no further and tore the paper into bits.

In the meantime, Johannes had quietly observed the dove, as he always called Agnes in speaking of her to

Berthold, and had concluded that in all likelihood her pretty little blond head was accessible to other than pious thoughts. He found her quite to his liking and decided to see what he could do. If he succeeded, he thought, he would play the philanthropist and turn her over to the helpless Berthold. If not, the intrigue in itself would justify his trifling pains and quite possibly he would make a charming new acquaintance. A born spy and adventurer, he always delighted in spinning threads and building bridges where it seemed difficult.

Cautiously and without haste, he made inquiries, convinced that sooner or later he would find a thread leading to the demure and unsuspecting maiden. He observed her, investigated her relatives, her home life, her duties and habits. Through comrades, through servants and girl friends, he found out what he wanted, for in his adventures Johannes always made friends and never enemies; the town was full of people who were only too glad to repay him for services rendered, and his well-ordered memory never forgot any of them.

And finally the thread was found. Johannes had a passing acquaintance with one of Agnes's girl friends, and another was friendly with one of his schoolmates. Johannes knew all about these friendships between students and burghers' daughters. They were not love affairs, but only hopeful beginnings; they seldom lasted long, and even more seldom led to any consummation. Often, with the help of obliging servants, the young people met in gardens or secluded lanes, sometimes alone, sometimes along with other couples; they maintained the proprieties, contenting themselves with the diffident pleasure of meeting in secret. A kiss was regarded as no mean pleasure and exploit. It was a first timid exploration of the outer courts of love, a halfway station between child's play and love.

Johannes now made his preparations. Everything went smoothly, and he looked forward with pleasantly mild excitement to his meeting with Agnes, although he expected no benefit for Berthold and not much for himself. For safety's sake he had told no one of his plans. Some days before, he had quarreled with Adam, who was ordinarily his confidant and helper in such matters. In their meetings, they had both remained sullenly silent. Of course Johannes was confident that when he got around to it he would patch things up quickly and easily, as he had done many times before.

But precisely because of the tension between them, Adam had watched him and had a pretty good idea of what he was plotting. He also knew that it could not be anything very serious, for Johannes was much too cautious to think of seducing a girl of good family, especially as he knew that the violent and irascible Berthold was in love with her. And even if that had been his intention, he would not have gone about it in this way, which could lead to nothing and necessarily involved witnesses.

And so, since the affair seemed harmless and since, what with the bad blood between them, Adam welcomed an opportunity to make a little trouble for Johannes, he went to Berthold, aroused him with vague hints, and finally, when he saw him bite, came out with the secret: Johannes would be meeting some girls the following afternoon in such and such a place, and a young lady in whom Berthold was interested would be present.

Displeased that Adam seemed to know of his love and not wishing to reinforce his presumptions, Berthold refrained from asking questions. He knew that Adam had a grudge against Johannes, and that prevented him from taking the communication very seriously. But lovers, especially unhappy ones, are always suspicious. He felt that it would be unjust to suspect Johannes, and yet he could not entirely dispel his suspicion. Though he did not thank Adam for his information, he decided to look into it.

When Johannes went to his rendezvous the next day, Berthold followed him at a distance. He saw him waiting at a street corner; he saw a comrade join him and the two of them walk along chatting. They went down to the Rhine. There they disappeared into a walled garden and closed the gate behind them. Berthold waited awhile. Then he climbed the wall at a place which was hidden from the garden by a tall elder tree.

From where he sat, he could easily watch the garden. He couldn't see the two students or anyone else, but he soon guessed that the company was in a small summerhouse surrounded by foliage, through which he could not see. Then he heard voices from within and recognized one of them as Johannes's, but he could not understand what was being said. From time to time he heard soft laughter. There was a large pear tree in the middle of the garden; around it beans, lettuce, and cucumbers were growing in narrow beds; some of the cucumbers, large and almost ripe, hung down over the sand path. Farther on, there were young fruit trees in a small grass plot, and here and there a small flowerbed. Roses, gillyflowers, and rosemary filled the still air with a mild, sun-warm fragrance.

Hidden by the elder, Berthold sat patiently on his wall, looking absently at the peaceful garden, the vegetables and flowers, the young trees and their motionless shadows, breathing the sun-drenched fragrance of the flowers and the familiar garden smells, which reminded him faintly of his home and early childhood. A weariness came over him and turned to sadness in his heart. There he sat, alone and excluded on his wall, an unbidden onlooker, while inside, his friend Johannes and other happy young people were enjoying themselves.

Time passed; he thought of going away, for he was beginning to feel ashamed of this dismal and inglorious spying. But the voices grew louder; he heard movement in the summerhouse, and then the other student came out with a girl. Her face seemed familiar and a moment later he recognized her as one of Agnes's friends. He was surprised and horrified to see her there, for he knew that

Johannes was an experienced lover and that, left alone with a girl, he would not content himself with sweet innocent words. Hardly able to breathe, Berthold waited.

He had waited only a few moments when his friend came out, and beside him, blushing and frightened, a slender girl with blond hair. When she turned to one side, he saw her face and recognized Agnes. His heart stood still; he felt as if it were being snatched out of his breast.

Pale and on the brink of unconsciousness, he nevertheless managed to keep himself in hand; making sure that he was well hidden, he looked down with burning eyes. He saw Johannes with his long eyelashes and his delicately smiling, girlish lips. Silent and with downcast eyes, Agnes was walking beside him. He saw Johannes's graceful movements as he turned toward her; he saw Johannes looking with a courtly, self-assured smile into her delicate, troubled face, and saw him speak to her, softly and cajolingly. And little mind as Berthold had for metaphors, he could not help thinking of the serpent, the tempter in the garden.

Without a sound, Berthold slipped down the wall on the outside and hid behind a damaged old boat that had been drawn up on the riverbank. He heard the flow of the water and the shouts of the bargemen, he saw lizards in the grass and wriggling little wood lice at play on the rotting floor of the boat, but all this was unreal, passing over him like a dream. The river flowed by, and with it flowed Berthold's past, a shadowy dream, washed away by gliding, indifferent waves, reduced to nothing and not worth thinking about. His decision had been made, and nothing else was real or alive.

Time passed, perhaps an hour, perhaps much less. Then the garden gate opened. Johannes's comrade came out, looked around, and went away. Berthold lay in wait. A little later the gate opened again and two girls came out. First they looked anxious; then, smiling with relief, they started back to town together. Berthold watched them go and followed Agnes's slender shape with his eyes. When the two of them were gone, he looked around. There was no one to be seen.

Again the gate opened, and Johannes came out. He closed the door, locked it, and put the key in his pocket. At that moment Berthold took a long leap and fell on him. Before Johannes could cry out, Berthold clutched his throat in both hands. He threw him to the ground, looked into his face, and tightened his grip. He saw him turn white, then red, saw his eyes bulge, saw the old smile on his lips freeze into an idiotic grimace. Desperately Johannes thrashed about him, but with unflinching hands Berthold held him fast. He did not utter a single word, nor did he strike Johannes or make any unnecessary movement. He merely tensed his fingers around the quivering, swelling throat, and waited for the end.

Then he looked around and wondered what to do with the body. The Rhine, he thought, but there it would be discovered too soon. And so he carried it to the old boat and shoved it underneath. Then he went home.

His state of mind was very different from when as a child he thought he had killed his playmate. This was a real murder with malice aforethought, and he felt no remorse. True, he regretted bitterly that it had to be his only friend. But since everything that had thus far been his life was shattered, he was almost glad that he had destroyed it so radically and that he was leaving no loose ends behind him. His friend had proved false, his love had been false and ridiculous, his calling had been a mistake, and now with his own hands he had strangled them all and put them behind him. Now he must try to live and to find a new career; perhaps it would be the right one next time.

But first of all he would have to save his skin. Well, he knew what awaited him if he were caught. He knew that once his crime was discovered he would have only enemies and death was certain. Johannes himself in his stories had often described arrests, trials, and ignominious executions with all their ghastly details. At the first moment, when he was still holding his dead friend in his arms and his mind was still full of the fair Agnes and the scene in the garden, he had thought of letting things take their course, of waiting to be arrested, of denying nothing. Better to die than to live the life of a fugitive, burdened with such memories. Now that everyone and everything had deceived and forsaken him, life no longer seemed worth all the struggle and sacrifice. But once he had left the corpse and started for town, life appeared to him on all sides with its old familiar face and such thoughts were forgotten. If the beadles were already after him and escape was no longer possible, he would defend his life with his last strength.

The cool courage of desperation made him cautious and circumspect. In case his quickly conceived plan should fail, he was determined to make his enemy feel his strength and to sell his life dearly. The thought calmed him, and he did what had to be done with cool deliberation.

It was not yet evening when he left the city at a slow, deliberate pace. He still had his black coat on, but under it he was dressed in peasant buckram, and he had provided himself with two talers. A brisk evening wind was blowing. When the bells began to ring in Cologne and Berthold looked back for a moment, he saw the city's towers gray and ghostlike in the evening mist. He had long since wrapped his black coat around a good-sized stone and thrown it into the river. He was bound for Westphalia, where he hoped to find a recruiting sergeant and to disappear in the shadow of the banners, in the turmoil of the great war.

Here, where Berthold starts on his way to the adventures of the Thirty Years' War, the manuscript breaks off.

FRIENDS

Friends

THE low-ceilinged tavern was full of smoke, beer fumes, dust, and noise. A few juniors were swinging sabers at each other, setting up momentary whirls in the dense tobacco smoke, a drunk was sitting on the floor, gibbering a senseless song, and some older students were playing dice at the end of the long table.

Hans Calwer motioned to his friend Erwin Mühletal and went to the door.

"Hey!" one of the dice players cried out. "Leaving so soon?"

Hans nodded but didn't stop. Mühletal followed him out. They descended the steep old wooden stairs and left the building, which by then was almost entirely silent. The wide, deserted market square received them with blue starlight and the cold air of a winter night. Breathing deeply and opening his coat, which he had just buttoned, Hans started for home. His friend followed without a word; he almost always walked Calwer home at night. But at the second intersection Erwin stopped. "I'm going to bed," he said. "Good night."

"Good night," said Hans curtly, and continued on his way. But after a few steps he turned around and called out to his friend.

"Erwin!"

"Yes?"

"Wait. I'll walk a way with you."

"All right. But I'm going to bed, I'm half asleep already."

Hans walked back and took Erwin's arm. But instead of heading for Erwin's room, he led him down to the river and across the old bridge to the long avenue of plane trees. Erwin offered no opposition. Finally he asked, "Well, what's up? I'm really tired."

"Are you? So am I. But not in the same way."

"All right. What is it?"

"To make a long story short, this is my last Wednesday at the tavern."

"You're out of your mind."

"No, *you're* out of your mind if that stuff still amuses you. Bellowing songs, guzzling beer because that was the thing to do, listening to idiotic speeches, letting twenty simpletons grin at you and slap you on the back—no, I've had enough and I'm through. Like everybody else, I was in a state of intoxication when I joined. But I'm leaving with a clear head and for good reasons. I'm getting out tomorrow."

"Yes, but . . ."

"I've made up my mind, and that's that. I haven't told anyone else. You're the only one it concerns at all. I wasn't asking your advice."

"Then I won't give it to you. So you're getting out. There's bound to be a bit of a row."

"Not necessarily."

"Maybe not. Anyway, it's your business. It doesn't really surprise me. You've always complained, and I'll admit that our crowd isn't very exciting. But I assure you, the other fraternities are no better. Or were you thinking of joining a Korps—on your allowance?"

"No. Did you really think I was getting out so as to join something else? If that was the way I felt, I might just as well stay put. Korps or Burschenschaft or Landsmannschaft—they're all the same. I'm sick of playing the clown to three dozen fraternity brothers. I want to be my own master. That's all."

"That's all, you say. I ought to advise you against it, but with you I know better. If you regret it in three weeks . . ."

"You really must be sleepy. All right, go to bed and forgive me for taking up your precious time with such nonsense. Good night. I'm going to walk some more."

Alarmed and somewhat irritated, Erwin ran after him. "You'll have to admit it's hard to talk to you. Why do you tell me these things if I'm not allowed to say anything?"

"I thought you might be interested."

"Good God, Hans, be reasonable. What's the good of being so touchy between friends?"

"You don't understand me."

"There you go again! Get some sense. You say six words, and the minute I answer, you claim that I don't understand. Now tell me plainly what you were driving at."

"I simply wanted to tell you I was getting out of the fraternity tomorrow."

"And what else?"

"The rest, I believe, is up to you."

Erwin began to see the light.

"Oh," he said with forced calm. "You're getting out tomorrow after taking plenty of time to think it over. And now you think I should run after you without a moment's hesitation. But, you see, I don't find the so-called tyranny of the fraternity so very oppressive, and for the time being I'm perfectly satisfied with some of the men. I'm all for friendship, but I refuse to be your poodle."

"I see. I can only repeat that I'm sorry to have taken up your time. Goodbye."

He walked away slowly, with the nervous, affectedly light step that Erwin knew so well. Erwin looked after

him, meaning at first to call him back. But from moment
to moment that became more difficult.

"Let him go!" he grumbled under his breath. He followed Hans with his eyes until he vanished in the darkness and the bluish snow-light. Then he turned around
and slowly walked the whole length of the avenue,
climbed the steps to the bridge, and headed for his room.
He was sorry for what had happened and all his thoughts
were with his old friend. But at the same time he remembered that in the last few weeks Hans had become
steadily more arrogant, more domineering, and harder to
please. And now he wanted with two words to make him
take an important step, just as in their school days he had
drawn him into his escapades without so much as a by-
your-leave. No, this was too much. He had been right in
letting Hans go. Maybe he'd be better off without Hans.
Throughout their friendship, it now seemed to him, he
had been the tolerated inferior who just tagged along; his
fraternity brothers had teased him about it often enough.

He was walking faster now, impelled by a spurious ela-
tion; he felt courageous and resolute. He quickly opened
the outside door, climbed the stairs to his room, and went
to bed without putting on the light. Surrounded by a gar-
land of blue stars, the steeple of the Stiftskirche looked in
through the window. The dying embers in the stove
glowed faintly. Erwin couldn't sleep.

Angrily he sought out memory after memory that fitted
his bitter mood. He summoned up an advocate inside him
to prove that he was right and Hans was wrong. The
advocate had assembled copious material. Sometimes he
resorted to unfair methods, bringing up nicknames and
terms of abuse that the fraternity brothers had coined for
Hans, or repeating arguments which Erwin had used in
past moments of indignation and which he had always
been ashamed of later on. Even now he felt rather
ashamed and occasionally cut the advocate short when he

became too acrimonious. But come to think of it, what was the good of forbearance now, why should he weigh his words? Overcome by bitterness, he refashioned his picture of their friendship, until nothing remained of it but a humiliating servitude.

He was amazed at the flood of memories that rose up in support of this view. There were days when he had come to Hans with serious worries and when, instead of taking him seriously, Hans had merely poured out wine or dragged him off to a dance. On other occasions, when he had been happy and full of alluring plans, Hans, with a glance or a few words, had made him feel ashamed of his good cheer. Once Hans had gone so far as to speak in positively insulting terms of the girl Erwin was in love with at the time. And actually it was Hans who had talked him into joining the fraternity in the first place; he had joined only to please him. All in all, he'd have preferred the Burschenschaft.

Erwin found no peace. More and more buried memories, reaching back to the remote twilight of their school years, kept rising to the surface. Always, in all their escapades, he had been the patient, long-suffering dolt. Whenever they quarreled, he had always been the one to apologize or to pretend to have forgotten all about it. And why had he done all that? What was there about this Hans Calwer that he should have kept running after him? Oh yes, a certain wit, a certain assurance in his manner, no doubt of that; he could be clever, and he knew what he wanted. But, on the other hand, he was dreadfully conceited; he was always doing things for effect, he looked down on everybody, forgot appointments and promises, but flew into a rage if anyone else failed to keep a promise to the letter. Oh well, that could pass, Hans had always been rather touchy, but his arrogance, his self-assurance, his eternal superciliousness, as though nothing were good enough for him—that was unforgivable.

One of these silly memories kept plaguing him. They had been thirteen or fourteen at the time. Every summer they had filched plums from a tree belonging to Erwin's neighbor. As usual, Erwin kept his eye on the tree and inspected it now and then. One afternoon he had gone to Hans and said with a joyful, mysterious air, "Hey, they're ripe." "What?" Hans had asked, with a look implying that he didn't know what Erwin was talking about and that his thoughts were busy with something entirely different. When Erwin, astonished and laughing, reminded him of the plums, he had said with an air of condescending commiseration, "Plums? Oh, you want me to steal plums? No, thank you."

Who did he take himself for? Anything to make himself interesting! That was the story of the plums, and it had been just the same with all their enthusiasms: gymnastics, declamation, girls, bicycling, and so on. From one day to the next, an occupation that had been taken for granted was disposed of with a shrug of the shoulders and a look of: What are you talking about? And now suddenly walking out of the fraternity. Erwin had wanted to join the Burschenschaft. Oh no, Hans wouldn't hear of it, and Erwin had given in. Hans and Hans alone had decided which fraternity to join, but he didn't say a word about that now. Sometimes of course Erwin couldn't help agreeing with Hans's jibes and complaints about fraternity life. But once you had joined, there was no excuse for breaking your word and walking out simply because you were bored. He in any case meant to do no such thing, and certainly not just to please Hans.

The hours sounded from the belfry, the fire in the stove had gone out. Little by little, Erwin calmed down, his memories blurred and faded, his arguments and recriminations died away, the stern advocate fell silent. But he still couldn't get to sleep. He was dejected. Why should he feel dejected? He need only have consulted his heart, which was more loyal than his mind. Undeterred by the angry accusations or weary silence of his mind, his heart was still beating sadly for his friend, who had walked away from him under the plane trees, in the pale moonlight.

Meanwhile, Hans walked through the park along the riverbank. As he strode from avenue to avenue, his pace steadied. From time to time, he stopped and looked attentively at the dark river and the sleeping town. He was no longer thinking of Erwin. He was mulling over what he would do next day, what he should say, and what attitude to take. He shrank from explaining his resignation, because his reasons were of such a nature that he could not state them and could not expose himself to counterarguments and attempts to dissuade him. No, he wouldn't try to justify himself. That was the only way—he would just have to let the wolves howl. Above all, no arguments, no discussion of matters that concerned no one but himself with men who simply didn't understand him. Word for word, he pondered what he would say. Of course he was well aware that he would say something entirely different next day, but the more thoroughly he explored the situation in advance, the better able he would be to keep calm. And that was the main thing: to keep calm, to ignore misunderstandings, to put up with reproaches, but above all to avoid arguments and not to play the part of a misunderstood victim, much less that of an accuser, a know-it-all, or a reformer.

Hans tried to visualize the faces of the Head and of the other fraternity brothers, especially those he disliked, who, he feared, might provoke him and ruffle his calm. He saw their looks of surprise and displeasure; saw them take on the countenances of the judge, the offended friend, the benevolent mentor; saw their expressions of coldness, disapproval, incomprehension, almost of hatred.

In the end he smiled as though the whole scene were

already behind him. With disbelief and a kind of curiosity, he recalled the day when he had joined the fraternity and that whole amazing first term. Despite his high hopes, he had arrived at the university with a fairly cool head. But then came that strange, intoxicating week during which older students had been friendly to him, drawn him into conversation, and listened to him with interest. They found him alert and clever and told him so; they praised his social grace, which he had always doubted, and his originality. And in his intoxication he had let himself be deluded. It seemed to him that he had come from alien solitude to like-minded companionship, to a place and a society where he could feel at home, and that he was not cut out to be such a solitary freak as he had always thought. Here the social life he had often missed, the desperately longed-for community in which he might lose himself, seemed near, possible, attainable, almost self-evident. This lasted for a time. He was happy, he felt saved, he was grateful and open to all, had a warm greeting for everyone, found everyone charming, took a whimsical pleasure in learning the rites of the tavern, and was even able to join with genuine feeling in some of their idiotic songs. Yet it didn't last so very long. He soon noticed how few of them were aware of the idiocy, how stereotyped and conventional the witty speeches and the friendly, easygoing manners of his fraternity brothers were. Soon he was unable to take them quite seriously when they held forth about the dignity and sanctity of the fraternity, its name, its colors, its banners, and its weapons, and soon he found himself looking with malignant curiosity on the elderly philistines who on visits to the university town would drop in on their "young fraternity brothers," tank up on beer, and with antique gestures join in the youthful merriment, which was still the same as in their own day. He heard what his comrades thought about their studies, about the university in general, about their future positions and careers. He saw what they read, how they judged their professors, and occasionally their opinion of him came to his ears. Then he knew that everything was the same as before, the same as everywhere else. He knew that he fitted into this community no better than into any other.

It had taken from then until today for his decision to mature. If not for Erwin, it would have gone more quickly. Erwin had held him back, partly with his affectionate ways, and partly because he felt responsible to Erwin for having drawn him into the fraternity. Now he would see how Erwin reacted. If he felt happier in the fraternity, Hans had no right to drag him into a different life. He had been irritable and unfriendly; this evening again he had been short with him. But why did Erwin put up with it?

Erwin was no mediocrity, but he was weak and unsure of himself. Hans looked back to the beginning of their friendship, when after prolonged bashful advances Erwin had finally won him over. Since then Hans had taken the initiative in everything: games, exploits, fashions, sports, reading. Erwin had welcomed his friend's weirdest ideas and wildest projects with admiration and understanding, and had never left him alone. But Erwin himself, it seemed to Hans, had done or thought very little. Erwin had almost always understood him, always admired him, and fallen in with everything. But their life together had not been an organic fusion of two individual lives; rather, Erwin had simply led his friend's life. It now occurred to Hans, and the thought frightened him, that in their long friendship he himself had not, as he had always thought, been the knowing, perceptive party. On the contrary, Erwin knew him better than anyone else had ever known him, but he knew Erwin very little. Erwin had always been his mirror, his imitator. Perhaps in all the hours when he was not with Hans, he had led an entirely differ-

ent life. How well he had gotten along with certain of
their schoolmates and now with certain fraternity
brothers with whom Hans had formed no relationship at
all, not even one of mutual aversion! It was sad. Could it
be that in reality he had had no friend at all, possessed no
share in someone else's life? He had had a companion, a
listener, a yes-man, a henchman, and no more!

He recalled the last words Erwin had spoken on this
wretched evening: "I refuse to be your poodle." So Erwin
himself had sensed the nature of their relationship; he
had played the poodle now and then because he admired
Hans and liked him. Undoubtedly he had long been aware
of this state of affairs and occasionally rebelled, but never
a word of all this to Hans. Unbeknownst to his friend, he
had led a second, very different life of his own, in which
his friend played no part.

Depressed by these thoughts, which wounded his pride
and made him feel impoverished, Hans tried to put them
aside. He needed fortitude and a cool head for the next
day; this was no time to worry about Erwin. And yet it
now dawned on him for the first time that in his present
situation only one thing really mattered to him: Would
Erwin follow him out of the fraternity or let him down?
The rest was a mere formality, the outward consummation of a process he had inwardly completed long ago.
Only because of Erwin did it become a venture and a test
of strength. If Erwin stayed behind, if Erwin gave him up,
Hans had lost the battle; then in his life and person he
would indeed be inferior to the others; then he could
never again hope to attach another human being to himself and hold him fast. And if that was so, this was a bad
time for him, much worse than anything that had gone
before.

Once again, as on a number of past occasions, he was
seized with helpless rage at all the imposture in the world

and at himself for having let himself be taken in by it time and time again, despite his better knowledge—most recently by the university and especially by student life. The university was an antiquated, badly organized school; it gave the student what appeared to be almost unlimited freedom, only to enslave him all the more completely in the end with a mechanical, cut-and-dried system of examinations, while doing nothing to protect him against injustices ranging from benevolent patronage to bribery. But what really plagued him was student life, the gradation of the fraternities according to origins and wealth, the speeches that made you think of flag-raising ceremonies and middle-class choral societies, the oaths of allegiance to the colors, the threadbare, utterly obsolete Old Heidelberg romanticism, the cult of the free-and-equal student side by side with worship of the razor-edged trouser crease. To think that all this continued to exist, and that he himself had fallen into so blatant a trap!

Hans remembered a student who had sat beside him now and then in a course in the history of Oriental religions. He wore a thick ancestral loden coat, heavy peasant boots, patched trousers, and a rough, knitted muffler—a son of peasants and a theology student no doubt. For his fashionable fellow students with their caps and ribbons, their galoshes and fine overcoats, their gold pince-nez and elegant thin canes, for these strangers from another world, he always had a kindly, almost admiring, yet somehow superior smile. He cut a rather comical figure, which usually struck Hans as pathetically touching, but at times he found the man impressive. Now he reflected that this nobody was closer to him than all his so-called comrades, and he envied him a little for the calm contentment with which he wore his isolation and his crude high boots. This was a man who like himself was all alone, yet he seemed to be at peace, impervious to the

humiliating need to resemble his fellows, if only in appearance.

With a sense of relief, Hans Calwer signed for the
small package brought him by the fraternity attendant,
which contained a laconic last letter from the fraternity
secretary, his song book, and a few of his belongings that
he had left at the tavern. The attendant was very stiff and
at first had even been unwilling to accept a tip. True, he
had been expressly forbidden to. Nevertheless, when
Hans offered him a taler, he took it, thanked him effu-
sively, and said amiably, "You shouldn't have done that,
Herr Calwer."

"What?" Hans asked. "Given you a taler?"

"No, you shouldn't have resigned. That's always a bad
thing to do. Well, I wish you luck, Herr Calwer."

All very unpleasant; Hans was glad to have it over
with. He had already given two of his three caps away.
The third he put in his traveling bag along with a ribbon
and a few photographs of fraternity brothers. Now he
deposited the song book with its tricolored escutcheon in
the same place and closed the bag. He was amazed at how
quickly it had gone. His appearance before the assembly
had been rather stormy, he had had to swallow certain
aspersions on his honor and character, but now it was all
over.

He glanced toward the door. What had plagued him the
most was his idling fraternity brothers' way of dropping in
at all hours, criticizing his pictures, littering the desk and
floor with cigarette ash, wasting his time and disturbing
his peace of mind, without bringing anything in return,
and refusing to take him seriously when he said he
wanted to work and to be alone. One morning, when Hans
was out, one of them had actually settled down at his desk
and taken a manuscript out of the drawer. It was his first

essay of any length and was titled rather pretentiously "Paraphrases on the Law of the Conservation of Energy." When word of it got around, Hans's comrades accused him of unpardonably excessive zeal, and it had cost him no end of lies and protestations to retrieve himself. Now they would leave him alone, he wouldn't have to lie any more. He was ashamed of those loathsome moments when he had held his breath behind his locked door while a comrade knocked, or when, laughing and concealing his heartache, he had listened to his fraternity brothers joking in their tavern jargon about matters that he took very seriously. That was all over now. Now he meant to bask in peace and freedom and go on working on his paraphrases. He would also rent a piano again. He had had a piano during his first month, but had returned it because it attracted visitors and because one of the brothers had come around almost every day and played waltzes. Now he hoped to enjoy quiet, pleasant evenings in the lamplight, with good books and good music. He would start practicing again to make up for the lost months. Then he remembered a neglected duty. The professor of Oriental languages had not yet heard of his resignation. Hans had met him through the fraternity, of which in his student days the old gentleman had been a member and co-founder. He called on him that same day.

The house was unpretentious, situated in a quiet suburb. Its small, comfortable rooms, full of books and old pictures, breathed the snug, withdrawn, yet not inhospitable life of good, kindly people.

The professor received Hans amid books and papers in a large study made by breaking down a wall between two rooms. "Good afternoon, Herr Calwer. What brings you? I'm receiving you here because I can't spare much time from my work. But since you've come at an unusual hour, I presume you have some special reason."

"Indeed I have. I'm sorry to have disturbed you, but now that I'm here, I hope you'll allow me to say a few words."

At the professor's bidding he sat down and told him his story.

"I don't know how you feel about fraternities, Herr Professor, or whether you find my reasons acceptable. In any case, nothing can be done, I've already resigned."

The frail, slender professor smiled.

"My good friend, what can I say? If you've done what you had to do, then it's all for the best. True, I take a different view of fraternity life. Our students have a great deal of freedom. To me it seems a good thing that you should subject your freedom to laws in these organizations, that in play, as it were, you should set up a kind of society or state to which the individual subordinates himself. Such a state, I believe, has its value, especially for those of you who are unsociable by nature. It provides you with a pleasant way of adapting yourselves to what everyone must learn later on, often at the cost of bitter sacrifices: to live with others, to belong to a community, to serve others, and yet to maintain his independence. Everyone must learn that sooner or later, and in my experience this sort of preparatory school makes it appreciably easier. I hope you will find other ways of accomplishing the same thing and that you won't be in too much of a hurry to immure yourself in the solitude of the scholar or artist. When you need such solitude, it will come by itself, there's no need to invite it. Your decision strikes me offhand as a defensive reaction to the disappointment that all social life is bound to provoke. I have the impression that you're slightly neurasthenic, and that makes your reaction doubly understandable. It's not for me to say any more."

A silence followed. Hans seemed embarrassed and not

fully satisfied. The professor looked at him kindly out of
his somewhat tired gray eyes.

"Surely," he said with a smile, "you didn't imagine that
your decision would seriously change my opinion of you
or lessen my regard for you? —Good. I'm glad you know
me well enough for that."

Hans stood up and thanked the professor warmly.
Then he blushed a little and said, "Just one more question, Herr Professor. It's my main reason for coming.
Must I stop seeing you or cut down on my visits to you? I
don't know what to think. I'm not pleading, only asking
for a hint."

The professor gave him his hand.

"There's my hint. Come when you like. Except on Monday evenings; true, Monday is open house, but that's
when the fraternity brothers come. Have I answered your
question?"

"Yes, and many thanks. I'm so glad you're not angry.
Goodbye, Herr Professor."

Hans left the house, went down the front steps, and
crossed the snow-covered garden to the street. The inter-
view had turned out pretty much as he had expected, yet
he was grateful for the professor's friendliness. If this
house had been closed to him, he would have lost his last
tie to the town, which he was unable to leave. From his
first visit on, the professor and his wife, for whom he felt
an almost loving veneration, had struck him as kindred
spirits. Both of them, he felt, were the kind of people who
took things hard and ought normally to have been unhappy. Yet he saw that they were not, though it was plain
that the professor's wife suffered from her childlessness.
These people, it seemed to him, had achieved something
which he too might hope to achieve: a victory over themselves and the world, and with it a warmth and depth of
feeling, such as one finds in invalids who have tran-

scended all but their bodily illness and whose endangered souls have fought their way through suffering to a purified, beautiful life. The suffering that draws others down has done them good.

Hans reflected with satisfaction that it was time for the evening pint at the Crown and that he didn't have to go. He went home, shoveled a bit of coal into the stove, strode back and forth humming softly, and looked out at the gathering darkness. He was easy in his mind; it seemed to him that good times lay ahead, modest hard work toward worthy ends, the frugal contentment of a scholarly life, in which personal existence runs along almost unnoticed, since passion and struggle and the heart's unrest have been relegated to the unearthly realm of speculation. Since he was obviously not meant for student life, he would study, not in order to pass some examination and attain to some post, but in order to enhance his strength and his yearnings by measuring them against great preoccupations.

He broke off his tune, lit the lamp, and sat down with his head in his hands, over a much-read volume of Schopenhauer, full of pencil marks and comments. He began with two sentences that he had already underlined twice: "This strange capacity for contenting oneself with words is more to blame than anything else for the perpetuation of errors. Leaning on words taken over from their predecessors, men have cheerfully overlooked obscurities and problems, which thus disregarded have propagated themselves down through the centuries from book to book, so that a thinker, especially if he is young, is driven to wonder whether he alone is incapable of understanding them, or whether he is indeed confronting something incomprehensible."

Like most highly talented individuals, Hans was forgetful. A new state, a new set of ideas could so take hold of him for a time that he utterly forgot everyday concerns which only a short while before had been living and present. This lasted until he had fully mastered and assimilated his new interest. Then his carefully cultivated memory of his life as a whole came back to him and all manner of sharp, clear images forced themselves, sometimes painfully, on his attention. At such times he suffered the bitter torment of all self-observers who are not creative artists.

He had quite forgotten Erwin. He had no need of him for the moment; content with his regained peace and freedom, he thought neither of the past nor of the future, but merely satisfied his longing—which in the last few months had become a craving—for solitude, reading, and work. He basked in the feeling that the days of noise and too many comrades had vanished almost without a trace.

With Erwin it was different. He had avoided a meeting with Hans and listened with stubborn impassivity to the news of his resignation and to the angry or regretful comments of his fraternity brothers. Because he was known to be the deserter's friend, he was subjected, during the first two days, to remarks that made him angrier than ever at Hans and more determined not to make up with him. Yet for all his determination, every unjust or malicious word about his friend galled him. Since he had no desire to suffer unnecessarily for his ungrateful friend, he instinctively avoided the solitude that would have made him think, and spent the whole day with his comrades, talking and drinking himself into a state of idiotic levity.

But that was no help. He was unable to banish his irksome friend from his heart. His artificial euphoria was followed by deep dejection, compounded of grief for his lost friend and dissatisfaction with himself. He felt ashamed of his cowardice and of his disingenuous efforts to forget Hans. One morning, ten days after Hans's resignation from the fraternity, Erwin went for a stroll with a group of his fraternity brothers. It was a sunny winter morning, the sky was blue, the air dry and crisp. The narrow streets of the old town were bright with the colored caps of students, and the hard wintry ground resounded with the hoofbeats of horses bearing sprucely clad riders.

Erwin and his comrades, ten or twelve of them all in resplendent brick-red caps, sauntered through the main streets, saluting with meticulous dignity when they passed friends sporting different colors, acknowledging the humble greetings of servants, innkeepers, and shopkeepers with easy condescension, looking in shop windows, stopping at busy street corners, and exchanging loud, uninhibited comments on the girls, women, professors, riders, and horses that passed.

They stopped outside a bookshop to inspect the display of pictures, books, and posters. Suddenly the shop door opened and Hans Calwer came out. All ten or twelve red caps turned scornfully away, or tried with frozen faces and unnaturally raised eyebrows to express non-recognition, rejection, contempt, in short, utter disregard of his existence.

Erwin, who had come close to bumping into Hans, flushed and turned from the showcase in a gesture of flight. Seemingly unruffled, Hans moved off without undue haste; he hadn't noticed Erwin, and the others didn't trouble him in the least. As he went his way, he took pleasure in the thought that the all-too-familiar caps and faces had upset him very little; he could hardly believe that only two weeks ago he had still been one of them.

Erwin was unable to hide his agitation and embarrassment.

"Nothing to get upset about," said his senior brother good-naturedly. Another grumbled, "That arrogant bastard! He wasn't even embarrassed! I felt like swatting him one."

"Rubbish," said the Head appeasingly. "His behavior under the circumstances was perfect. *N'en parlons plus.*"

Erwin stayed with his comrades until the next street crossing. Then he left them with a brief excuse and went home. Up until then it hadn't so much as occurred to him that he might meet Hans on the street at any moment, and in the course of these ten days he actually had not laid eyes on him. He didn't know whether Hans had noticed him, but the ridiculously undignified incident had left him with an uneasy conscience. It was just too silly; his best friend hardly two steps away and he couldn't even bid him good morning. In his first defiant days he had gone so far as to promise his senior brother that he would have no "unofficial dealings" with Hans Calwer. Now it was beyond him how he could have made such a promise, and he would have broken it without a qualm.

But Hans hadn't looked as if he were grieving for a lost friend. His face and gait had been calm and untroubled. Erwin could see that face so clearly: the cool, intelligent eyes; the thin, somewhat arrogant lips; the firm, clean-shaven cheeks; the clear, oversized forehead. That was how he looked in their early school days, when Erwin had admired him so fervently, hardly daring to hope that this noble, self-assured, quietly passionate boy might someday be his friend. Well, Hans had been his friend, and Erwin had let him down.

Yes, he had forcibly repressed his grief over his breach with Hans and deluded himself with spurious merriment. He passed judgment and found himself guilty, forgetting that Hans had often made it very hard for him to go on being his friend, that he himself had often doubted Hans's friendship, that Hans might have come to see him or written to him by now. He also forgot that in his rebellion against playing the poodle he had wanted to break off their unequal relationship. He forgot everything but his loss and his guilt. And as he sat despairing at his small, uncomfortable desk, tears welled from his eyes and fell on his hand, on his yellow gloves and red cap.

In reality it was Hans who had drawn him step by step from the land of childhood into the realm of knowledge and responsibility. But now it seemed to Erwin that his life had been an unbroken joy up to the moment of this loss. He thought of all his follies, of all the things he should have done and hadn't, and he felt tainted and fallen. And much as he exaggerated in this hour of sorrow and weakness, relating everything in some vague way to Hans, there was a certain truth in his feelings. For without wanting to be or quite knowing it, Hans had been his conscience.

Thus Erwin's real sorrow and real sense of guilt coincided with his first attack of the nostalgia for childhood, which occasionally overcomes nearly all young people and which, according to the circumstances, can take on all manner of forms, from common hangover to authentic, absurdly beautiful, absurdly meaningful Weltschmerz. In this hour, the young man's defenseless, unresisting soul mourned his friend, his guilt, his folly, and the lost paradise of childhood; he mourned them all in one, for the cool, discerning reflection, which might have told him that the root of all the evil was his own soft, unstable, overtrustful nature, was absent.

For this very reason, the attack did not last long. Exhausted by tears and despair, he went to bed early and slept long and soundly. Waking the next morning with the blissfully rested feeling of a healthy animal, he tried to revive his memories and spread new shadows around him. But then he was child enough to seek consolation with comrades over a liqueur-seasoned breakfast at one of the pastry shops. Surrounded by fresh faces and gay con-

versation, waited on by a pretty, quick-witted, and loqua-
cious young girl, he leaned back in melancholy contentment, popped diminutive rolls into his mouth, and,
drawing on several liqueur bottles, mixed himself a curious beverage that didn't actually taste good but royally
amused him and his friends, and created a light, pleasant
fog that blotted out his thoughts. That morning his fraternity brothers were all agreed that Mühletal was a jolly
good fellow.

In the afternoon Erwin attended a lecture, during
which he dozed off; then, quite revived by a riding lesson,
he went to the Red Ox, where there was a new waitress to
be courted. He had no luck, for the young lady was surrounded by a swarm of cadets. Nevertheless, he ended his
day contentedly at a café.

This went on for quite some time. He lived very much
like a sick man who, in his lucid hours, sees clearly what
is wrong with him but hides it from himself by forgetful-
ness and the pursuit of pleasant distractions. Though he
can laugh, talk, dance, drink, work, and read, he is unable
to dispel a vague dejection that seldom rises to the level of
consciousness. And intermittently, in sudden flashes, it
becomes clear to him that death has settled in his body
and is secretly at work.

He walked, rode, fenced, drank with his comrades, and
went to the theater, a dashing, healthy young fellow. But
he was not at peace with himself and carried within him a
sickness which, he well knew, was gnawingly present
even in his best hours. On the street he was often taken
with a sudden fear of meeting Hans. And at night, when
he slept after a tiring day, his restless soul walked the
trails of memory, knowing full well that Hans's friendship
was his most precious possession and that it was useless
to deny it or try to forget it.

Once in Erwin's presence a comrade laughingly remarked to the others that many of Erwin's phrases were

borrowed from Hans. Erwin said nothing, but he couldn't bring himself to join in the laughter and soon excused himself. Clearly he was still dependent on Hans, forced to admit that much of his life was unthinkable without him.

In the meantime Hans had attended the Orientalist's lectures, often sitting beside the rustic-looking student. He had watched him closely despite his awkward appearance and taken more and more of a liking to him. He had seen that his neighbor took notes in neat, effortless shorthand, and envied him this skill, which he himself had always been disinclined to acquire.

One day he sat watching him, while at the same time following the lecture. With pleasure he noted the attentiveness and understanding reflected in the man's quietly mobile features. Several times he saw him nod, once he saw him smile. It was a face that aroused not only his respect but his admiration and affection as well, and he decided to make friends with him. After the lecture, Hans followed the loden coat at a distance to see where the young man lived. To his surprise, the rustic student did not stop in any of the old streets, where most of the cheaper student lodgings were situated, but continued on to a modern, well-to-do neighborhood with wide streets bordered by gardens and villas. More curious than ever, Hans reduced the distance between himself and the man in the loden coat, who strode on and on, soon leaving the last villas and garden gates behind him. The imposing, well-kept street gave way to a wagon track leading through gently rolling farmland. The houses became fewer and fewer. The neighborhood was quite unfamiliar to Hans.

Hans followed for a quarter of an hour or more, gaining steadily on the loden coat. When he had almost caught up with him, the other heard his steps and turned

around. He looked at Hans questioningly but serenely out
of his clear, friendly brown eyes. Hans lifted his hat and
bade him good day. The other returned his greeting and
they both stopped.

"Taking a walk?" Hans asked finally.

"I'm going home."

"My goodness, where do you live? Are there any more
houses out here?"

"Not here, but half an hour farther on there's a village,
Blaubachhausen. That's where I live. But you must know
the place?"

"No, I've never been out here before," said Hans. "May I
walk a way with you? My name is Calwer."

"By all means. My name is Heinrich Wirth. I know you
from the Buddhism class."

They went on side by side, and involuntarily Hans
adjusted his gait to his companion's more regular stride.
After a short silence Wirth said, "You used to wear one of
those red caps."

Hans laughed. "Yes," he said. "But that's all over now.
It was a misunderstanding, though it lasted a term and a
half. Anyway, a hat's better in this wintry weather."

Wirth looked at him and nodded. Then he said, almost
shyly, "It may sound funny, but I'm glad."

"Why?"

"Oh, no special reason. But I sometimes had a feeling
that you weren't right for that kind of thing."

"You mean you've been watching me?"

"Not exactly. But I couldn't help seeing you. At first it
bothered me to have you sitting next to me. I thought,
One of those stuck-up fellows you hardly dare to look at.
Some of the students are like that, you know."

"Oh yes, indeed they are."

"Well, then I saw I'd been unfair to you. I saw you'd
come to listen and learn something."

"But so do the others."

"You think so? Not many, I'd say. The only thing most of them care about is passing their examinations."

"But even for that they've got to learn something."

"Yes, but not much. It's the attendance record that counts. What you can learn in a course on Buddhism doesn't come up in the examination."

"That's true. But on the other hand—begging your pardon—the purpose of the universities isn't spiritual uplift. If you're interested in Buddha from a religious rather than a scholarly point of view, you can get what you need from a small paperbound volume."

"Yes, of course. But that's not what I was getting at. Incidentally, I'm not a Buddhist, as you may have supposed, though I am fond of the Indian thinkers. —Look, do you know Schopenhauer?"

"Pretty well, I think."

"Good. Then I can explain myself briefly. At one time I was almost a Buddhist, or at least what I took to be a Buddhist. Schopenhauer helped me out of it."

"I don't quite understand."

"Well, the Indians find salvation in knowledge. Their whole ethic is simply an exhortation to gain knowledge. That appealed to me. But then I was in a quandary. Could it be, I wondered, that knowledge isn't the right way, or was it only that I hadn't acquired enough knowledge? That could have gone on and on, and it would have broken me. But then I went back to Schopenhauer. His ultimate insight, after all, is that cognition is not the highest activity and consequently that cognition alone cannot lead to the goal."

"What goal?"

"There you're asking a good deal."

"Right you are. We'll come back to it another time. But I don't quite see why that helped you. How could you know whether Schopenhauer was right or the Indians?

Two opposing doctrines. You were equally free to choose either one."

"No. The Indians went a long way in their pursuit of knowledge, but they had no theory of knowledge. It took Kant to supply that. And now we can't get along without one."

"That's true."

"Good. And Schopenhauer builds entirely on Kant. So I was bound to have confidence in him, just as an aeronaut has more confidence in Count Zeppelin than in the tailor of Ulm, simply because real progress has been made since then. So you see, the scales were not quite evenly balanced. Still, the crux of the matter was elsewhere. Let's say I was confronted by two opposing truths. One of these truths I could grasp only with my reason; as far as my reason was concerned, it was perfect. But the other raised an echo inside me; I was able to understand it in my whole being, not only with my mind."

"I see. Besides, there's no point in arguing about it. So since then you've been satisfied with Schopenhauer?"

Heinrich Wirth stopped in his tracks.

"Good God!" he exploded, though without losing his smile. "Satisfied with Schopenhauer! How can you say such a thing? Of course, I'm grateful to the guide who saved me from losing myself in detours. But that won't stop me from making further inquiries. My goodness! How can a man be satisfied with one philosopher? That would be the end."

"But not the goal?"

"No, certainly not."

They looked at one another with mutual pleasure. They didn't resume their philosophical discussion, for each of them felt that the other was concerned with something more than words and that they would have to know each other better before they could discuss such matters any further. Hans felt that he had unexpectedly found a

friend, but he could not tell whether the other took him
seriously in return; indeed, he vaguely suspected that for
all his seeming openheartedness Wirth was much too
sure of himself, too set in his ways, to give himself easily
in friendship.

It was the first time he had felt such respect for a man
scarcely older than himself and felt himself to be on the
receiving end without rebelling.

Beyond the black, snow-spotted fields the light-colored
roofs of a hamlet could be seen amid bare fruit trees. The
lowing of cows and the rhythmic sound of threshing came
to them across the silent deserted fields.

"That's Blaubachhausen," said Wirth. Hans thought he
would take his leave and turn back. He felt sure that his
new friend wouldn't want him to see his no doubt
wretched lodgings, or else that this village was his home
and he lived with his father and mother.

"Well, here you are," he said. "I'll leave you now and try
to get back in time for lunch."

"Don't do anything of the kind," said Wirth affably.
"Come and see where I live. You'll see that I've got a very
nice place and that I'm not a tramp. You can eat in the
village. Or be my guest if you can make do with milk."

The invitation came so naturally that Hans gladly accepted. They made their way to the village by a sunken
lane bordered by bushes. Outside the first house there was
a watering trough. A boy was waiting for his cow to drink
her fill. The cow turned her head and looked at the new
arrivals out of big, beautiful eyes. The boy ran up to them
and held out his hand to Wirth. Otherwise the wintry
street was deserted and still. Coming from the city's
bustling streets and lecture halls, Hans was amazed to
find himself in this lost village, and he was also amazed at
his companion, who seemed at home in both places and
who took this long, lonely walk to town and back once or
perhaps even twice a day.

"You have a long way to go," he said.

"An hour. It seems a lot less when you're used to it."

"You live all alone out here?"

"Not at all. I live with a family of peasants and I know half the village."

"I mean, you probably don't get many visitors—students, friends . . ."

"You're the first this winter. But during the summer term there was one fellow who came out fairly often. A theology student. He wanted to read Plato with me. We actually did start in. We kept it up for three or four weeks, but then his visits fell off. It was too far, and he had other friends in town. He lost interest. Now he's gone to Göttingen for the winter term."

He spoke calmly, almost with indifference, and Hans had the feeling that other men with their friendship and breaches of friendship could no longer affect this hermit very deeply.

"Are you studying theology too?" he asked.

"No, philology. Apart from the Buddhism class, I'm taking courses in Greek cultural history and Old High German. Next year, I hope, there'll be a Sanskrit seminar. Otherwise I work by myself. I spend three afternoons a week at the library."

They came to the farmhouse where Wirth lived, a tidy structure of white stucco and red-painted timbers separated from the street by a small orchard. Chickens were running about; on the far side of the yard, grain was being threshed on a large threshing floor. Wirth led his visitor into the house and up a narrow staircase smelling of hay and dried fruit. In the half-darkness of the windowless hallway he opened a door and called Hans's attention to the old-fashioned raised threshold, for fear that he might trip.

"Come in," said Wirth. "This is where I live."

Despite its peasant simplicity, the room was much

larger and more comfortable than Hans's room in town. It
had two broad windows. In a rather dark corner was a
bed, and beside it a small washstand with an enormous
gray and blue earthenware pitcher. Near the windows,
receiving light from both of them, was a large pinewood
desk covered with books and papers and a plain wooden
stool. The outer wall was taken up by three tall bookcases,
full from top to bottom, and by the opposite wall stood a
brownish-yellow tile stove in which a good fire was burning. Otherwise the sole furnishings were a clothes cupboard and a small table, which was bare except for an
earthenware jug full of milk and a wooden dish with a
loaf of bread on it. Wirth brought in a second stool and
bade Hans be seated. "If you care to join me," he said,
"let's eat right away. The cold air makes you hungry. Or
I'll take you over to the inn. Just as you please."

Hans preferred to stay. He was given a blue-and-white-
striped mug without a handle, a plate, and a knife. Wirth
poured milk into his mug and cut him a chunk of bread.
Then he served himself, cutting his bread into long strips,
which he dipped into his milk. When he saw that his
visitor was unaccustomed to this way of eating, he left the
room and came back with a spoon for him.

They ate in silence, Hans not without embarrassment.
When he had finished and declined another helping,
Wirth went to the cupboard and brought out a magnificent pear. "Here's something more for you; I wouldn't
want you to be hungry. Take it, I have a whole basketful.
They're from my mother, she's always sending me good
things."

Calwer couldn't get over his amazement. He could have
sworn that Wirth was a poor devil, studying theology on a
scholarship. Not at all. He was engaged in studies that
held out little promise of a profitable career, and his
imposing library made it clear that he could not be poor. It
wasn't one of those pitiful collections, inherited or made

up of random gifts, that people drag from place to place but make no use of. No, these were good books in good simple bindings, some of them new and all evidently acquired within the space of a few years. One bookcase was devoted to the literature of all nations and ages, from the ancients down to Hebbel and even Ibsen; one shelf was full of unbound volumes, including several of Tolstoy, a good number of pamphlets and Reclam paperbound books. The other bookcases contained scholarly works in various fields.

"What a lot of books you have!" Hans cried out in admiration. "Shakespeare! And Emerson! And there's Rohde's *Psyche!* Why, it's a real treasure trove."

"I suppose it is. If there's anything you'd care to read, take it home with you. It would be better if one could live without books, but it can't be done."

After an hour's time, Hans prepared to leave. Wirth advised him to go back a different way, which led through prettier country, and started out with him to keep him from getting lost. As they turned into the main street of the village, Hans had a feeling that he had been there before. And when they came to a modern hotel with a large garden, he suddenly remembered. It had been early in his first term, just after he had joined the fraternity. They had driven out here in landaus and sat in the garden, under the chestnut trees. Already half drunk when they arrived, they had made a good deal of noise. Now he was ashamed. Perhaps on that very day Wirth had been reading Plato with the faithless theology student.

As Hans took his leave, Wirth asked him to come again, and he gladly promised to do so. It occurred to him only later that he hadn't given Wirth his address. But then he was sure to see his new friend at the Orientalist's lectures. All the way home, he thought about Wirth. His curiosity was aroused. Wirth's rustic dress, his living out there with peasants, his noonday meal of bread and milk, his mother who sent him pears—all that was of a piece, but it didn't fit in with his imposing library or with the kind of things he said. Undoubtedly he was older than he looked and rich in experience. His simple, free-and-easy manner of speaking, of making friends, of giving himself in conversation while maintaining a certain reserve, seemed almost worldly in contrast with his appearance and mode of life. But what struck Hans most of all was the clear, serene, self-assured look of his warm, brown, handsome eyes.

What he had said about Schopenhauer and Indian philosophy, though not new, sounded as if it had sprung from his own experience, not like something he had read or learned by heart. And in Hans's recollection, the words he had spoken about his "goal" lingered with the infinitely moving resonance of a bass chord.

What goal? Perhaps the same as his own, though in his case present only as a dark intimation, but in Wirth's clearly perceived and pursued with deliberation. Yet it seemed to Hans that each man has his own goal, that each man's goal is different, and that apparent agreements are bound to be deceptive. Nevertheless, it is possible for two human beings to go a long way together and be friends. And he felt that he desired this man's friendship, that for the first time in his life he was prepared to yield, to subordinate himself to another, to recognize another man's superiority with willingness and gratitude.

Night was falling when he reached the city. Tired and chilled through, he went home and had his landlady make him tea. She told him that a student had been there twice and asked for him. The second time, he had asked her to let him into Hans's room and had waited there for over an hour. He had left no word. She didn't know his name, but from her description Hans knew it had been Erwin.

The next day he met him outside the auditorium. Erwin looked pale, as if he hadn't slept. He was wearing his colors and was in the company of his fraternity brothers.

When he recognized Hans, he averted his face and ostentatiously looked the other way.

Hans thought of going to see him but couldn't make up his mind. He knew Erwin was weak and impressionable, and felt sure that he could reassert his influence if he tried. But would it be good for either of them? Perhaps it would be best for Erwin to forget him little by little. He had plenty of other friends and without Hans he would become more independent. It grieved him not to have a friend any more, and he found it strangely painful to think that one who had become a stranger to him should know him so well and share so many of his memories. But wasn't that preferable to forcibly preserving so one-sided a relationship? And he admitted to himself that he was relieved in a way to be rid of responsibility for his all-too-dependent friend.

He forgot that only two weeks past he had felt quite differently. At that time it was a humiliating defeat that Erwin should prefer the fraternity to his friendship; now the thought left him cold. This was partly because of his momentary satisfaction with life, but far more, more than he himself knew, because of his newborn admiration for Heinrich Wirth and his hope of finding in him a new friend whom he would love in an entirely different way. Erwin had been a playmate; the other, he hoped, would truly share his life and thoughts; he would be a mentor, a guide and a companion.

Meanwhile, Erwin was in a bad way. His comrades couldn't help noticing his uneven, irritable temper, and some of them sensed that Hans was the cause of it. They sometimes told Erwin as much, and one day one of them was indelicate enough to speak of his friendship with Hans as a "love affair" and to ask him if, now that Hans, thank God, was out of the way, he didn't think it was high time he fell in love with a woman, as was usual among healthy young men. Erwin flew into a blind rage and bloodshed was narrowly averted. He flung himself on the other, who was with difficulty torn from his grip. His older comrades could find no other way of calming him than to make the offender apologize. But since the apology was as forced and lacking in conviction as the older comrades' insistence on it, the rift remained unhealed. Now Erwin had an enemy he was obliged to see every day, and what was worse, the condescending pity with which the others seemed to treat him made it impossible for him to behave naturally. Formerly his jolly-good-fellow act had been solely for his own benefit: now he put it on for the others as well, but not very successfully.

It was on the day of the insult that he had tried to see Hans. His failure had left him resentful—why hadn't Hans been in his room?—yet at the same time he found a certain morose satisfaction in the thought that the moment of unappeased pain and anger that would have enabled him to act boldly and so set himself free had gone by. Now he let things take their course, and their course was downhill. In the presence of his comrades, he kept up appearances, making a special effort at fencing class and at riding school. But he could do no more. He felt ill at ease with his comrades, who always seemed to be observing him and going out of their way to spare his feelings. On the other hand, he couldn't bear to be alone for very long and couldn't keep his mind on his studies. He began to spend his days at cafés and taverns—here a few mugs of beer, there a jug of wine or a glass of liqueur—with the result that he went about in a daze. Though never really drunk, he was seldom entirely sober, and in next to no time he had taken on certain of the habits and gestures specific to drinkers, which on occasion seem delightfully droll but in the long run became dismal and disgusting. There can be a kind of beauty in getting drunk now and then because you are happy or angry; it can even restore the soul; but the permanent befuddlement of the toper, who destroys himself slowly, in the easiest, laziest possible way, is always a wretched, loathsome sight.

Christmas vacation brought a salutary interruption. Erwin went home to his family. Feeling ill, he stayed on an extra week and let his mother and sister fuss over him. At first they were horrified at the change in him, but then they were delighted when his repentance over the life he had been leading and the need for shelter and protection inherent in his unstable character expressed themselves in outpourings of tenderness.

He had thought that Hans Calwer would also spend his vacation in his hometown and half expected a reconciliation, or at least a heart-to-heart talk. In this he was disappointed. Calwer, whose parents were dead, had gone on a trip instead. With his morbid lack of initiative, Erwin let it go at that. On his return to the university, he resumed his old life. In his sober moments, it became clear to him that this state of affairs could not go on; at heart he knew he would ultimately give up his red cap and go back to Hans. But in his state of self-pity and weakness, he let himself drift, hoping that the decision that could only come from within would be forced on him from outside. And then came a new folly, which soon became a dangerous servitude.

As is the way with demoralized students, lacking either real work or real friends, he began to look for distraction in run-down bars which, strictly speaking, were out of bounds for him. Here he fell in with a society of seedy students and drunks. Among them, side by side with utter dolts, there were a few gifted men who, in the obscurity of sordid back rooms, played the parts of melancholy revolutionary geniuses. Since all their ingenuity was spent in projecting meaning into their meaningless existences, they could, under favorable circumstances, make an impression of great originality. Their hallmarks were malicious wit, flamboyant phrases, and unvarnished cynicism.

When, soon after Christmas, Erwin first met a group of
these men in a shabby bar in the outskirts, he avidly
welcomed their society. He found them infinitely cleverer
than his fraternity brothers, yet at the same time noticed
that, as a member of a respected fraternity, he enjoyed a
certain esteem despite all their jokes at the expense of the
student organizations.

It goes without saying that he was exploited on this first
occasion. His new companions pronounced him "more or
less acceptable," though still "wet behind the ears," and
did him the honor of letting him pay for their evening's
drinks.

All this didn't amount to much and ordinarily he would
have lost interest after a few evenings. But once he had
shown himself to be a good fellow, willing to pay for an
occasional round of drinks, they took him to the Blue
Hussar, an "amazing café," where, they assured him,
undreamed-of pleasures lay in wait. The splendor, of
course, was imaginary; the place was dark and dingy, a
wretched dive with a ramshackle billiard table and bad
wines, and the waitresses, though accommodating
enough, were by no means as seductive as poor Mühletal
had hoped. Nevertheless, he savored the diabolical quality
of the atmosphere and, like the innocent that he was, took
a certain pleasure in his feelings of guilt over doing something forbidden.

Then on his second visit to the Blue Hussar, he met
Fräulein Elvira, who was the proprietress's daughter and
the guiding spirit of the place. Her beauty and a deplorable lack of principle gave her power over the young men;
they all revolved around her and she ruled them with an
iron hand. When she took a liking to one of them, she sat
on his lap and kissed him, and if he was poor she gave
him free drinks. But when she was out of sorts, she made
it plain even to her favorite that no jokes or liberties were

in order. If one of the customers displeased her, she sent him away, and from then on the house was closed to him, at least for a time. She refused to admit anyone in an advanced state of drunkenness, even if he was a friend. Toward bashful neophytes who had not yet lost their air of innocence, she took a motherly attitude; she wouldn't let them get drunk and prevented the more hardened customers from making fun of them or filching their money. Then sometimes she was sick of it all; she would disappear for the evening or sit in an overstuffed chair reading novels, and no one was allowed to disturb her. Her mother gave in to all her moods and was satisfied if they passed without a storm.

When Erwin Mühletal saw Fräulein Elvira for the first time, she was sitting in her overstuffed sulking chair, leafing nervously and absently through a crudely bound volume of some illustrated weekly, without so much as a glance at the customers and their goings-on. Her lovely soft hair—the careless disarray of her coiffure was only apparent—was arranged so as to half conceal the upper part of her pale, mobile, moody face, and her eyes were curtained by long lashes. Her unoccupied left hand rested on the back of a big gray cat which was staring sleepily out of green slanting eyes.

When their wine was served, Erwin and his companions began to play dice. It was only then that she raised her eyelids and surveyed the newly arrived guests. She looked almost directly at Erwin, who was embarrassed by her unabashed scrutiny. Then she withdrew behind her magazines.

But an hour later, when Erwin felt that he'd had enough and rose to leave, she stood up, showing her slender, supple figure. He bade her good evening, and she nodded to him with an almost imperceptible, yet encouraging smile.

He went away with his head in a whirl, unable to forget

her tender, ironic, promising glance and her supple, lady-like figure. He no longer had the unerring, innocent eye that is drawn only to health and purity, but he was still inexperienced enough to mistake acting for the real thing and to see, perhaps not an angel, but at least an alluringly demonic woman in the catlike Fräulein Elvira.

From then on, whenever he could detach himself from the fraternity, he went to the Blue Hussar, and there, according to Elvira's mood, he would spend a few excitingly happy hours or suffer painful humiliation. His desire for freedom, to which he had sacrificed his only friendship and which in the long run had also found the laws and duties of his fraternity burdensome, now succumbed without resistance to the moods and whims of an imperious coquette who, to make matters worse, held court in a loathsome dive and made no secret of the fact that, though choosy enough about her lovers, she was quite capable of having several successively or simultaneously.

And so Erwin went the way that many a customer of the Blue Hussar had gone before him. On one occasion Fräulein Elvira might make him treat her to champagne; on another she might send him home on the ground that he needed sleep; or she might be invisible for two or three days, and then again she might overwhelm him with goodies and lend him money.

Intermittently, his heart and mind rebelled, giving him desperate days full of self-accusation and resolutions which he knew he would never carry out.

One evening, when he was wandering about unhappily after finding Elvira in one of her bad moods, he passed Hans's place and saw light in his window. He stopped and looked up, full of nostalgia and shame. Hans was sitting at the piano, playing a passage from *Tristan,* and the music echoed through the dark, silent street. For perhaps a quarter of an hour, Erwin walked back and forth listening. When the piano fell silent, he seriously considered going up. Then the light went out in the room and he saw his friend leaving the house in the company of a tall, unfashionably dressed young man. Erwin knew that Hans didn't play *Tristan* for just anyone.

So he had already found a new friend!

Hans sat beside the brown tile stove in Wirth's room in Blaubachhausen, while Wirth paced the floor.

"All right," said Wirth. "I can tell you in a few words. As you must have noticed, I come of a peasant family. But my father was a special kind of peasant. He belonged to a religious sect that's rather widespread in our part of the country, and spent his whole life—or so it seemed to me—searching for the way to God and the right way to live. He was well off, you might almost say rich. He had a large farm and ran it well enough to make it gain rather than lose in value despite his kindliness and generosity. But farming wasn't his main interest. What meant far more to him was what he called the spiritual life. That was what took up most of his time and energy. He went to church regularly, but he didn't set much store by it; he looked for wisdom among the members of his sect, in biblical exegesis and lay preaching. His room was full of books: Bible commentaries, studies of the Gospels, a Church history, a history of the world, and whole piles of religious literature, some of it mystical. He didn't know Böhme and Eckhart, but he read the German theologians, a few of the seventeenth-century pietists, especially Arnold, and some of Swedenborg.

"It was almost heartbreaking to see him trying to find his way through the Bible with a few of his fellow sectarians, always chasing after some light he thought he had glimpsed and always losing himself in a maze. The older he grew, the more convinced he became that his goal was right but that his way of pursuing it had been wrong, that it couldn't be reached without methodical study. I began to share his interests when I was very young, so he placed his hopes in me. He wanted me to study. Then, he thought, pious searching combined with true science would lead me to the goal. He felt sorry about his farm, and my mother even more so, but he made the sacrifice and sent me to school in the city, though as his only son I should have taken over the farm. In the end he died before I even got to the university, and maybe it was just as well that he didn't live to see how I've turned out, that I'm neither a reformer nor a Bible scholar, nor even a good Christian in his sense of the word. In a somewhat different sense I am one, but I don't think he'd have understood.

"After his death the farm was sold. My mother tried to persuade me to go back to farming, but I had already made up my mind, and she resigned herself. She came to live with me in town, but she only stuck it out for a year. Since then she's been living in our village with relatives, and I spend a few weeks with her every year. What grieves her most is that I'm not studying for a career, that she can't look forward to my becoming a pastor or a doctor or a professor someday. But she knows from her experience with my father that when a man is driven by the spirit no pleas or arguments can move him. When I tell her I've given the people here a hand with their harvesting or threshing or wine pressing, she sighs. Ah, if only I were doing all that on our own farm instead of wasting my time with strangers."

He smiled and stopped pacing. Then he sighed a little and said, "It's all very strange. Come to think of it, I'm not so sure I won't die a peasant. One fine day I may just buy a piece of land and learn to plow again. If a man has to have an occupation and if he doesn't happen to be a genius, there's nothing better, after all, than tilling the soil."

"Why do you say that?" Hans cried out.

"Why? Because a peasant sows and harvests his own food, because he's the only man on earth who can live by the labor of his hands, without turning his labor into money day after day and then, by devious ways, turning his money into food and clothing. Also, because his work always has meaning. Almost everything a farmer does is necessary. What other people do is seldom necessary; most of them might just as well be doing something else. No one can live without bread and the fruits of the soil. But most people could live perfectly well without most trades and what they produce, or without books and learning, for that matter."

"I suppose so. But all the same, when the peasant is sick he goes to the doctor, and when his wife needs consolation she goes to the pastor."

"Some do, but not all. In any case, they need the consoler more than the doctor. Healthy peasant stock doesn't get many diseases, and for them there are home remedies. Peasants accept the fact that they're going to die someday. Most of them, I admit, need the pastor or some other adviser. And for that very reason I have no intention of reverting to the peasant before I'm capable of giving advice, at least to myself."

"So that's your goal?"

"Yes. Do you know of another? To find a way of coping with the incomprehensible, to have a consoler within yourself, that's all there is to it. One man is helped by knowledge, another by faith; some need both, and most aren't helped much by either. My father tried in his own way and failed; at least, he never found perfect peace."

"I don't believe anyone does."

"Oh yes, they do. Think of Buddha! Think of Jesus! They achieved what they did by such human means that one can't help thinking it must be within everyone's reach. I'm convinced that a good many people no one ever heard of have achieved the same thing."

"Do you really think so?"

"Certainly. The Christians have their saints and their blessed. And the Buddhists have many Buddhas who achieved Buddhahood, perfection and perfect redemption for themselves. In that, they are equal to the great Buddha; the only difference is that he took the further step of communicating his way of redemption to the world. The same with Jesus. He didn't keep his beatitude and inner perfection to himself, but preached his doctrine and gave his life for it. If he was the perfect man, he must have known what he was doing. Like all the great teachers, he explicitly taught the possible, not the impossible."

"I suppose so. I haven't thought about it very much. One can comfort oneself by attaching all sorts of meanings to life, but that's a delusion."

"My dear Herr Calwer, that won't get us very far. Delusion is a word; you can just as well substitute myth, religion, presentiment, or philosophy for that matter. What is real? You, I, this house, this village? Why? Obviously there's no answer to these riddles, but are they so important? We feel our own selves, our bodies, come into contact with other bodies, and our minds with riddles. The problem isn't to demolish the wall but to find the door. Doubt in the reality of things is a state of mind; you can settle down in it, but you won't if you think. Because thought doesn't stand still, it moves. And once we recognize that there's no solution to a problem, we stop trying to solve it."

"But if we can't explain the world, why should we bother to think?"

"Why? So as to do what's possible. If everybody resigned himself to not thinking, there'd be no Copernicus and no Newton, no Plato and no Kant. Anyway, you're not serious."

"No, not in that sense. I only mean that, of all theories, ethical theories are the most dangerous."

"That's true. But I wasn't talking about theories. I was talking about men who devote their lives to solving problems—in other words, to redeeming mankind. But we're still too far apart. When we get to know each other better, we'll be sure to find an area of understanding."

"I hope so. We really are far apart, or rather, you're far ahead of me. You've already begun to build, while I'm still tearing down and making room. I've learned nothing except to distrust and analyze. I don't even know whether I'll ever be able to do anything else."

"Who knows? Yesterday you played for me. With a few passages you gave me a conception of a great work of art. That's something more than analysis. —But come now, let's go out a while before it gets dark."

They went out into the cold, sunless January afternoon. Over rough, frozen paths, they climbed a hill from which, standing among fine-branching birches, they looked out on two narrow valleys, the nearby town, and distant hills and villages.

When they spoke again, it was about personal matters. Hans told Wirth about his parents, his fraternity days, and his studies. It turned out that Wirth was almost four years older than Hans. Hans walked along beside him, feeling almost afraid at the thought that this man had chosen him as a friend, but that it was too soon for them to form a true friendship and that it might not be possible for a long time to come. It seemed to him that they were fundamentally unlike and that friendship with Wirth could not be based on mutual adaptation, on a blending of their natures, but that in full awareness of the differences between them they would both have to make concessions of their own free will and grant each other certain rights.

At the same time, Hans felt less sure of himself than ever. Since his awakening to consciousness, he had thought of himself as a distinct individual, apart from the herd and markedly different from all others, and at every stage he had suffered from being too young. But now, with Wirth, he felt himself to be half baked and really young. He realized that his superiority to Erwin Mühletal and other comrades had given him a false self-assurance which he had abused. In his dealings with Heinrich Wirth, a bit of wit and mental dexterity were not enough. He would have to take himself more seriously, to be more modest, to stop representing his hopes as achievements. This friendship would not be a game and a luxury; he would have to muster all his strength and measure it against another's. For Wirth all the problems of life and thought amounted in the end to ethical tasks, and Hans felt far from comfortable in the realization that this was a much more serious preparation for life than his own aestheticism.

Wirth's thoughts were less troubled. He sensed Hans's need for friendship and welcomed him wholeheartedly. But Hans was not the first to approach him in this way, and he steeled himself in advance to the likelihood that Hans too would fall away from him. Perhaps Calwer was just one of the many who "took an interest in his aims," and interest was not what Wirth needed; no, what he needed was living companionship, sacrifice, devotion. What he otherwise demanded of no one, he would have to demand of a friend. All the same, he was drawn to Hans by a gentle but compelling affection unmarred by any purpose. Hans had something that he lacked and therefore prized: an innate feeling for beauty, a love of art for art's sake. Art was the only sphere of the higher life which to his regret had remained alien to him, but which, he dimly suspected, held out a promise of salvation. Accordingly, he didn't see Hans as a disciple who would learn what he could from him and go his way, but hoped, and felt it to be possible, that he would learn from Hans and find a guide in him.

Still busy with their thoughts, they took their leave of one another. They tried to take a cordial tone but were unable to. They had come together too quickly; both instinctively dreaded the moment of surrender and perfect openness without which acquaintance cannot become friendship.

When he had gone a hundred yards or so, Hans turned around and looked back, half hoping that Wirth, too, would look back. But Wirth was plodding back to his village through the early dusk with the firm and even step of a man who had found himself, who could go his hard road as unswervingly by himself as with a companion, and was not easily turned aside by inclinations and desires.

He walks as if he were wearing armor, Hans thought to himself, and felt a burning desire to strike this tower of strength a secret blow, to find an unguarded cleft in his armor and wound him. He decided to wait and to say nothing until this man, so sure of himself and conscious of his goal, should one day show himself to be weak and human and in need of love. Though Hans didn't know it and wasn't even thinking about it, his hope and yearning and suffering in that moment were not very different from the patient yearning with which long ago, in his boyhood, he had courted Erwin. But he wasn't thinking of Erwin now; he seldom thought of him. He didn't know that Erwin was suffering and going astray on his account, and through his fault.

Erwin was still in love with Fräulein Elvira, or so he thought. Nevertheless, he went about his life of vice with a certain caution and his moments of stock-taking and good resolutions had become more frequent. Though numbed and helpless for the time being, his true nature rebelled in secret against his sordid associations. The capricious Elvira made it easier for him, for more often than not she treated him harshly and gave two or three other regulars precedence over him.

At times it seemed to Erwin that the worst was over, that he knew the way back to self-respect and well-being. All that was needed was a firm decision, a brief period of stubborn self-control, possibly a confession. But unfortunately such a change didn't come of itself, and the pitifully inexperienced young sinner soon discovered to his horror that bad habits once acquired cannot be cast off like a shirt, and that before a child knows what fire is and learns to avoid it, he must be seriously burned. He thought, of course, that he had been burned enough and been made sufficiently unhappy, but in that he was very much mistaken. Unsuspected blows were still in wait for him.

One morning, when he was still in bed, he received the visit of his senior brother, a jolly, personable student whom he had formerly been fond of. But his relations with the fraternity as a whole had become so strained and artificial that he seldom met privately with any of its members. Consequently, this unexpected visit made him uncomfortable and aroused his suspicion.

Sitting up in bed and affecting a yawn, he cried out, "Hello there!"

"How are you doing, son? Still in bed?"

"I was just getting up. Have we got fencing this morning?"

"You must know that as well as I do."

"Yes, I suppose so."

"Now listen to me, son. Surprisingly enough, there seem to be a few things you don't know. So I'd better enlighten you."

"Does it have to be now?"

"Yes, I think so. I'd have spoken to you before, but you're never home. I wouldn't want to go looking for you at the Golden Star."

"At the Golden Star? What's all this about?"

"Don't play innocent. You've been seen at the Golden Star twice. You know you're not allowed to go there."

"I never wore my colors."

"I should hope not. But you're not supposed to go there at all, or to the Whale either. And you're not supposed to associate with that medical student Häsler, whom no decent person looks at, or with Meyer, who was thrown out of the Rhenish Brotherhood three terms back for cheating at cards and who backed out of two challenges."

"Good Lord, I had no way of knowing that."

"I'm glad to hear you didn't know. It makes your preference for those gentlemen's company a little less humiliating to your fraternity brothers."

"You know perfectly well why I've been keeping away."

"Yes, of course. The business with Calwer . . ."

"And the way I was insulted . . ."

"I beg your pardon, only one man insulted you, a boor, I admit, and he apologized."

"Then what should I do? All right, I'll resign."

"That's easily said. But if you're a decent fellow, you won't. Don't forget you're not Calwer. His situation was different. True, his resignation came as a blow to us, but—I have to hand it to him—the man was irreproachable. Your case is a bit different."

"You mean I'm not irreproachable?"

"No, son, I'm sorry to say you're not. But now do me a favor, calm down. My visit isn't official, as you might think, I've come purely out of friendship. So be reasonable! —You see, if you were to leave us now, it wouldn't be right. You've behaved badly and you ought to straighten that out first. It wouldn't take much. A few weeks of unexceptionable behavior, no more. But then your silly ideas will pass, too. Look here, other men have been through it. What do your little excesses amount to? Much worse things have been straightened out. And be-sides—I may as well tell you—if you thought of getting out now, things might be made unpleasant for you."

"Why?"

"Don't you see? We might steal a march on you."

"Throw me out, you mean? Because I've been in the Golden Star a couple of times?"

"Yes, strictly speaking it's not sufficient grounds, but if necessary we might do it. It would be harsh and unjust, but there'd be nothing you could do about it. And that would be the end of you. It may be amusing to drink a beer now and then with those derelicts, but to become dependent on them—no, that would be ruinous, even for a stronger character than yours."

"Then what should I do?"

"Nothing at all. Just keep away from those places. Don't worry, you won't be called in for questioning. I'll tell them you recognize that your conduct hasn't been all it should be and that you promise to turn over a new leaf immediately. That will be the end of it."

"But what if I don't fit in with you? What if I'm not happy in the fraternity?"

"That's your affair. All I know is that others have felt the same way and got over it completely. And so will you. Or if you feel you have to, you can still resign. But not now; it just wouldn't be right."

"I can see that. I'm grateful to you for trying to help me, I really am. All right. I won't go to the Star any more and I'll be on my good behavior. Is that enough?"

"I think so. But just this. Please bear in mind that I . . . well, you see, I've taken this stupid business pretty much on myself. I wanted to spare you an official repri-mand. You realize, of course, that I can't do it more than once. If ever again you . . ."

"Of course. You've already done more than . . ."

"Good. And now pull yourself together. Come around more often, even if there's nothing social going on. Come out to the café with us, join us in our strolls, and do your best at fencing. Then everything will be all right."

Erwin was hardly of that opinion. To his mind, everything was worse than ever. He had no hope of completing his university career as a satisfactory fraternity brother, or any desire to. He would stay in the fraternity only until it became possible to resign in dignity and honor, perhaps until the end of the term.

From then on he faithfully avoided the forbidden taverns and their regulars, and he didn't miss them. With the sole exception of the Blue Hussar. After a few days he went back, more or less in the intention of making it a farewell visit. But he had reckoned without Elvira. Instantly seeing the lay of the land, she was so friendly that he came again the next evening. She had no difficulty in coaxing the secret of his preoccupations out of him. She insisted on his staying in the fraternity. Otherwise, she said, she wouldn't see him any more.

And so, feeling like a thief, he crept back to the ill-reputed café night after night. Soon he was as hopelessly in the girl's power as ever. And once she was sure of him, she gave free rein to her moods and caprices. Whereupon, moved by anger and bitterness, he made a violent scene. The result was not what he had bargained for. She let him rage and then quietly produced a shabby little notebook in which she had marked down his drinking debts and the occasional loans she had made him, which he had long since forgotten. When in the past he had offered to repay them, she had laughingly declined. Now it all added up to a staggering sum. Champagne and expensive wine that he had not expressly ordered had been drunk on convivial evenings; his drinking companions had cheerfully cooperated, time and again holding out their glasses for more. Now all these bottles, meticulously listed, stared him in the face, grinning malignantly. The total was so enormous that he couldn't possibly pay it out of his monthly allowance, not even in installments. And unfortunately, this was not his only debt.

"Is it correct or isn't it?" Fräulein Elvira asked with majestic serenity. She fully expected him to protest. If necessary, she would have canceled a good part of the debt. But Erwin did not protest.

"Yes, I guess it's correct," he said humbly. "I'm sorry, it must have slipped my mind. Of course I'll pay you as soon as possible. Can you wait a little?"

Her success so much exceeded her expectations that she was touched and took a motherly tone. "I didn't mean any harm," she said gently. "I only wanted to remind you that you owe me something more than harsh words. If you're a good boy, my little notebook will stay right where it is, I don't need the money, and one of these days I may just throw it in the fire. But if you make me angry with your complaints, I might take it into my head to discuss your little bill with your fraternity brothers."

Erwin stared at her in horror.

"Come, come," she said, laughing. "You needn't be afraid."

That came too late. He was afraid. He knew he had fallen into a trap and that from then on he would be at the mercy of a coldly calculating woman.

"That's good," he said with an idiotic smile. And, sadly and humbly, he left. Up until then, he realized, his despair had been childishly absurd. Now suddenly he saw what a bit of lightheadedness could lead to, and the company into which he had fallen so innocently for all his guilty conscience appeared to him in a glaring, merciless light.

Now something would have to be done. He couldn't go on with a noose around his neck. Suddenly the squalor

and wrongness of the last few months, which only yesterday had seemed harmless and held out a semblance of
charm, engulfed him like a noisome swamp.

Like every young man with a certain amount of flighti-
ness in his nature, Erwin had formerly, in moments of
morning-after depression, toyed with the thought that if
all the joy went out of life he could take a revolver and
put an end to it all. Now that he was in real trouble, even
this feeble consolation had taken flight; the possibility
didn't so much as enter his head. He had no thought of
committing a final act of cowardice; no, he must take full
responsibility for his deplorable follies and if possible live
them down. He had awakened from a dreamlike, irresponsible twilight state, and it never occurred to him for
one moment to fall asleep again.

He spent the night making plans. He looked for a way
out, but with still greater urgency his thoughts kept returning, with horror and amazement, to his incomprehensible behavior. Had he become an entirely different man
in a few weeks' time? Had he been blind? Yet, horrified as
he was, he knew that his fear was retrospective, that the
danger was past. The main difficulty was his debt; that
must be paid immediately at all costs. The rest would take
care of itself.

By morning his plan was made.

He went to see his senior brother and found him shav-
ing. Aghast at Erwin's appearance, the other thought
something dreadful must have happened. Erwin said he
was obliged to leave town for a day or two and asked to be
excused from his fraternity obligations.

"A death in the family?" his comrade asked sympa-
thetically. In his haste, Erwin leapt at this offer of a
white lie. "Yes," he said quickly. "But I can't tell you
anything now. I'll be back the day after tomorrow at the
latest. Please make my excuses at fencing. I'll tell you all
about it when I get back. Many thanks and goodbye."

He went straight to the station. In the early afternoon he arrived in his hometown, where, taking a circuitous route so as to avoid his mother's house, he made his way to the office of his brother-in-law, who was part owner of a small factory and the only person to whom Erwin could turn for money.

The brother-in-law was not a little surprised to see him. Erwin came right out with his financial difficulties and the brother-in-law stiffened. He took him to an adjoining room and there they sat facing one another. Feeling very uncomfortable, Erwin looked into the unassuming, eminently respectable face of his sister's husband, in whom he had never taken any particular interest. But sooner or later he would have to lay himself bare, to do penance, and there was no point in putting it off. Screwing up his courage, he threw himself on the other's mercy and made a full confession. Interrupted by terse questions from the astonished businessman, it took a good hour.

An embarrassed pause followed. Then the brother-in-law asked, "What will you do if I can't give you the money?"

Erwin had gone so far in his confession that he was near the breaking point. He was almost beginning to regret that he had said so much. He felt like saying, "That's none of your business." But he controlled himself and held back the words. Finally he said hesitantly, "There's only one way. If you can't give it to me or if you don't want to, I'll have to go to my mother and tell her everything. You know how much that will hurt her. Besides, it would be hard for her to raise the money right away, though of course she'd do it. I could also go to a moneylender, but I thought I'd try someone in the family first." The brother-in-law stood up and nodded once or twice thoughtfully.

"Well," he said finally. "Of course I'll give you the money. At the usual rate of interest. You can sign the receipt in the office before you go. There's no point in my giving you advice, is there? I'm sorry this has happened to you. Will you have tea with us later on?"

Erwin thanked him but declined the invitation. He wanted to take the train back that same afternoon. His brother-in-law also thought that would be best.

"As you wish," he said. "I'll write out a check."

The philosophical "Paraphrases on the Law of the Conservation of Energy" had been completed in accordance with Hans's original idea, but they had ceased to give their author any real satisfaction. He was already very much under the influence of Wirth, the rustic thinker, whose way of grappling with problems, though more one-sided, was far more direct and consistent than his own. He had thought of showing him the manuscript, but had soon decided not to, for he felt sure that Wirth would regard it as a piece of futile aestheticism. And little by little he had come around to the same way of thinking. It now struck him as little better than a feuilleton, written in a self-complacent style, as though he had gone out of his way to make himself interesting. He couldn't bring himself to destroy the carefully written pages, which he had just reread, but he rolled them up, tied a string around them, and put them away in a corner of his cupboard. He was in no hurry to see them again.

It was evening. His reading and painful self-criticism had first stirred him up, then made him sad. For he saw that he was not yet ready to produce anything really good, and at the same time he was tormented by an urge to express his secret thoughts and to put his meditations into finished, conclusive form. He had often felt that way as a schoolboy. He wrote poems and essays; twice a year he looked them over and destroyed them; yet his longing to produce something of lasting value had become steadily stronger. He tossed his cigarette stub into the stove, stood for a while at the window letting in the winter air, and finally went to the piano. For a while he groped and improvised. Then, after a moment's thought, he took out Beethoven's Sonata 23 and played it through with increasing care and fervor.

When he had finished and was still leaning over the piano, there was a knock at the door. He stood up and opened it. Erwin Mühletal stood there.

"Erwin!" Hans cried out, surprised and somewhat disconcerted.

"Yes, it's me. Can I come in?"

"Of course you can. Come in, come in!"

He held out his hand.

They sat down at the table. Now, in the lamplight, Hans saw that the face he knew so well was strangely aged. "How have you been?" he asked, to make a beginning. Erwin looked at him and smiled.

"Pretty well. I don't know if my visit is welcome, but I thought I'd try. I wanted to tell you a few things and possibly ask a favor of you."

Hans listened to the familiar voice and was surprised at how happy it made him and how much lost well-being, which he had almost ceased to miss, it gave him. Once again he gave Erwin his hand.

"It's good of you to come," he said cordially. "We haven't seen each other in so long. I really should have gone to see you. I hurt you. But now you're here. Have a cigarette."

"Thank you. It's cozy here. And you've got a piano again. And the same good cigarettes. —Were you angry with me?"

"Angry? Of course not. God knows how it happened. That stupid fraternity . . . oh, I'm sorry."

"Go right ahead. I'll probably be getting out soon."

"Really? Not because of me, I hope. But then I suppose you've had a good deal of unpleasantness on my account."

"Yes, but that's all over. If you have time, I'll tell you the whole story."

"Please do. And don't spare me."

"Oh, you hardly figure in it, though I thought of you the whole time. I should have got out when you did. You were kind of brusque at the time and that made me obstinate. This time, I decided, I wouldn't follow you through thick and thin. But you know all that. From then on I had a bad time of it, but I myself was to blame."

Then he told his story. Hans was surprised and horrified to hear what his friend had suffered while he, hardly giving Erwin a thought, had been managing quite well without him.

"I don't know how it happened," he heard him say. "That kind of life isn't really in my line. But the fact is, I wasn't myself. I was running around in a fog the whole time, and I just let things slide. But now comes the climax. It happened at the Blue Hussar café, you've probably never even heard of it."

Then he told the story of Fräulein Elvira. It struck Hans as so sad and at the same time so ridiculous that Erwin couldn't help laughing at the look on his face.

"What now?" Hans asked when he had finished. "You need money of course. But where are you going to get it? You can have mine, but it's not enough."

"Thank you. The money is taken care of." And happily Erwin told that part of the story, whereupon Hans pronounced the brother-in-law a very decent fellow.

"But how can I help you?" he asked then. "Didn't you say there was something I could do for you?"

"Yes, indeed. A big favor. Could you go to that place and pay their stupid bill for me?"

"Hmm, yes, of course I could. Only I wonder if you shouldn't do it yourself. It would be a kind of triumph for you, and a perfect exit."

"Yes, I suppose so. But I believe I'd rather not. I'm

pretty sure it's not cowardice; it's just that I couldn't bear the thought of seeing that dive or even the street again. Besides, I thought, if you go, you'll see the place with your own eyes, you'll have a kind of illustration to my story. Then you'll be able to share the memory of my Blue Hussar period with me."

That seemed reasonable to Hans and he undertook the errand with a certain curiosity. When Erwin produced the money and counted out the bills and coins on the table, Hans laughed. "Good God!" he cried out, "that's a fortune!" And he added more seriously, "You know, it's a shame to pay all that money. I'm sure Elvira charged you triple. She'll make a good profit and be perfectly happy if you give her half of this. No, it won't do. I could take a policeman with me in case of trouble." But Erwin wouldn't hear of it.

"You may be right," he said calmly. "I'd thought of it myself. But I'd rather not. Let her have her money. Of course she's overdoing it, but once it's all paid up, I'll be free. And another thing: I'm completely cured now, but I was in love with her for a time."

"Pure imagination!" said Hans angrily.

"Perhaps. I was, though. And I'd rather have her take me for a decent fool than for a cheat like herself."

"There's something in that." Hans admitted. "Don Quixote was the noblest knight of all. It's foolish of you, but nice. All right, I'll attend to it tomorrow and give you my report."

They parted in good spirits. Hans was glad of the opportunity to work off a bit of his guilt by doing something for his friend. On the following morning, he went to the Blue Hussar, where Elvira, after keeping him waiting for quite a while, received him with extreme distrust. Intimidated by her grand manner, he soon abandoned a halting attempt to take her to task for her underhanded maneuver and contented himself with handing her the money and demanding a receipt, which for safety's sake he got her mother to sign as well. With this document in hand, he went to Erwin, who laughed with joy and relief as he took it.

Then with a note of embarrassment he said, "May I ask you a question?"

"Yes, of course. What is it?"

"Who is the student who sometimes comes to see you in the evening, the one you played *Tristan* for?"

Hans was both disconcerted and moved to hear that Erwin had taken such an interest in his life as to listen outside his window.

"His name is Heinrich Wirth," he said slowly. "Maybe you'll meet him one of these days."

"Is he your friend now?"

"Yes, in a way. I met him in one of my classes. He's a remarkable man."

"Really? Well, maybe I'll see him here sometime. Would you mind?"

"Of course not. I'm glad you'll be coming to see me again."

But in his secret heart he did mind a little. The note of jealousy in Erwin's question displeased him, for he had no intention of letting Erwin influence his relations with Wirth. But of this he said nothing and his pleasure at their reconciliation was genuine enough to stifle all misgivings for the present.

There followed a period of calm, especially for Erwin, who went about with the happy feeling of one who had recovered from an illness and begun to take a milder and fairer view of his comrades and their demands. He was pretty sure that his fraternity brothers knew he was seeing Hans Calwer again. He was grateful to them for not holding it up to him and took all the more pains to fulfill his obligations. He never missed a meeting, renewed his friendship with his senior brother, and joined in the tavern gatherings. Since he no longer seemed bored and disgruntled but participated with cheerful good will, his comrades soon found him sufficiently improved and treated him with renewed cordiality. All this was balm to him; he recovered his balance and sense of humor, and before long his comrades were pleased with him and he with himself. He no longer thought it absolutely necessary that he resign; in any case, he was in no hurry.

Hans, too, was happy with this state of affairs. Erwin came to see him two or three times a week. He had become more self-reliant and showed no sign of falling back into his old state of dependency. This in turn made Hans feel freer. He had no regrets that their relationship was no longer as close as it had been.

Toward the end of the term, Erwin came to see him and spoke of his life in the fraternity. This, he said, was the time to decide whether to resign, which he could now do honorably, or to remain a color student of his own free will. If he stayed on, he would soon become a senior.

When Hans told him with a smile that the colors became him and advised him to go on wearing them, he cried out with enthusiasm, "You're right! You see, if you had said one word, I'd have resigned on the spot; you still mean more to me than the whole shebang. But it does amuse me, and now that I've lived through my junior stage and the fun is really starting, it would be too bad to leave. So if you have no objection, I'll stay in."

The old inseparable bond between them was gone, but so on the other hand were the misunderstandings, quarrels, and storms. Their friendship, which had once been so passionate, became peaceful, easygoing, and a bit superficial. They accepted each other with tolerance, left each other in peace, and ceased to talk everything over between them. Yet when they met, they felt they belonged together.

At first Erwin had expected something more, but the cheerful good fellowship of his fraternity brothers compensated in good part for what he failed to obtain from his friend, and an unconscious pride convinced him that in becoming less dependent on Hans he was taking a step in the right direction. As for Hans, he was all the more pleased with this state of affairs because of his increasing preoccupation with Heinrich Wirth.

One evening shortly before the end of the term, Erwin met Wirth at Hans's. He closely observed the man who had aroused his jealousy and, despite Wirth's friendliness, didn't really take to him. He was put off by the rustic philosopher's exterior, his unyouthful dignity, and his vegetarian way of life. Perceiving Erwin's critical attitude, Hans was thoroughly annoyed with him. Erwin went out of his way to provoke Wirth by talking with exaggerated enthusiasm about student goings-on. Then, when Wirth not only listened to him patiently but even encouraged him with questions, Erwin changed the subject to abstinence and vegetarianism.

"What do you get out of your asceticism?" he asked. "Other people drink and eat well and it doesn't seem to give them any ailments."

Wirth laughed good-naturedly. "If that's how you feel about it, just go on drinking. The ailments will come later on. But even now it would do you good to lead a different kind of life."

"What good? You mean I'd save money? That doesn't interest me very much."

"Why should it? I have something else in mind. Take me. For three years now I've been living in my way, which you call ascetic, and I hardly feel the need of women any more. I used to suffer a good deal from that. Most students do, I think. The health and strength you build up by riding and fencing you throw away in the taverns. That seems a pity to me."

Erwin was beginning to feel uncomfortable. He had no desire to go on with the argument and contented himself with observing, "You make us sound like a lot of cripples. What's the good of health if you have to keep thinking about it? Young people ought to be able to stand a little wear and tear."

Hans put an end to the conversation by opening the piano.

"What should I play?" he asked Wirth.

"Oh, you know I don't know anything about music. But that sonata you played the other day—I'd be glad to hear it again."

Hans nodded and opened a book of Beethoven. While playing, he turned his head from time to time in an attempt to catch Wirth's eye. Erwin could see he was playing for Wirth alone, courting him with his music. And for this he envied the uncouth rustic. But when Hans had finished playing and the conversation started up again, Erwin spoke with polite gentleness. He saw that this man had gained power over his friend, and he also saw that if Hans had to choose between them, it wasn't Wirth he would sacrifice. Erwin didn't want to drive him to any such choice.

Wirth's influence on Hans struck Erwin as unfortunate. He felt that Hans was already too crotchety, too much given to brooding, and that Wirth took him still further in a direction that could be dangerous as well as ridiculous. Hans had always been something of a dreamer and a solitary thinker, but formerly he had had a kind of freshness and elegance that saved him from absurdity. Now, it seemed to Erwin, this Wirth was leading him astray, deliberately trying to make him into more of a recluse and problem-monger than ever.

Wirth remained friendly and calm, but Hans, who felt the tension in the air, was annoyed with Erwin and let him see it, taking a condescending tone that Erwin was no longer willing to put up with. Exasperated in his turn, he soon took his leave.

"Why were you so rough on your friend?" Wirth asked when he had gone. "I liked him."

"Really? I thought he was being unbearable. Why did he have to provoke you like that? It was stupid."

"There was no harm in it. I can take a joke. I'd have been the stupid one if I'd got angry."

"He wasn't getting at you, he was getting at me. He doesn't want me to associate with anyone but him. When he runs around all day with twenty fraternity brothers."

"My goodness, you're really wrought up. That's something you should get over, at least with friends. Your friend was disappointed in not finding you alone, and he showed it a little. Apart from that, I thought he was charming. I hope I get to know him better."

"All right, let's forget it. I'll go a ways with you if you don't mind."

They went out into the dark street and crossed the city. Here and there voices could be heard singing in chorus. Soon they were in the open country. A soft breeze was blowing in the mild, starless March night. On the north slopes of the hills an occasional patch of snow glowed faintly. The wind blew lazily over the bare branches. The distant countryside was cloaked in black, impenetrable night. As usual, Heinrich Wirth's stride was firm and serene, while Hans's gait was nervous and he kept changing his step. From time to time he stopped and peered into the blue-black night.

"You're upset," said Wirth. "Forget your little irritation."

"It's not that."

Wirth made no answer.

For a time they walked on in silence. In a farmyard far in the distance, dogs barked. A blackbird was singing in a thicket nearby.

Wirth raised his finger. "Hear that?"

Hans only nodded and quickened his pace. Then suddenly he stopped.

"Herr Wirth, tell me the truth. What do you think of me?"

"I can't tell you that."

"I mean—do you want to be my friend?"

"I think I am your friend."

"Not yet entirely. Oh, Herr Wirth. I think I need you. I need a guide and comrade. Can you understand that?"

"I can. You want something different from what other people want. You're looking for a way, and you think I might be able to show you the right one. But that's something I don't know. I think every man must find his own way. If I can help you to do that, good. But then you'll have to go my way for a stretch. It's not yours, and I don't think it will be a very long stretch."

"Who knows? But how do I start going your way? Where does it lead? And where will I find it?"

"That's simple. Live as I live. It will do you good."

"What do you mean?"

"Live in the fresh air as much as you can. Work out of doors if possible. I can find you such work. Apart from that, eat no meat, drink no liquor, tea, or coffee, and stop smoking. Live on bread, fruit, and milk. That's the beginning."

"You want me to become a vegetarian? Why?"

"Because it will stop you asking why all the time. If you live sensibly, a great many things that once looked like problems become self-evident."

"You think so? Maybe you're right. But it seems to me that practice should follow from thought, not the other way around. Once I see the advantage of that kind of life, I'll be ready to take it up. How can I go into it with my eyes closed?"

"That's up to you. You asked for advice, and I gave you the only advice I know. You want to start with thinking and end with living. I do the opposite. That's what I meant by my way."

"And if I don't take it, you won't be my friend?"

"It wouldn't work. We could have conversations, we could talk philosophy, but it wouldn't be anything more than a pleasant exercise. I'm not trying to convert you. But if you want to be my friend, I have to be able to take you seriously."

They started to walk again. Hans was confused and disappointed. Instead of warm encouragement, instead of cordial friendship, he had been offered a kind of nature cure, which struck him as irrelevant and almost ridiculous. "Stop eating meat and I'll be your friend." But when he thought of his earlier conversations with Wirth, of the earnestness and assurance that had made such a powerful impression on him, he was unable to put him down as a mere vegetarian and apostle of Tolstoy.

In spite of his disillusionment, he began to ponder Wirth's proposal and to think how forsaken he would feel if he were to lose the one man to whom he felt drawn and who, he was convinced, had it in his power to help him.

They had gone far. As they approached the first houses of Blaubachhausen, Hans held out his hand to his new friend and said, "I'll try your advice."

More to oblige Wirth than out of conviction, he embarked on his new life the next morning. He found it much harder than he had imagined.

"Frau Ströhle," he announced to his landlady. "From now on I won't be drinking coffee. Please bring me a quart of milk every day."

"Why, what's wrong? Are you sick?" Frau Ströhle asked in surprise.

"Not really. But milk is more wholesome."

She did his bidding without another word, but she wasn't happy about it. Clearly, her lodger had a screw loose. So young and always with his nose in a book, playing the piano all by himself, resigning from such a fine fraternity, hobnobbing with that shabby-looking philosopher, and now this milk drinking—it wasn't normal. At first she had been glad to have such a quiet, unassuming lodger, but this was going too far. She would rather have had him come home dead drunk now and then like other students and found him asleep on the stairs. From then on she kept a suspicious eye on him, and what she saw was not to her liking. She saw that he had stopped going out to eat at the restaurant, that he was sneaking packages into the house. And when she came in to do his room, she found his table littered with nuts, apples, oranges, prunes, and scraps of bread.

"Gracious!" she cried out, and it was all up with her respect for Hans Calwer. Either he was crazy or they had stopped sending him money. And when he told her a few days later that he was planning to live elsewhere next term, she only shrugged her shoulders and said, "As you wish, Herr Calwer."

In the meantime, Hans had rented a room in a farmhouse next door to Wirth. He planned to move into it after the spring vacation.

The milk drinking and fruit eating were no great hardship to him, but in leading this life he felt he was acting a part that had been imposed on him. He missed his cigarettes painfully, and at least once a day a moment came when despite his resolutions he lit one and with a guilty conscience smoked it at the open window. After a few days he felt ashamed and gave all his cigarettes, a large boxful, to a delivery man who had brought him a magazine.

While Hans was spending his days in this way and feeling none too cheerful about it, Erwin did not show himself. That last evening had left him out of sorts, and he had no desire to see Wirth again. Besides, it was the last week before the spring vacation and he was kept very busy, for his comrades now treated him as a promising new senior and he had certain preparations to make for his graduation from juniorship to the ranks of the respected seniors, who ruled the roost and set the tone.

So it came about that he didn't drop in on Hans until the last day of the term. He found him packing and saw at a glance that he was not planning to keep his room, for the piano was gone and the pictures had been taken down.

"Are you moving?" he asked in surprise.

"Yes. Sit down."

"Have you got another place? —Really? Where?"

"Out of town. For the summer."

"Where?"

"In Blaubachhausen."

Erwin jumped up. "You don't mean it! You're joking."

Hans shook his head.

"Then you're serious?"

"Yes indeed."

"To Blaubachhausen! With Wirth, I suppose. With that kohlrabi eater. —Hans, be reasonable. Don't do it."

"I've already taken the room and I'm going to move in. What do you care?"

"Good God, Hans! Leave him to his phantoms. Think it over. Got a cigarette?"

"No, I've stopped smoking."

"Aha! There you have it. And now you're going out to live with that hermit and sit at his feet? I must say, you're not as proud as you used to be."

Hans had dreaded the moment when he would have to tell Erwin of his decision. Now his anger helped him over his embarrassment.

"Thanks for your kind opinion," he said coldly. "I could imagine what you'd think. But tell me this: Have I ever asked you for advice?"

Erwin's temper rose. "No, unfortunately. But if you

insist on making a fool of yourself, you can count me out."

"I'll be glad to."

"I mean that seriously. If you want to go out there to live with that shabby saint, they won't let me go near you."

"Who's asking you to? Stick to your fraternity monkeys."

Erwin had had enough. He might have struck Hans if he hadn't been deterred by a last vestige of feeling for him. He left without saying goodbye and slammed the door behind him. Hans's anger had died down, but he didn't call him back.

After all, he had committed himself to conquering that stubborn, silent Wirth by submission, and now he was determined to go through with it. At heart he sympathized with Erwin; even to himself this discipleship of his seemed rather preposterous. Yet he was resolved to attempt this arduous path, to sacrifice his freedom and his will, to be subservient for once. Possibly this was the way he had not yet found, the narrow bridge to knowledge and contentment. As when in a moment of intoxication he had joined an organization to which he was not suited, so now he was driven by weakness and dissatisfaction to seek a human bond that would give him strength.

Anyway, he felt sure that after sulking a while Erwin would come back.

In that he was mistaken. In view of what Erwin had suffered on his account after his resignation from the fraternity, Hans would have had to reinforce their ties if he was to keep a lasting hold on him. Erwin had expected more from his return to Hans. Moreover, at the Blue Hussar, at his brother-in-law's office, and especially among his fraternity brothers since then, he had learned a few things, unsuspected by Hans, which had set him free from Hans's unconditional domination. Amid all the foolishness of fraternity life, he had quietly become a man. Though himself unaware of it, he had overcome his sense of Hans's superiority and discovered that, for all his intelligence, the friend he so much admired was not a hero.

In short, Erwin didn't take the new rupture too much to heart. He regretted it and thought he was partly to blame; but deep down he felt that Hans had it coming to him, and soon he stopped thinking about it altogether.

When pleasantly tired from the end-of-term celebration and attendant festivities Erwin returned home for his Easter vacation in all his glory as a senior brother, his mother and sisters were delighted with him. He was radiantly happy, even affable and entertaining. He paid visits in a splendid new summer suit, played dominoes with his mother, brought his sisters flowers, won the hearts of his aunts with little attentions, and was at pains to make himself agreeable to everyone he met.

For this there was a good reason. On the very first day of his vacation, Erwin Mühletal had fallen in love. A young girl was staying at his uncle's house, a friend of his uncle's daughters. She was pretty and vivacious; she played tennis, sang, and talked about the Berlin theater. Though she liked the young student well enough, she refused to be impressed. The challenge only redoubled his efforts. He did everything in his power to charm and oblige her, and in the end the haughty damsel's heart was softened. Before his vacation was over, they were secretly engaged.

He spoke of Hans only once, when his mother asked after him. Then he said coldly, "Calwer. He's stupid. Now he's gone in for abstinence. He's living with some kind of freak, a Buddhist or theosophist or some such thing, who only gets his hair cut once a year."

The spring term began magnificently. The parks burst

into bloom, filling the whole town with the smell of lilacs and jasmine. The days were a brilliant blue, the nights summery-warm. Colorful groups of students swaggered through the streets, rode horseback, or, playing the part of coachmen, drove the new juniors about town. At night, singing could be heard from open windows and gardens.

Hans saw little of this joyful life. He had moved to Blaubachhausen. Every morning he walked to town with Heinrich Wirth to attend a Sanskrit class. At noon he dipped bread into his milk. Then he went for a walk or tried to help with the farm work. At night when he collapsed on his hard straw tick, he was dead tired, but he didn't sleep well.

His friend didn't make things easy for him. He was still only half convinced of Hans's seriousness, and was determined to put him through a hard course of training. Without departing from his serene calm, without ever commanding, he compelled him to live as he did in every way. He read the Upanishads and Vedas with him, studied Sanskrit with him, taught him how to handle a scythe and mow hay. When Hans was tired or irritable, he shrugged his shoulders and left him alone. When Hans grumbled and questioned his new mode of life, Wirth smiled and said nothing, even if Hans grew angry and insulting.

"I'm sorry you find it so hard," he said once. "But until you experience the hardship of life in your own skin, until you learn what it means to be free from the charms and pleasures of the flesh, no progress is possible. You are traveling the same road as Buddha and all those who have been serious about attaining knowledge. Asceticism in itself is worthless and has never made a saint, but as a preliminary stage it's necessary. The ancient Indians, whose wisdom we revere, and to whose books and teachings Europe is now trying to return, were able to fast for forty days or more. Only when we have fully transcended our bodily needs, only when they cease to be important, can a serious spiritual life begin. You're not expected to become an Indian penitent, but you will have to acquire the peace of mind without which pure meditation is impossible."

Often Hans was so exhausted and miserable that he was unable to go to work or even to remain with Heinrich. Then he would stroll across the meadows behind his house to a hillock shaded by a few pine trees. There he would throw himself down in the grass and lie for hours. He heard the sounds of the farm work, the sharp, high clang of scythes being sharpened, the soft swish of the mowing; he heard dogs barking and children shouting, and once in a while he heard the boisterous songs of students driving through the village. He listened patiently and wearily, and envied them all, the peasants, the children, the dogs, the students. He envied the grass, its silent growth and easy death, the birds and their hovering flight, the light-flying wind. How easily and unthinkingly they all spent their lives, as though life were a pleasure.

Sometimes he was haunted by a sadly beautiful dream —those were his best days. Then he thought of the evenings he had once spent at the professor's house and of the professor's lovely, quiet wife, whose image lived in him and called forth his yearning. Then it seemed to him that the people in that house lived a serious and authentic life, that their sacrifices and sufferings were necessary and meaningful, whereas he, in his hope of coming closer to the meaning of life, was without necessity subjecting himself to artificial sufferings and sacrifices.

These thoughts came and went with the wind, unbidden and dreamlike. When his fatigue and numbness of soul wore off, his thoughts went back to Heinrich Wirth, and then he felt himself subjected to the gaze of those serenely commanding, silently questioning eyes. He couldn't get away from the man, and he was beginning to wish at times that he could.

For a long while he refused to admit even to himself that he had expected something different from Wirth and that he was disappointed. The Spartan diet, the farm work, the absence of all comfort were painful to him, but would not have sobered him so soon. What he missed most were the evenings at the piano, the long restful days of reading, the twilight hours spent quietly smoking. Years seemed to have passed since he had heard good music, and sometimes he would have given everything just to sit for an hour, freshly bathed and well dressed, among congenial people. True, he could have had all that very easily; he had only to walk into town and call on the professor, for instance. But he couldn't bring himself to do it. It wouldn't be right to nibble at the good things he had solemnly forsworn. Besides, he was always tired and listless; this unaccustomed life disagreed with him, for if a drastic cure is to be beneficial, it must be undertaken of one's own free will, out of inner necessity.

What made him suffer most was that his master and friend viewed all his exertions with silent irony. He never mocked him, but he watched. He said nothing, but seemed well aware that Hans was on the wrong track and was tormenting himself to no purpose.

At the end of two hot, wretched months, the situation became unbearable. Hans had stopped grumbling; his unhappiness expressed itself in morose silence. For some days he had taken no part in the farm work. Returning from the university toward noon, he spent the rest of the day lying forlornly in his meadow. Wirth decided that the experiment had gone on long enough.

Always an early riser, he appeared in Hans's room one morning when Hans was still in bed, sat down beside him, and looked at him with his serene smile.

"Well, Hans?"

"What's up? Time to go to class?"

"No, it's just past five o'clock. I wanted to have a little talk with you. Am I disturbing you?"

"Well, yes, at this time of day. I haven't slept much. What's wrong?"

"Nothing. Let's just talk a little. Tell me, are you happy?"

"No. Far from it."

"That's easy to see. My advice to you is to take a nice room in town, with a piano . . ."

"Stop making jokes."

"I know you're not in a mood for jokes. Neither am I. I'm serious. —Look, you've tried to go my way, and I must say you've tried hard. But it won't work, and I think you should stop torturing yourself. You're bent on sticking it out, you've made it a point of honor. But you can't, and there's no more use in trying."

"Yes, I believe you're right. It was foolishness, and it's cost me a beautiful summer. And you've had your fun looking on. You hero! And now that you've had enough and it's begun to bore you, you condescend to call off the torture and send me away."

"Don't be bitter, Hans. It may look that way to you, but I don't have to tell you that things are never what they seem. It's true I expected this to happen, but I never got any fun out of it. I meant well by you, and I think you've learned something after all."

"No doubt about that. I've learned plenty."

"Don't forget, you wanted to do it. Why shouldn't I have let you do what you wanted, as long as there seemed to be no danger? But now you've had enough. I don't think either of us need regret what's happened so far."

"And what now?"

"You'll have to answer that for yourself. I'd hoped you might be able to adopt my way of life. It didn't work—

what was voluntary in my case is a dismal strain in yours. It would destroy you. I'm not saying your will wasn't strong enough, though I believe in free will. You're different from me. You're weaker, but also more sensitive. Things that are luxuries for me are necessities for you. For instance, if your music had been just another of your affectations, you wouldn't miss it so much now."

"Affectations! You have a fine opinion of me."

"I'm sorry. I meant no harm by the word. Let's say self-deceptions. That was true of your philosophical ideas. You were dissatisfied with yourself; you abused and tyrannized your friend, who's a very nice boy. You experimented with the red cap, then with your studies of Buddhism, and finally with me. But you never really sacrificed yourself. You tried to, but you didn't succeed. You still love yourself too much. Forgive me for saying all this. You thought you were in great distress, you were prepared to give up everything to find peace. But you were unable to give up yourself, and perhaps you'll never be able to. You tried to make the greatest sacrifice, because you saw I was happy in doing so. You wanted to go my way, but you didn't know that it leads to Nirvana. You wanted to enhance and sublimate your own life. I can't help you do that, because my goal is to stop having a life of my own and to merge with the totality. I'm the opposite of you and I can't teach you anything. Think of it this way: you've gone into a monastery and you've been disillusioned."

"You're right. It's something like that."

"So the only thing to do now is to leave and seek your salvation somewhere else. It's been a detour, that's all."

"But what about the goal?"

"The goal is peace. Perhaps you're strong enough and artist enough—then you'll learn to love your shortcomings and draw life from them. I can't do that. Or, who knows, someday you may succeed in sacrificing yourself and giving yourself entirely. Then you'll have come back to my way, whether you identify it with asceticism, Buddha, Jesus, Tolstoy, or whatever. It will always be open to you."

"Thank you, Heinrich. You've been a friend. Tell me just one more thing: How do you see your future life? Where will your way lead you in the end?"

"I hope it will lead to peace. Someday, I hope, it will lead me to the point where, in full possession of my consciousness, I shall nevertheless rest in God's hand, as carefree as a bird or a plant. Someday, if I can, I shall communicate something of my life and knowledge to others, but for myself I seek only to overcome fear and death. That will be possible only if I cease to regard my life as a distinct individual life; only then will every moment of my life have its meaning."

"That's a good deal."

"It's everything. It's the only thing that's worth wishing and hoping for."

On the evening of the following day there was a knock at Erwin's door. "Come in," he called, thinking it was a fraternity brother whom he was expecting. When he turned around, there was Hans. Erwin was surprised and embarrassed to see him.

"You?"

"Yes. Forgive me if I'm disturbing you. The last time we met, we parted in anger."

"Yes, I know. But . . ."

"I'm sorry. It was my fault. Are you still angry?"

"No, of course not. But, forgive me, I'm expecting a visitor . . ."

"Just a moment. I'm going away tomorrow. I'm not quite well. And I won't be coming back here next term."

"I'm sorry to hear it. What's wrong? Nothing serious, I hope."

"No, nothing serious. I just wanted to know how you've been getting along. Well, by the looks of you."

"Oh yes. But you don't even know . . ."

"What?"

"I'm engaged. It happened this spring. It hasn't been announced yet, but I'm going to Berlin next week for the celebration. My fiancée is from Berlin."

"Congratulations! Lucky man! Now I suppose you'll buckle down to your medicine."

"Oh, I've been doing all right. But starting next term I'm really going to work. What are your plans?"

"Maybe Leipzig. But I'm disturbing you?"

"Well, you see, don't be offended—I'm expecting a fraternity brother. You know how it is, it would be embarrassing for you, too . . ."

"Oh. I'd forgotten about that. Well, by the time we meet again, all that will be water under the bridge. Goodbye, Erwin."

"Goodbye, Hans, and no hard feelings. It was good of you to come. You'll write me once in a while? —Thank you. And have a good trip."

Hans went down the stairs. He was going to pay a farewell visit to the professor, with whom he had had a long talk the day before. Out in the street, he cast a last look up at Erwin's window.

As he walked away, he thought of the hard-working peasants, the village children, the fraternity brothers with their brick-red caps, and of all the happy people whose days slip through their fingers unregretted. And then he thought of Heinrich Wirth and himself and all those for whom life is a problem and a struggle and whom in his heart he hailed as his friends and brothers.

THE FOURTH LIFE

The Fourth Life

First Version

DURING the reign of one of the many obstinate, gifted, and for all their faults almost lovable dukes of Württemberg, who for several centuries fought perseveringly and victoriously, but also capriciously and childishly, with the Estates over money and rights, Knecht was born in the town of Beutelsperg, some ten or twelve years after the peace of Rijswijk freed the duchy from the devils who, at the instigation of Louis XIV, had long plundered, devastated, and despoiled it in a truly bestial manner. The peace, to be sure, was short-lived, but the able duke, in league with Prince Eugene of Savoy, then at the height of his fame, mustered his forces, inflicted several defeats on the French, and finally drove them out of the country, which for almost a hundred years had known more war than peace and more misery than happiness. The people were grateful to their enterprising prince, who, taking advantage of their gratitude, imposed a standing army on the country, so restoring the customary and normal state of hate-love between prince and people, which had been kept warm by endless friction and harassment.

Knecht's father's house was situated on the edge of the town, at the top of a steeply sloping street, pervaded by the deep bell strokes of the blacksmith's hammer and the smell of singed horses' hoofs and consisting of two rows of half-timbered houses with tall, pointed gables fronting on the street. Each house was separated from the next by a dark, musty areaway. Most of the houses had manure piles in front of them, some enclosed in a neatly plaited straw border, for most of the burghers were not only artisans, merchants, or officials but also owned fields, meadows, and woods, and kept cattle on the ground floor of their gabled houses or in separate barns. Even in the opulent capital city of Stuttgart, this neighborly symbiosis of town and country, man and beast, still survived with all its natural charm; in June the streets were fragrant with hay, in September with fruit and cider; wise but quarrelsome geese made their way from the houses to the river in the morning and came back again in the evening; in the autumn and winter, fir and beech logs were unloaded from wagons outside the houses, where they were sawed and split into firewood by the houseowners or their hired hands. Beutelsperg was a pretty little town surrounded by strong walls. Ferns grew in the chinks between the stone blocks, and the area directly inside the walls was occupied almost entirely by gardens, for the most part grass plots studded with walnut, apple, and pear trees, as well as two of the plum trees, which later became so popular, grown from slips which the survivors of a Swabian regiment had brought back from Belgrade in 1688, thus earning the praises of the local fruit growers for many years to come. From the Gothic church, whose steeple had been damaged in the Thirty Years' War and thus far had been replaced only by a makeshift wooden roof, the stately buildings of the Old City extended in irregular rows around the cobbled marketplace, among them the proud Rathaus, dating from the days of Duke Ulrich, with its double flight of outside stairs. Beyond the marketplace, less impressive streets curved down to the river, ending at the Upper and Lower Mills. On the far side of the bridge, a long single row of houses, the sunniest in the whole town, twined its way between the river and the mountain slopes. The Knechts' modest house was not on this street but in the highest part of the town, above the market and the church. Behind it, a swift little brook flowed through a narrow ravine and emptied into the river not far from one of the mills.

The Knecht house resembled all the others on the street, except that it was smaller and simpler than most. The ground floor was occupied by the stable and a store-room for provisions or hay. A steep wooden staircase led to the second floor where, in three rooms, the family lived, slept, ate, came into the world, and died. The kitchen was also on the second floor, and upstairs under the roof there was yet another tiny room. At the back of the house, facing the ravine, there was a small covered balcony that reached up to the second floor. Between the second floor and the roof there was a loft where firewood was kept and washing hung up to dry. In the ground-floor barn there were no cows, only goats and a few chickens. Under the staircase, a trapdoor led to the cellar, a windowless hole cut out of the soft rock. Here a barrel of cider was kept, and cabbage and turnips were stored for the winter.

In this little house Knecht was born. His father plied a none-too-profitable but uncommon and respected trade; he was a fountain master. He was responsible to the town council for keeping the public fountains clean and sup-plied with water. True, there were two or three springs in the town that flowed unaided, and quite a few of the local housewives carried their pitchers day after day to one of these springs, even if it was a long way off, and filled them with pure, cold water. But the other fountains and the watering troughs were fed by distant springs in the woods, whence the water was conveyed into the town by wooden pipes. To fashion these pipes (hundreds of which were needed in the course of the year) from halved lengths of heartwood with semicircular grooves; to fasten them together so as to form conduits running sometimes above, sometimes below the ground; to keep them clean; to locate damage and repair it—this was the work of the fountain master. In times of urgency, after floods, for example, he worked with several journeymen who were supplied by the township. The town council was pleased with Knecht's father: he was a good, reliable worker, though perhaps somewhat taciturn and eccentric, as men tend to be who work by themselves and spend most of their time deep in the woods. The town children regarded him as a man of mystery, a friend of the water sprites, making his home in dark, remote spring chambers that no one could see into, that gave out strange, primeval gurglings, and were thought to be where babies came from.

The boy Knecht had great respect for his father. There was only one man he looked up to with greater awe, who seemed to him still nobler, higher, and more awe-inspiring. This was the rector, the highest Evangelical authority in the town and district, an imposing figure of a man: tall, erect, invariably clothed and hatted in black, with a serene, bearded face and a high forehead. Young Knecht's veneration for the rector was in part his mother's doing. She had grown up in a parsonage—a poor country parsonage, to be sure—and like her sister, who was married to a parson, she held faithfully to her pious memories of her childhood home. She read the Bible and raised her son in a spirit of pious obedience to the Lutheran church and the pure doctrine that had been faithfully observed in the duchy since the days of Brenz and Andreä. She referred to the devotees of the Roman Church as papists and servants of the devil, and was also rather suspicious of Protestants with slightly different beliefs, especially the Zwinglians and Calvinists. This cast of mind determined the spirit of the Knecht household, and in this spirit the child was brought up. Father Knecht played only a silent part; he went to church every Sunday and took com-

munion several times a year. That was the extent of his
religious needs; theological needs, such as his wife's, he
had none. But the church and the Knecht household had
one need and interest in common, and that was music.
When the congregation sang, both parents enthusiastically lent their voices, and when they sang hymns or folk
songs at home, as they often did in their free time, father
Knecht sang the second voice skillfully. Even before
young Knecht and his sister Benigna were of school age,
they too joined in, and three- or four-part songs were
neatly rendered. Father Knecht inclined more to folk
songs, of which he knew a great many, while his wife
preferred hymns. When he was away from home, the
more worldly-minded fountain master indulged in other
kinds of music, and these too helped to enrich the moments when he stopped to rest from his usually solitary toil. Then he would sing or whistle his folk songs,
marches, and dances, or pipe on some instrument that he
himself had fashioned (his favorite was a thin little
wooden flute without stops). In his younger days he had
played the pipe or cornet at dances, but when he became
engaged to the parson's daughter in the year 1695, she
had made him promise never to do so again, and though
by no means as deeply and passionately convinced as his
wife that inns and dance floors were hotbeds of sin, he
had kept his promise. In later years Knecht remembered
the rare occasions when his father had taken him, then a
little boy, to his places of work outside the town. When
his work was done, his father had taken out his high-
pitched wooden flute and played tune after tune, while
the youngster sang the second part. After his father's
death, the image of his father making music with him
deep in the woods became one of his tenderest memories,
taking on the heavenly radiance and magic peculiar to
childhood memories and to certain dreams.

Knecht's mother, as we see, played a far larger part

than his father in the spiritual conduct of the household
and in the education of the children. Through marriage with this intelligent and pious woman, the fountain
master's nature had undergone a certain sublimation; his
life had been transposed into a different, more spiritual
key. He had won a wife who, in addition to her piety, was
also interested in improving his mind and who even knew
a little Latin. In return, he had forsworn certain of the
habits of his younger days; in particular, he had given up
drinking in the taverns and playing in a dance band. On
the whole, this sublimation of his nature was successful.
It was only natural and in no way reprehensible that
when he was alone with himself or the children he should
sing only his beloved folk songs, to the neglect of hymns,
which he got enough of on other occasions. On the other
hand, he paid for the ennoblement of his life with certain
little foibles, one of which was not so little but a considerable burden and embarrassment to himself and others;
indeed, one might even call it a vice or disease. Though
for months on end he scrupulously observed his duties as
a fountain master, husband, father, and churchgoer, and
led the life of an exceptionally abstemious and upright
burgher and Christian, once or twice a year he departed
from his good behavior (which was evidently something
of a strain on him) and let himself go. On such occasions,
he would drink and loll about in taverns for a whole day
and sometimes as much as two or three days, and then
creep quietly back home, a picture of contrition. For years
glances were exchanged over these unfortunate happenings, but never a word was spoken. True, the discipline
governing Knecht's life had a chink in it—these rare fits
of intemperance, which served as a kind of escape valve
for the undisciplined residue of his animal instincts. Yet,
even in his days of vice, even when he seemed to have
thrown it off, this discipline remained strong and never
set him entirely free. For when the urge to drink himself

into a stupor came over him, the fountain master not only avoided his house but kept away from the town altogether, and from all the places where he was ordinarily to be seen. Even when he was so drunk that he seemed to have lost all willpower and sense of responsibility, he never set foot in his usual haunts and never confronted his own diurnal life, so to speak. He made his sacrifice to the night side of his nature in concealment, either taking his liquor out into the country with him or drinking in obscure taverns on the outskirts, where there was no danger of meeting a burgher of his rank. And he never went home drunk, but always cleansed, sobered, and repentant. Consequently, it was years before the children heard of his escapades, and even then they long refused to believe what they heard.

Thus, from both parents the boy inherited a love of music; from his father a certain unstable balance between spirit and nature, between duty and indolence; and from his mother a devotion to religion and a taste for theology and speculation. Unconsciously, he felt a strong kinship with his father, who taught him to love solitude and the woods. Father Knecht's stringently disciplined life in his wife's shadow made him a kind of guest in his own house. This the boy sometimes sensed, and it filled him with a tenderness close to pity. On the other side stood his mother, with her world of order and piety, and behind her the church, that transcendent home. Though only a small church, it was then the only one he knew, and side by side with the smiling memories derived from his life with his father there were others, no less beautiful, no less beloved and sacred: his mother and her fine voice, the spirit of her Bible stories and hymns, the priestly figure of the rector, and the atmosphere of the town church, to which his parents began taking him when he was still a very small boy. Among the memories that the Sunday hours spent in this church left with him, three were most prominent: the rector, tall and imposing in his black vestments, striding to the pulpit; the long-sustained waves of organ music flooding the sacred place; and the high vault over the nave, which he gazed at dreamily during the long, solemn, and largely incomprehensible sermons, fascinated by the strangely living ribwork, so old and stony and immobile, which, when he fixed his eyes on it, breathed life and magic and music, as though the organ music wove itself into these sharp, angular ribs and both together strove upward toward an infinite harmony.

In the course of his childhood, the boy conceived varying pictures of his future. For a long time it seemed right and self-evident that he should become what his father was, that he should learn his father's trade from him and become a fountain master, taking care of the springs, keeping the spring chambers clean, laying the wooden pipes, and, when he stopped in the woods to rest, playing tunes on flutes he himself had made. But later on it struck him that there could be no more desirable aim in life than to stride through the town like the rector, clad in black dignity, a priest and servant of God, a father to the congregation. True, this implied talents and powers that it would be presumptuous to impute to himself. And then came still other desires and possibilities, especially to make music, to learn to play the organ, to direct a choir, or at least to become a harpsichordist, flutist, or violinist. These were his childhood dreams; the earliest and most innocent of them—to become what his father was— waned with the waning of his childhood.

Knecht's sister Benigna, a few years younger than himself, a beautiful, rather shy and self-willed child, showed unerring sureness in her singing, and later in playing the lute. And in her feelings as well she was surer and more decided than her brother. From the first, she was drawn closer to her father than to her mother, and as she grew older she took his part more and more. She became his favorite and comrade, learned all his folk songs, even those that were not sung at home in her mother's presence, and was passionately attached to him. But it should not be thought that these two were the fountain master's only children. Six or more were born, and at times the small house was bursting with children; but only two grew to maturity, the others died young and were mourned and forgotten; they will not figure in this story.

Among the greater and lesser impressions, events, and encounters of Knecht's boyhood, there was one experience which affected him more deeply than all the rest, and had lasting reverberations. It was the experience of only a moment, but it had symbolic force.

Knecht hardly knew Rector Bilfinger as a man of flesh and blood; he knew him more as a heroic figure or archangel, for the high priest seemed to live and stride in a remote, inaccessible sphere. Knecht knew him from church, where with voice and gesture, standing either at the altar or high up in the pulpit, he directed, admonished, counseled, comforted, and warned his Christian flock, or, as an intermediary and herald, conveyed their pleas, their thanks, and their cares to God's throne in prayer. There in church he seemed venerable, holy, and also heroic, not a human individual, but only a figure, representing and embodying the priestly office, transmitting the divine word and administering the sacraments. Young Knecht also knew him from the street; there he was nearer, more accessible and human, more a father than a priest. Greeted respectfully by all who passed, the rector strode along, tall and imposing, stopped to chat with an old man, allowed a woman to draw him into conversation, or bent down over a child. Then his noble, spiritual countenance, no longer official and unapproachable, radiated kindness and friendliness, while love and trust came to him from every face, house, and street. The patriarch had several times spoken to young Knecht. He had felt the patriarch's big hand around his little one or on his head, for Bilfinger esteemed Frau Knecht both as a parson's daughter and as a zealously pious member of the congregation; he often spoke to her on the street and had visited the Knechts at home on occasions of illness and at the deaths of the children.

And then suddenly an unforgettable moment gave the priest and patriarch, the preacher and demigod, a new face in the boy's eyes, and inspired him with new feelings toward the rector, which brought him both dismay and happiness.

The rector lived not far from the church in a well-built stone house, set slightly back from the street. Eight or ten wide stone steps led to a massive walnut door with heavy brass fittings. On the ground floor there were no dwelling rooms, but only a large empty vestibule with a stone floor and a low-vaulted assembly room. Here the parish elders conferred now and then, and here too the district clergy gathered every few weeks for a few hours of ecclesiastical sociability interspersed with lectures and disputations. The rector and his housekeeper lived on the second floor. Thus, his daily life was invisible to the outside world, and this dignified seclusion was eminently suited to him, though he owed it to chance: the rectory had formerly been the official residence of the count's bailiff, and some of the old townspeople still spoke of it as "the bailiff's." Often, when the boy Knecht was in the neighborhood, he stopped to look at the distinguished, mysterious house; once or twice he had crept up the cool front steps, touched the shiny brass on the weather-darkened old door, examined the ornaments on it, and even glanced through a crack into the silent, empty vestibule, at the back of which a flight of stairs could be seen. Other, ordinary houses allowed a glance at the life of their inhabitants—you could look through a window and see someone sitting inside; you might see the house owner or his hired man or maid at work, or children at play—but here everything was hidden; the domestic life of the rector, who was a widower and whose house was kept by a taciturn old relative, was carried on in a silent, invisible higher sphere. The back garden with its fruit trees and berry bushes had high hedges around it, so that it too was well concealed; only the next-door neighbor might occasionally see the rector strolling about on summer days.

A maiden aunt of Knecht's mother occupied two rooms in a house on the hillside directly above the rector's garden, and sometimes when Frau Knecht went to see her she took the children along. One autumn day, while the two women were busy talking, the boy stood at the window. Rather bored and disgruntled at first, he soon became fascinated by the view of the rector's garden far below, where the trees were defending their last withered leaves against the October wind. One could also see the rectory, but on the first two floors the windows were all closed and nothing could be made out behind the curtains. Up above, however, it was possible to look into the loft. Here there were a pile of firewood and a clothesline with a few pieces of washing on it. Looking obliquely downward, the boy could see, adjoining the loft, a rather bare attic room. He saw a large box full of papers and along the wall a pile of cast-off household articles: a chest, an old cradle, and a ramshackle armchair with torn upholstery. With unthinking curiosity, Knecht gazed into the cheerless room. And then suddenly a tall figure appeared: the rector himself, in a long black frock coat, his gray hair uncovered. Knecht waited tensely to see what the venerable gentleman might have to do in this obscure corner of the house.

Several times Rector Bilfinger strode back and forth across the room. His face was careworn; clearly he was prey to grave and sorrowful thoughts. He stopped with his back to the window and slowly his head drooped. Thus he stood for a while; then suddenly he fell to his knees, folded his hands, pressed them together, raised and lowered them in prayer, then remained on his knees, bowing his head to the floor. It was immediately evident to Knecht that the rector was praying. Shame and guilt weighed on the boy's heart, but he couldn't tear himself away from the sight. Breathless and aghast, he stared at the kneeling man, saw the entreaty in his hands and the repeated bowing of his head. At length with some difficulty the rector stood up; again he was tall and erect. For a moment Knecht could see his face: though there were tears in his eyes, it shone with tranquil, pious happiness. It was so beautiful, so incredibly lovable, that the boy at the window shuddered inwardly and the tears came to his eyes.

Knecht managed to hide his tears, his agitation, indeed his whole experience. This was his first and, for a time, most intense reaction to his experience: he had a secret; all alone he had witnessed something ineffable and great, but secret, and he knew from the first that he would never be able to confide this secret to a living soul. But this was only one of the deep and moving aspects of a vision which long remained a source of fantasies, of secret thoughts, emotions, and dreams. Indeed, if anyone had asked Knecht at the end of his career what had been the most crucial event in his life, he might well have evoked those moments when, standing at his aunt's window, he had looked out over the bleak autumnal garden and seen the rector kneel down and pray in his attic room. What deep meaning there was in that vision! What developments it provoked! How many faces it had! He, a child of seven, had seen a big, grown man, an old man, pacing the room, anguished and needful of help, had seen him kneel down, had seen him pray and weep, struggle, humble himself, and implore. And that man was not just anyone; he was the rector, the venerated and somewhat feared preacher, the man of God, the father of all his parishioners, to whom all bowed low, the living embodiment of all human and priestly dignity and nobility! This was the man Knecht had seen anguished and despondent, kneeling in the dust with the humility of a child, bowing down to One before whom he, so great and so revered, was no more than a child and a grain of dust! The first two thoughts that sprang from Knecht's vision were these: how truly pious this man must be, and how great, how kingly and powerful God must be, that such a man should kneel to Him in supplication! And more: his supplication had been heard; it had borne fruit; the tearful face of the suppli-cant had smiled, had glowed with release, appeasement, consolation, and sweet trust. In his reflections over the months and years, Knecht never exhausted the substance of these moments; it flowed like a living spring and turned the thoughts of the boy, who had often dreamed of becoming a rector in a black frock coat and buckled shoes, to Him whose servant the rector was and from whom he had received his office, his importance, and the honor in which he was held. And yet before Him, before the Lord, the rector was not only a servant, a minister; no, he was His child; he appealed to God as a child appeals to his father, humbly, but full of candor and trust. And for Knecht, the child who had witnessed that prayer, the rector was at once diminished and magnified; he lost something of his proud dignity, but to make up for it, he grew in nobility and sanctity; removed from the common, natural order of things, he entered into an immediate bond with the heavenly Father. Knecht himself had often prayed, and not always because he was told to or from habit. But such prayer had hitherto been unknown to him; he had never known such affliction and such urgency, such devotion and entreaty, such humility and resignation, nor had he ever seen a supplicant rise to his feet with such an aura of joy, reconciliation, and grace.

For the first time Knecht saw something very different from official dignity in the life and calling of a clergyman; behind preacher and sermon, behind church, organ music, and congregation, he for the first time gained an intimation of the power which all this was made to serve and glorify, the God who is at once the commander over kings and the father of every man.

These reflections developed only slowly in the child. Some of them never rose to consciousness and were never spoken, but all the religious thoughts and feelings that arose in Knecht throughout his lifetime were rooted in these moments. And it was not only because he was a child that his thoughts took so long to mature. There was still another reason: the secrecy of his experience gave him an oppressive feeling of loneliness. He could not share his great moment or rejoice in it with others; there was something shameful about it, for he had witnessed the kind of episode that shuns and excludes all witnesses; he had seen something that was not meant to be seen. From then on, he not only felt greater veneration and love for the rector but also feared him and felt ashamed in his presence as never before. And because of this secret sense of shame, his thoughts, though drawn again and again to his vision, sought at the same time to avoid it, and he tried to forget what could not be forgotten. Knecht was a quiet, modest child with little self-confidence. If not for the resilient, musical aspect of his nature, his secret would have injured him, and even so, it weighed heavily on his mind.

Each year there was school from autumn to spring; apart from reading and writing, the children learned Bible verses and hymns. School was monotonous but never tiring. Knecht learned to read music at an early age—without effort, from his parents. While still a child, he read and reread the few books his parents owned. The most important and inexhaustible was the Bible. A passage was read aloud every morning, after which a hymn was sung. In addition to the familiar hymns, which he sang a hundred times and soon knew by heart, there were many others; these were printed in a small (in 16°) parchment-bound book entitled *The Soul's Harp or Württemberg Hymn Book*. The boy loved this pretty little book. On the parchment cover was stamped a narrow gold border, inside which was a delicately drawn and colored stamping of a potted plant with five different flowers and three different leaves. Inside the book, before the title page and the duke's patent, there were two pages of copperplate engravings. On one, King David was shown playing a gracefully curved harp, the top of which was ornamented with an angel's head surmounted by five Hebrew letters. On the second, the Saviour sat by the side of a well, talking with a woman, and the well was Jacob's well in the town of Sipar in Samaria, and the woman was the Samaritan woman who came to draw water at the sixth hour, when Jesus, weary from his journey, was resting by the well. And Jesus said unto her, "Give me to drink," and she replied, "How is it that thou, being a Jew, asketh drink of me, which am a woman of Samaria?" (John 4:9). The bottom of the page showed the ducal coat of arms with its three antlers, the fishes of Montbéliard, and other emblems, and a tiny engraving of the city of Tübingen. The book contained more than three hundred hymns, written by Dr. M. Luther, Duke Wilhelm of Saxony, Clausnitzer, Rinkhardt, Rist, Heermann, Nicolai, Paulus Gerhard, Johann Arnd, Goldevius, and many other poets, some of whom had splendid foreign-sounding names such as Simphorianus Pollio. When young Knecht sang these hymns with his parents, what really mattered to him was the harmony, the interweaving of parts; he was aware of the religious content only insofar as it determined the mood. It was only when he

read the books by himself that he dwelt on the words;
then he delighted in the joyful expectation of the Advent
hymns and the festive exuberance of the Christmas
carols, the bitter grief of the Passion hymns and the
jubilation of the hymns of Resurrection, the anguish of
the penitential chorales, the rich images of the Psalms,
the freshness of the morning songs and gentle sadness of
the evening songs:

> *All you who long for bed*
> *Weary in bones and head,*
> *Now go and lay you down.*
> *When your time has run*
> *And your work is done,*
> *You will be bedded in the ground.*

Before he was old enough to read the Bible, the words
of these hymns nourished and delighted his soul. They
were his plays and his novels. Through them the sufferings, death, and glory of Jesus became a part of his intimate experience; they gave him his first reading of the
human heart with its fears and exaltations, its courage
and wickedness, its transience and striving for eternity,
his first knowledge of life in this world, where evil so
often triumphs, and of the kingdom of God, which
reaches into this world in exhortation and judgment:

> *From wrath and envy keep thy soul,*
> *In mildness never fail,*
> *For though the godless get more gold,*
> *Their wrath is no avail.*

In this little book, two hundred years of German
Protestantism were preserved. Some of the pieces, such as
the Kyrie eleison litany, translated by Luther himself,
were even older and carried a note of still more venerable
and mysterious antiquity. Much of the older Christian
knowledge and faith, on which Christians had fed before
Luther, was gone; a good part of the older religion was

now condemned as papist idolatry and worldly vanity. This was a narrowed Christianity, diminished in power and splendor, and yet there was youth, life, passion, and struggle in this narrowed faith, which was still being persecuted and bloodily repressed in France, Moravia, and elsewhere, and had its heroes and martyrs.

It gave Knecht's mother pleasure to see him reading her little book and later the Bible, and when he asked questions, she answered patiently. She was glad that one of her children should show religious leanings, and she made up her mind to help him in every possible way if he should someday decide to become a theologian and preacher. And as far as was in her power, she taught him the rudiments of Latin.

It is not very often that a boy chooses a vocation that is capable not only of occupying his faculties but also of transforming the dream that lies dormant within him into reality, that will not only feed him and bring him honor but also magnify and fulfill him. Many conditions must be met before so fortunate a choice can be made and followed through. Perhaps we are overinclined to draw hasty conclusions from the careers of the so-called geniuses of the past, and to comfort ourselves with the belief that men endowed with true talent and strength of character have always found themselves and won their proper place in the world. This is a cowardly, philistine assumption, possible only if one shuts one's eyes to the truth. For all their great achievements, many of the most famous geniuses never really fulfilled themselves, and moreover, innumerable highly gifted men were prevented by circumstances from taking up the career that was right for them, or took it up too late. Some men, it is true, have not only borne up bravely under a botched, unhappy life, but have even achieved nobility in their acceptance of it, their *amor fati,* but this is beside the point.

In the case of young Knecht, the possibility of a happy,
fulfilled life in keeping with his talents seems quite conceivable. Without great ambition, he had the makings
more of an artist than of a scholar. From both parents he
had inherited a considerable musical talent. If only he
had grown up amid a somewhat higher musical culture,
in a city blessed with concerts, theaters, proficient music
teachers, etc., he would have found no difficulty, even
without great sacrifices on the part of his parents, in
becoming an accomplished musician. But such a possibility occurred neither to his parents nor to himself. In the
midst of musical eighteenth-century Germany, there
seemed to be no opening for the boy's talent. There were
no doubt excellent musicians at the court in Stuttgart, and
in some few cities musicians may have been employed as
organists or choir masters, but these were rare exceptions
and all this was far away. As a boy Knecht never dreamed
that it might be possible to acquire a serious musical
education that might enable him not only to earn a living
but even to achieve fame as a musician. True, there were
musicians in every small town in Swabia—the fiddlers
and pipers who played at festivals and dances. But they
were regarded as little better than vagabonds; they drifted
from place to place in search of scant earnings, offered
their services at every wedding, church fair, and Sunday
dance; they were looked upon as drunkards and debauchees, and no self-respecting burgher would have
dreamed of letting his son take up their trade. As a young
man, father Knecht himself, though not a professional
musician, had played with dance bands on holidays. In
the seclusion of the woods, he still piped all the dance
tunes he had learned then, but on the day of his betrothal
he had solemnly renounced his place among the happy-go-
lucky musicians. The boy, who had learned to play the
flute when he was very young, and the lute some years
later, would have shaken his head in disbelief if anyone

had asked him if he planned to become a strolling musician. Yet if he had known as a child that it was possible to study music with esteemed musicians, and then to become an organist in one of the great churches, kapellmeister at an opera house, or even a chamber musician, it seems more than likely that he would never have nurtured any other dream for the future. As it was, music always occupied first place in his heart, but not in his consciousness, for he did not know that there were men who held music sacred and devoted their lives to it, just as others devoted their lives to the service of the duke, the church, or the town council. He knew three kinds of music: playing and singing at home with his family, which was glorious, and it was unthinkable that he would ever let himself be deprived of it, but it was only a pastime, something one did when there was no work to do; then there was church music, which for all its splendor was a mere handmaiden of religion, condemned to fall silent the moment the preacher opened his mouth; and finally, the music of the fiddlers and pipers, the three-penny music played at weddings and fairs, which, for all the brilliance of an occasional performer, was not to be taken seriously.

Yet every man, even in childhood, is a composite being, living under complex conditions and deriving from multiple sources. Knecht was a healthy child with a generally sunny disposition, and he grew up in a tolerably peaceful and happy household. Yet this happy home was not without its shadows and tensions, which also involved the children, whether they suspected it or not. Here was father Knecht, strong, handsome, skilled in his craft, musical, a simple, childlike man; but in his youth he had shown a penchant for dance floors and taverns, and it was not for nothing that he had felt the need to marry a woman superior to himself in station, character, and intellect—a gamble that had been largely but not entirely successful. If his proficiency in his work had not given him a certain independence and won him general esteem as a citizen and provider, he would have cut a sorry figure beside his wife. As for his wife, whom both husband and son loved and awesomely admired, she never forgot that her husband was of lower station than her father had been, and tended to overestimate the class to which she no longer belonged. Consequently, she was ambitious for her children; she would have liked to see her son become a rector or even a prelate or professor, and her daughter at the very least a parson's wife. Though there was no great harm in all this, it was a source of tension, and it was fortunate that along with the conjugal love between the fountain master and his wife, a kindly spirit, the good fairy of music was also present in the household.

If young Knecht's choice of profession and hopes for the future presented a problem, it was not rooted solely in his personal circumstances or those of his parents. An individual is not an end in himself; he is born not only into a family but also into a country, an epoch, and a culture, and long before he could have known it, Knecht too was surrounded by movements, problems, yearnings, conceptions, misconceptions, and dreams arising from the time and place in which he lived. Some of these in time were to mean so much to him and become so much a part of his own nature that he not only accepted them passively as a part of the outside world but identified himself with them in his own thoughts, yearnings, struggles, and responsibilities. With his musical gift, what he desired most in the world was harmony, wholeness; he longed to become an integral part of something great, to dedicate his person to an ideal, to something unquestionably noble and good. All his life he pursued this yearning within the forms and constellations he had been born into. In this light, it is significant that at an early age he developed a passionate attachment to religion and the church, and

that after a few indecisive school years it was decided that
he should become a theologian.

Despite misgivings and objections on his father's part,
he was taken out of school at the age of nine or ten and
entrusted to the aged Preceptor Roos, who in the course of
his career had taught a good many boys Latin and prepared them for the higher schools. To defray the costs,
the rector contributed the sum of fifteen florins out of an
endowment fund which he administered. For Knecht
these last summer weeks before the onset of his studies,
the last weeks of childhood freedom, were to become a
precious memory, often looked back upon with sadness. A
chapter in his life was ended. For a time the boy was the
center of attention; consultations were held and plans
were made, with him as their object; he felt honored and
important. But now, for a little while, before the new life
which he anticipated with curiosity and a certain dread
began, he was still a child, allowed to go out with his
father for half days or even whole days, to watch him at
his work and to help him. His father made him a present
of a new flute. He had also been given a pair of brand-new
deerskin breeches, which his little sister Benigna thought
wonderfully becoming. Otherwise, she thought it silly that
her brother should study and become a blackcoat; she had
hoped her father wouldn't allow it. Sometimes, when the
weather was good and her father had to inspect the water
pipes in the woods, she too was taken along. When they
were tired out from walking, they sat down to rest on the
moss under the fir trees, and after they had eaten their
bread and milk and berries, they sang two- or three-part
folk songs such as "All My Thoughts" or "Innsbruck, I
Must Leave Thee." In a clear, cold brook amid rocks and
ferns, young Knecht's father taught him to watch for
trout, which the father would then catch in his hands;
and the children gathered flowers and berries to take
home to their mother.

All the neighbors knew that the boy was to learn Latin and become a student; they called out to him, praised him, congratulated him, gave him a bun, a handful of quills, a piece of cherry cake. The blacksmith, whose anvil sounds filled the street, called him into his sooty smithy with its blazing forge fire, held out his big horny hand, and said, "So you're going to study Latin and be a minister? Look here, son, I don't give a hang for that, and neither does the Saviour; He didn't know any Latin Himself. Don't forget, when you tie on your bands and climb up in the pulpit, that your father was an honest craftsman, which is as good or better than a scholar. Now don't fret, I don't mean any harm, but it's too bad. Well, that's that, and now wait a second." With that he walked out of the smithy and came back after a while with a goose egg, which he gave to the boy. During the blacksmith's absence, young Knecht hadn't given a thought to his words, but had taken a small hammer from the workbench and several times, with long pauses in between, tapped lightly on the anvil, listening with delight to the sweet, full tones.

The short holiday was over. One day, in the cool of the morning, his mother brought the young scholar to Preceptor Roos. She took with her a basket full of peas and spinach as a gift to the preceptor, left young Knecht in the preceptor's sitting room, and returned home with an empty basket and no son. Roos was an old man; his hand trembled so that it took him quite some time to get a proper hold on his slate pencil or pen, but then, slowly and carefully, he wrote out row after row of beautiful, perfectly shaped letters and figures. He had once been famous and feared as a teacher; two of his pupils had become prelates and one a court astronomer; six had become rectors, and many had grown up to be town parsons, village parsons, or Latin teachers. In his old age, he was still a passionate and irascible teacher, but the atmosphere in his sitting room was calmer than in his old Latin school, where he sometimes seemed to devote whole days to thrashing, scolding, and running furiously back and forth. All his pupils had feared him, some had hated him; many years ago one of them, in self-defense, had bitten him so hard on the left hand that the scar was still to be seen. Though he had given up the thrashings, or almost, he was still a strict and domineering master. But on the whole Knecht was well treated, for from the start he had an ace in the hole, or rather, two aces. In the first place, the preceptor admired Knecht's mother, whose father he had known, and his weakness for her sometimes expressed itself in the forms of an older, more chivalrous day. In the second place, the old man was not only a teacher but also a musician; he had played the organ for years and directed the chorus of the Knörzelfingen Latin school, and though it was originally as a favor to Frau Knecht that he took on a pupil in his retirement, he soon grew fond of the boy, because he could read music and sing in perfect pitch and time. And so, something that no one had thought of came to pass. Young Knecht's musical education was continued and his hours in the schoolroom, which were not always peaceful or pleasant, were followed by music lessons, in which scoldings were rare and moments of festive joy frequent.

At the start Latin was his main subject. In addition to mastering the grammar, it would be necessary to learn, not only to translate correctly and fluently, but also to speak, write, and debate in Latin, and to compose Latin hexameters, distichs, and odes—a goal which, though in his first year it seemed far beyond his reach, Knecht nevertheless attained in the end. There was also a bit of arithmetic. As for Greek, that wouldn't begin until his third year. A whiff of scholarship carried over into the music lessons, as, for example, when they translated a number of German hymns into Latin and took to singing them in that language.

Every morning Knecht spent five hours in the school-room, and most afternoons two or three hours, this, of course, quite apart from music. The preceptor owned a harpsichord, which on days of good humor he sometimes let the boy play. He also borrowed a violin for him and taught him the fingering. Knecht practiced at home until he was proficient enough to play sonatas and suites with his teacher. Yet for years the boy was unable to satisfy his most ardent desire, to learn the organ. The old man no longer had the strength for it, young Knecht was too little, and the day wasn't long enough.

The course of study imposed on Knecht was cruelly exacting and cannot have failed to harm him in some degree. Undoubtedly it robbed him of a good part of his childhood, and yet, contradictory as it may appear at first sight, the childlike quality that stayed with him in his mature years is largely attributable to his schooling. For though his one-sided concentration on study banished him prematurely from the freedom, innocence, and natural aimlessness of childhood, on the other hand it isolated him from many of the major and minor experiences which ordinarily expand a child's knowledge of life and gradually build up in him the thoughts and feelings of an adult. The world of learning was ageless and masculine, and those who entered into the republic of scholarship excluded themselves from naïve life. True scholars, it has been observed, are often precocious in childhood and early youth, but this precocity manifests itself only in the conscious, intellectual side of their nature and is accompanied by an almost childlike unworldliness that lasts as long as they live. Knecht did not escape this fate, but he had an easier time of it than many of his contemporaries. We know from his own account of his childhood that the future prelate Oetinger, a man distinguished by piety,

learning, and true wisdom, was driven to despair and
even to blasphemy by his teacher's brutal severity. Such
children were no weaklings; they endured a good deal.
Knecht had a much easier time of it than his future
instructor at the Tübingen Stift, and not only because of
his preceptor's advanced age. We believe that his true
guardian angel was music. For music has a profound,
magical healing power, and even more than the other arts
it can serve as a substitute for nature. It was music that
saved Knecht's soul from intellectual aridity.

Moreover, Preceptor Roos, himself preserved by his
music from the extremes of pedantry, had learned to
moderate the rigid school discipline with little distractions
and to give his pupil a breathing spell when his attention
threatened to flag. He would not have favored the numerous educational systems that were to crop up at a later
day, the combination of work and play, the individual,
humanizing methods of teaching. No, he was a sergeant
of erudition; he knew and loved his training manual, and
would rather have driven himself and his pupil mad than
deviate a hair's breadth from it. No sentimentalities for
him. But little by little, in the course of a long, hard
career, he had found out that uninterrupted strain is
likely to make a student dull and recalcitrant, and that
children subjected to severe discipline are often astonishingly grateful for small rewards such as the timely gift of
a few minutes or a bit of variety. Early in his school
career, Knecht became acquainted with one of the preceptor's little vagaries. The boy had been writing words with
a goose-quill pen. When it seemed to him that the pen
was blunted, he held it out to his teacher and asked him to
sharpen it.

Roos took the quill, which was indeed in a sad state,
and reached for his penknife ("Someday, *volente Deo*,
you will also learn how to whet one of these knives").
His hand trembled so that for a long minute the under-

taking seemed hopeless, but in the end he applied the sharp little knife to the quill, cut off the tip, and proceeded to show young Knecht how one went about making a new point. This was the beginning of a new, sometimes agonizing, sometimes delightful branch of instruction—pen sharpening—which from time to time came as a welcome interruption to a lesson that was growing tedious. On one occasion, the pupil cut the quill, tried it, cut it again, tried it again, and seemed unable to complete the operation. After chuckling over the boy's efforts, the old man told him the story of Oknos, the rope plaiter, whose rope the she-ass kept gnawing away as fast as he could plait it. Knecht was to remember the story as long as he lived.

Knecht was sometimes allowed to help with the housework, and to him this was a holiday. True, the old man, to his pupil's regret, forbade his widowed daughter, who kept house for him, to employ Knecht for daily kitchen and garden chores; it could be done only occasionally and unofficially. But when there were special tasks that exceeded a woman's strength and intelligence, Roos took command and Knecht's services were welcome. And so it was that he helped to unload and pile up firewood, to put up fruit or sauerkraut, and to press pears for cider.

Still, the temple of knowledge, in whose vestibule the boy underwent his hard novitiate, remained a temple. It had the loftiness and somewhat stilted grandiloquence of late baroque, and was suffused more with the light of reason than with mystical twilight. Religious exertions were never expected of the child, for the preceptor himself did not overdo his piety. He gave the church its due, attended services on Sunday, and saw to it that his pupil learned his catechism and his hymns. Apart from that, he let God rule His own kingdom. It was in music that he found the necessary emotional counterweight to the rather colorless sobriety of scholarship. He himself had composed cantatas in his younger days, and he had two chests full of manuscript scores, for the most part church music from Palestrina down to the contemporary organists Muffat and Pachelbel. With a certain awe, Knecht observed that the older manuscripts, many of which the preceptor had copied with his own hand, were as brown and withered as antique books. There were also some very old books which the old man occasionally leafed through and explained to Knecht, of liturgical songs with Latin texts and stiff, rhomboid notes inscribed in four rather than five lines. The whole treasure trove was at his disposal. He would take a book or a few manuscript sheets home with him over Sunday and copy them carefully. He spent every groat he could lay hands on for paper. He himself would line it and then make copies of chorales, dances, arias, madrigals, motets, cantatas, passacaglias, etc. Thus, at an early age, he amassed a store of food for the soul that would last him all his life.

On Sunday when, amid the breathing silence that filled the church after the organ had fallen silent, Knecht saw Rector Bilfinger appear in the pulpit, he was often stricken with consternation at the realization that he had forgotten his secret for whole days. Sometimes he was so engrossed in thinking about it that he missed half the sermon. Now that he was studying Latin, he saw the rector in a new light, for he too was destined to become a clergyman, a priest, and he had set foot on the lowest rung of the ladder, at the top of which he saw the man he so revered. Yet he did not feel that he had come closer to the rector, and for this his secret was again to blame. He knew that the way which led to the priesthood and pulpit was noble and arduous, but he also knew that all in all there was no secret to it; you need only study Latin, then Greek and Hebrew, etc., long and diligently, and then one day you got there. But even if you achieved the title and the dignity and perhaps even the ability to preach, what

was most sacred and miraculous would still be lacking;
you would still be barred from the secret into which he
had once by chance cast a forbidden and alarming glance,
a secret that had no place at the altar or in the pulpit, but
dwelt in attic rooms and lonely hidden places: direct,
childlike communion with God. He knew from hearsay
that all men, even the old and venerable, can and should
regard themselves as children of God. He had heard tell
of the communion of saints and knew that it was given to
some to achieve sainthood; among these young Knecht
unhesitatingly numbered the rector, and in his own
mother as well he discerned a shimmer of holiness. But
he knew that he himself was worlds removed from sainthood, more remote from it than a little Latin scholar
from a rector.

Meanwhile, Latin occupied Knecht's days and thoughts,
not leaving much time for brooding. When he had done
his translating, learned his vocabulary and conjugations—
all of which earned him a privileged, respected, almost
hieratic place at his father's table—he sank gently back
into the old familiar world from which his studies had
estranged him: then he played with little Benigna, listened with deep feeling to his father's pure, deep, radiant
voice as the family sang together, helped his mother clear
the table, or watched her as she sat with her sewing
basket, patiently darning and mending. He felt instinctively that what with his prolonged daily absence, the
hours spent writing and studying in respected silence at
the cleared table, and his preoccupation with new and
alien concerns, he was somehow slipping away from his
home, becoming disloyal and unfair to his family; and his
little sister told him the same thing much more clearly
and directly. Since Knecht had started going to the preceptor's house, coming home late, and sitting with his
papers at the table, where no one was allowed to disturb
him, she had felt deprived of her brother and betrayed by

him, and she made no attempt to hide her feelings. She hated the preceptor, she hated Latin, she hated books and exercises; she hated having to keep still and wait for her distinguished brother to finish his work. She rebelled against the tyranny of Latin and sometimes avenged herself with little acts of sabotage: once she hid her brother's grammar for several days; once she lit the hearth fire with one of his copybooks; once she threw his inkwell from the balcony down into the ravine. And when Knecht's work was done and he called his sister to come and play or to go out with him to meet their father, she was either nowhere to be found, or so hurt, hardened, and hostile that it took no end of wheedling and pleading to bring her around. She loved him and fought for his love, and when he was nice to her she always melted in the end. But more and more Benigna turned against her mother, who, she firmly believed, was to blame for all this. The more severely her mother treated her, the more her mother harped on the importance of religion and study, the more the child withdrew from her and the fonder she became of her father and his warmer, simpler, more natural world, of wanderings in the woods, flute playing, dances, and folk songs. It was she, the child with the unruly red-blond hair, who insisted that the family should go back to singing folk songs and secular arias along with the hymns. Time and time again, she would strike up a folk song, and when her mother protested that they all preferred hymns, she would say, "It's you that wants to sing hymns all the time, you and no one else! I'm sure father likes the other songs better, and my brother likes them too. If you don't let us sing them, I won't join in the hymns." And indeed, she kept silent during the hymns until the religious tradition was breached and the singing of secular songs was resumed in the Knecht household. Far from being gentle and yielding like her father and brother, she had a strong, stubborn character. Like her mother, she had a will of her own, but not the same will as her mother's. Her mother was too intelligent and too pious not to break off the battle before it went too far, but a battle it was, and if for the time being outright unpleasantness was avoided and peace always restored in the end, the guardian angel of the household was song, music. The mother gave in, the father conciliated; a number of folk songs that were not too frivolous or too worldly were taken back into the repertory. Conflict and anger were still in the air, but the family sang, and often young Knecht accompanied the singing on the fiddle. He was always glad to sing with his sister; he brought her music, taught her to read notes and to play a small flute. This was his answer to the little girl's love and jealousy, and thanks to music she gradually became reconciled to her brother's studies and even to the preceptor.

And so Knecht grew. Dreaded difficulties that had once seemed insuperable had somehow been overcome. He spoke Latin very nicely and read Cicero with ease. He had started Greek and even learned to cut pens quite tolerably. In addition he copied out whole notebooks full of music. And then one day old Roos dismissed him. The learned old man was so grieved to be losing the pupil—no doubt his last—with whom he had shared his study for several years, that to hide his emotion he spoke more gruffly than usual. As they stood beside the desk, the old man delivered a parting sermon; he wanted to make it friendly and affectionate, for he was very fond of the boy, but dread of the leave-taking put a lump in his throat. It cost him a brave effort to speak, and the result was an unintended harshness. "You've been doing tolerably well in Latin for the last year, I can't deny it, but what does a young flibbertigibbet know of the pains it has cost his teacher? And when it comes to Greek, you still have a long way to go. Preceptor Bengel will be amazed at some of those second aorists you invent. Oh well, it's too late to find fault now. So here you are, running away from me without a care in the world; you think the worst is over, but other teachers will have their work cut out for them before you're fit to be seen. You don't really deserve it, but I've got a farewell present for you. Here!" With this he picked up a book of old French chansons and slapped it down on the desk. When Knecht, close to tears, tried to take his hand to thank him for the precious gift, he rebuffed him and started in again. "No need of thanks. What does an old man need all this music for? You can thank me by studying properly and making something of yourself that won't disgrace me. These chansons aren't bad. Those fellows knew something about part writing. And oh yes, so you won't be unfaithful to Musica, I've put aside two organ pieces for you, modern things by a man named Buxtehude; no one ever heard of him in these parts, but he knows how to write music and has ideas." Again he slapped a book down on the desk, and when he saw that young Knecht was getting ready to cry, he thumped him on the back and bellowed, "*Vade, festina, apage,* a big boy doesn't cry!" With that he pushed him out the door, which he slammed, but immediately opened again and cried out, "It's not forever, you milksop. We'll be seeing each other again, child. In your vacation you'll come over and make music with me. You're not nearly as good at the harpsichord as you seem to think. Practice, child, practice!" And then he shut the door for good.

Before embarking on a new phase of his life, Knecht was on vacation again. He had been admitted to one of the cloister schools that prepared Swabian theologians for the university. Again he felt that his mother was proud of him, while his father said little and Benigna, anticipating her loneliness, cursed his impending departure. She was quite a big girl by then and wore her hair in pigtails. In those vacation days she and her brother played a good deal of music together, and once she said to him, "Maybe you really are going to be a blackcoat; I never really believed it up to now."

"Stop saying blackcoat all the time," Knecht scolded. "What have parsons ever done to you to make you so down on them? Our own grandfather was a parson."

"Oh yes, and Mother is still proud of it and gives herself airs and thinks she's better than anybody else, but that doesn't stop her from eating the bread our father earns with his hard work."

Her blue-green eyes flashed angrily. He was aghast at the hatred with which she spoke of her mother.

"Good Lord, you mustn't talk like that!" he said imploringly. She gave him a furious look, evidently on the point of putting it even more forcefully. But suddenly she turned away and started to taunt her brother by hopping around him on one foot, singing to the tune of a hymn, "Blackcoat, blackcoat, you're a silly goat." And then she ran away.

Knecht was on vacation again, and in many ways it was like the time before his school days with old Roos. Once again Schlatterer, the tailor, made him new clothes, but now, instead of deerskin breeches, it was a black seminarist's suit. When he tried it on under his mother's supervision and looked down at himself, he felt strangely solemn; it annoyed and even angered him that his mother should show such unabashed pleasure in these new black clothes. He remembered his sister's blackcoat jingle, he thought of his father and the days when he had sung with him in the woods. It was a bewitched, disagreeable moment. Everything that was dear to him seemed to have gone out of his life; the future looked alien, black, and solemn, worthy of Benigna's jibes. It was only a moment, only a brief spasm, and then even the expression on his mother's face, that exasperating look of triumph, was gone. She looked at him affectionately and said, "The next time you get new clothes, maybe it will be for Tübingen."

It was the same in many ways. Again he was on vacation. But the last time the smell, the sound, the taste had been different. That would never come again. His father was no longer a magician from the woods; his sister was no longer a gentle child; even his mother, with her pride in Knecht's black suit and her scanty Latin, had lost something; the whole world had become more disenchanted and at the same time more difficult. Only the beauty and magic of music had remained and, if anything, had grown stronger, but little by little this music, which had held the Knecht household together for so long, was drawn into the sphere of problems and difficulties. Knecht's musical world had grown larger and more varied from year to year, and his parents could no longer keep up with him. To his father music was a natural gift and need. He was always glad to hear music or to play; but to read notes, to study the complicated scores, whether of old polyphonic choral music or of modern organ pieces as his son did, struck him as outlandish; it smacked of schoolwork like Latin and Greek. His wife could go along if she pleased, he wanted no part in it. But his wife didn't really go along; to her, religion meant more than music, and she was beginning to be afraid that the opposite might be true, not only of her daughter, but of her son as well. And of that she could not approve. Music was a good thing; there was no harm in enjoying a good polyphonic song, yet what really mattered in the end was not the singing itself but *what* you sang. If your singing ceased to be edifying, if it no longer served to glorify God, if you made music for its own sake, to display your talents or to wallow in feeling, you were abusing a divine gift, perverting and reversing the values. Music that ceased to be a form of worship was worthless; it could only intoxicate and corrupt the soul— like the erudition which delights in itself and, instead of serving God and His Word, presumes to explain the world.

The existence of such erudition was known to her from conversations with theologians. Of course she did not doubt her son's piety and fear of God; he had never given her cause to. But in little Benigna she saw, or so she thought, signs of what the profane gifts of a fine voice and a good understanding of music could lead to if they were not sanctified by subordination to something higher. Though her son was far more docile and reverential than her daughter, they both had a good deal of their father in them; it was disturbing to see how passionately Benigna worshipped her father and took his part, and how she tried to turn her brother away from his mother.

As for Knecht's attitude toward religion, his mother had no cause for worry; he was on the threshold of what may properly be termed the "pious" period of his life. But he was never one to show his piety in unmistakable signs and gestures. All his life he found those pious men, whose humility or love of Christ or gift of awakening the heart could be read in their eyes, gait, posture, and even in their manner of greeting, admirable but at the same time irritating.

With his admission to the cloister school a new life began for him in many respects, though Latin, and now to an even greater extent Greek, still filled his days and often followed him into his dreams. The course of study was no less rigorous than with Preceptor Roos, yet there were differences. Knecht no longer sat facing his teacher in a small room; here he was one among many. Three dozen boys lived, studied, and played with him. At least in regard to theological learning, these young men were the flower and hope of the duchy, either the pick of the Latin schools or the sons of learned pastors, whose own fathers had begun to prepare them for the ministry when they were still small children.

These well-trained Latinists were all dressed in black,

and indeed the cloister schools still had an air of monasticism, though they were no longer monasteries and no longer belonged to Catholic orders, having been wrested away from the papists and transformed into homes of the pure doctrine and of Lutheran learning. For a good three hundred years these Protestant "cloisters" have supplied Swabia with its parsons and with no end of illustrious scholars, while the woods, fields, mills, and land titles belonging to the cloisters have provided the Swabian treasury with roughly a third of its total receipts. These receipts, it was originally stipulated, were to be used primarily for the maintenance of the churches and the training and remuneration of the ministers, and by and large this was done, though occasionally, when one of the God-appointed dukes was too pressed for money, he would plunder the entire treasury without stopping to ask what would be left for the propagation of the pure doctrine.

And so Knecht, not without tears, left his home for the first time and entered the Denkendorf "cloister." In Denkendorf he found what he would have found at any of the other cloister schools: strict discipline, stimulating friends, excellent instruction in Greek, Hebrew, and French. But he also found something more and extremely rare: a gifted and in every other way extraordinary teacher. The teacher's name was Johann Albrecht Bengel, and he was not only the preceptor of the school, but also the Denkendorf preacher. When Knecht became his pupil, Bengel, though by no means an old man, was already famous as a teacher. Though a great scholar, he had managed with his self-effacing humility to evade all advancement. For almost thirty years he served as preceptor at Denkendorf; only then did he rise, quickly, though with no pushing on his part, to the highest offices and dignities. But even as an unassuming preceptor he exerted a quiet but profound influence for many years, and not only on his own students, for many of whom he remained throughout his lifetime a mentor, confessor, and consoler. Indeed, his reputation as a great scholar and incorruptible guardian of the Word extended even to foreign lands.

In his first conversation with Knecht, he asked him, "What is your father?" "A fountain master." Bengel looked inquiringly into Knecht's face and then said softly, choosing his words in his deliberate way, "Become what your father is, a good fountain master. In the spiritual sense; that is what I myself try to be. The word of God and the Lutheran doctrine are the fountainhead from which our people draw the water of life. To keep this fountainhead pure is obscure work; no one talks or thinks about it, but few occupations are so holy and important." For years, in the few hours that his two offices left free, Bengel had been working faithfully and patiently on an edition of the original Greek text of the New Testament, carefully tracking down the purest, oldest, most reliable sources, scrupulously weighing and testing every word. Not a few of his pious friends thought it a sinful waste that an able minister and teacher should spend precious days and years on a work of niggling and all in all superfluous scholarship, but he never swerved from his purpose, and it was characteristic of the man that he should have appointed himself the task of "keeping the fountainhead pure." The church to which Bengel belonged did not recognize canonization, but Bengel stood high on the list of its secret saints.

When this teacher with the serene, bony face and kindly eyes came to the classroom bright and early for the morning prayer and his first lesson, he had spent several hours of the night over his Bible text and his wideranging, partly scholarly, partly pastoral correspondence and had begun the new day with an examination of conscience and a prayer in which he entreated God to give him perseverance, patience, and wisdom. He brought with him not only a serene alertness and cool intelligence but also an aura of gentle devotion and inspiration to which few of his pupils were impervious. Like other Lutheran churches, the Swabian church had developed a rigid and rather pharisaic orthodoxy, and the clergy had taken on a certain upper-caste arrogance. Bengel was one of the first disciples and models of a new kind of Christianity known as pietism. Over the years, this vigorously spontaneous movement, like all other movements, was to slacken and degenerate. But then it was in its springtime, and there was something of its freshness and delicacy in the aura of this man, who by nature inclined far more to clarity, moderation, and order than to sentimentality and mysticism.

There was little or no difference between the teaching methods of Bengel and those of Preceptor Roos. With Bengel, however, study and erudition were no longer ends in themselves but wholly directed toward a supreme goal —divine worship. The ancient languages, to be sure, had their profane authors and humanistic charms; Bengel himself took pleasure in speaking Latin and Greek; but for this great philologist, all philology culminated in theology; it was an introduction to the world of God, a manner of teaching men to revere it and be faithful to it. When, as occasionally happened, a student didn't seem to be getting ahead, the preceptor would admonish him not only to study harder but with equal urgency to pray, and when it seemed necessary, Bengel himself prayed with him. What with his earnestness, modesty, and utter lack of professorial arrogance, his attitude toward his pupils was that of an equal, and sometimes he almost humbled himself before them. In a talk with a former student, he once said that he looked up to each one of his pupils with respect, for in each of them he saw something better and nobler than himself, and that when he gazed at those young faces he was often profoundly grieved at the thought of how pure and untainted these souls still were, while he himself had already squandered and bungled so much of his life.

In his two years at Denkendorf, Knecht remained true to music. He continued to practice the violin, and with the help of an enthusiastic schoolmate organized a double vocal quartet. But more important than this or his studies was Bengel's influence. This venerable man, it seemed to him, was a true child of God; trust in God emanated from him like a gentle, joyful light. Several of his pupils, who were especially devoted to their teacher, decided among themselves to take his path, to purify themselves each day with prayer and self-examination, so as to become vessels of grace. Knecht was one of them. The friends read Arnd's *True Christianity*, copied and discussed Bengel's Sunday sermons, confessed their trespasses, omissions, and evil thoughts to each other, and vowed to imitate Christ. They took it for granted that conversion and salvation must begin with contrite awareness of one's sinful nature. Though the trespasses of these young men, including Knecht, amounted to very little, they found it necessary to ascribe them to original sin and to be horrified at them. In their own hearts they detected the universal depravity, self-seeking, and lukewarmness of man, and in the depth of their affliction set all their childlike hope in the miracle of Jesus, who had sacrificed himself to overcome this very sinfulness and so opened the way to God's heart to each one who accepts the Saviour's sacrifice in loving faith.

Sometimes it worried Knecht that this feeling of sinfulness was neither as intense nor as lasting in him as it seemed to be in some of his comrades. Sometimes he felt tired and his zeal flagged; sometimes it struck him as useless and exaggerated to torment oneself so, and in secret he agreed with some of the other pupils' jokes at the expense of the pietist group. But in this relapse, this slackening of his feeling, this backsliding into the ways of the world, this flirtation with the lusts and habits of the old Adam, he soon recognized the well-known wiles and snares of the devil and resisted them. Sometimes he even suspected his love of music and the hours spent practicing the violin, but he could not bring himself to give them up. In all other respects he was very strict with himself, for he was determined to go the whole way, to transform and ennoble his whole life; to penetrate to the center, no longer to belong to himself and lead his own life but to make himself entirely into an instrument of God. What sacrifice, what heroism would be too great if he could become what the Apostles had been, if he could become like Preceptor Bengel? He and his friends studied the Bible, the catechism, the hymn book, the works of Arnd and Arnold; even the works of pagan antiquity were searched for methods of self-mastery. Cicero's *De Officiis* was pored over, the maxims of Isocrates learned by heart, though his eloquent Greek might have been worthy of a profounder philosopher; it was only later that they gained a slight knowledge of Plato. On the other hand, a rumor and shimmer of the secular philosophy that was then modern had penetrated the cloister. The more secular-minded students had heard the name of Leibniz and rejoiced in what they sensed to be the dawn of a radiant new spirit; to prepare themselves for it, a few of the more energetic among them took up such extracurricular studies as algebra and plane geometry. This secular-minded group included two of the best students in Knecht's class; they gave themselves airs and regarded themselves as an intellectual aristocracy. Their chief criticism of Bengel and his emulators was that their piety was merely a means by which inferior minds could escape from their studies to religion. For Bengel himself had said on several occasions that talent and industry were not

enough for a future theologian, and that a deficiency in
reasoning power or memory could well be compensated
by superior love of God and fervor in prayer. This the
secular-minded students denied categorically; they joked
about the poor in spirit, who were unable to turn out an
elegant Greek period and hated mathematics as an artifice
of the devil, but made up for their incompetence by praying until they had callouses on their knees. It must be
said, however, that in those days the secular-minded were
not alone in striving for high intellectual achievement,
and that Swabian pietism in its beginnings cannot be
identified with the dunce's fear of strict intellectual discipline. Though the new piety was very much a matter of
feeling, though it had a profound and fruitful influence
on the common people, its Swabian leaders and models in
those early days were far from shunning the sciences.
Some of them were distinguished mathematicians and
logicians, and nearly all of those who later combated
pietism started out as its pupils, and not bad ones at
that.

At vacation time Knecht returned home, where he
found his mother sympathetic to all his interests and
concerns, his father lovingly silent, his sister somewhat
reserved and estranged from her learned brother, but
always ready to make music with him. Now he often took
her with him on his visits to old Roos; she was learning to
play the harpsichord and Roos couldn't praise her enough.
Knecht did not discuss religious matters with Roos. But he
had several conversations with Rector Bilfinger, who,
every time they met on the street, encouraged the young
scholar to visit him. Though he was not nearly as old as
Roos, his health was failing; his hair was white, his walk
had become gingerly, and a curate replaced him in the
pulpit. He had Knecht read to him from the Greek New
Testament, questioned him about what he had read, in-
quired of Bengel, and sent him greetings. Once, at the end

of Knecht's vacation, the rector was unwell and received
him in bed. He prayed with the boy and blessed him. "If
you think of me at Denkendorf," he said in leave-taking,
"include me in your evening prayer, as I too shall remember you in my prayers. I'm an ailing old man and you're a
spry young student, but before God we're both poor sin-
ners and it's pleasing to Him that we should pray for each
other. My prayer for you is that He should make you grow
and improve and become a staunch *minister divini verbi*,
and you, I hope, will pray that He forgive an old man his
failings and help him to die a brave death."

When Knecht next returned home, the rector was still
alive but could no longer receive visitors, and soon there-
after he died. Knecht forgot neither his words of admonition nor his request, and whenever he thought of the
rector, he remembered his childhood secret as the first
call to reach him and open his heart to the divine. Organ
music, hymn singing, Sunday sermons, and dreamy gaz-
ing at the living mathematics and silent music of the
Gothic church vault, his mother's instruction and stories
had gone before; then came the secret, the vision of the
man praying in his attic room, but never had the two
worlds—the solemn, official world of church Christianity,
held in common by all, and the hidden, more profound
and mysterious Christianity of that solitary prayer—come
together and fused into one. In the course of Knecht's
years at Denkendorf, they moved closer to one another. In
the figure of Bengel they seemed to be united; by emulat-
ing him, Knecht thought, he might succeed in becoming a
priest and at the same time a child of God, a scholar and
at the same time a man of simple heart. To be a true
scholar, Bengel had once said, was to serve the word of
God; the innermost essence of scholarship was unceasing
praise of God.

Almost every day Bengel took one of his pupils aside
for a few moments, half an hour or a whole hour, accord-

ing to the circumstances. Knecht too was often alone with him; sometimes Bengel called him into his study and sometimes they went for a walk under the trees. Some of their conversations were carried on in Latin, not the specifically religious ones but those dealing with learned matters and general morality. Knecht, who was shy, said little as a rule. But once he summoned up his courage and spoke of his love of music, admitting that if he had been free to choose he would rather have become a good organist or harpsichordist than a theologian. Then he asked whether his love of music was sinful. Bengel comforted him. Music, he said, was no more sinful than any other art; like scholarship it could lead to self-indulgence and vanity, but God gave the gift of music to praise Him and to thank Him with. "I myself am not musical," he said. "You have a noble gift that I lack; you must be grateful for it and not neglect it. But my advice is to take the same attitude toward music as I do toward the writing of books. The writing of books is also an art, and for many it is a passion; many a famous writer has been overpowered by his passion and driven to hell. When I am writing a book and the desire comes over me to strive for gain or celebrity or the praise of my fellow scholars, there is one thought that always sets me right. A maker of books, I tell myself, should never write a single word that he would have to regret in the hour of death. That goes for you too. When music threatens to intoxicate you, resolve never to make music in such a way as to regret it in the hour of death. Artists and scholars should both be instruments for the praise of God; as long as we are that, our art will be sanctified by Him and pleasing to Him." Then Knecht asked another question by trying to explain his feelings about the cleavage between the two kinds of religion, the official and the private, church religion and personal religion, the sermon from the pulpit and the prayer in the attic room.

"There is indeed a big difference," said the teacher, carefully choosing his words, "and in the next few years, *delecte fili,* you will see that this difference is what makes theology necessary and important. Theology is service to the Word, and in theology the Word is of first importance, for the Word is the core and foundation of revelation, and to accuse theologians of quarreling over words is in my opinion more praise than blame. We *should* quarrel over words; we *should* hold words sacred and defend them, but God's words, not our own. Remember, son of the fountain master, to keep the fountainhead pure! As for your misgivings, they point to the core and center of our holy calling, the priesthood. Alone with himself, a believer may invoke the Saviour by any name he pleases, the most solemn or the most familiar; there are some who address Jesus as their brother and even give Him playful nicknames, 'my little Jesus' and the like. Though I regard such endearments as unnecessary and would not countenance them in my presence, it seems perfectly possible that a man who prays in this way when alone in his room will find salvation. But what a man does in the solitude of his room is a very different matter from what he does in the company of others. If I, as a responsible servant of the Word, were to employ playful words of that sort in the pulpit, I should be committing a mortal sin. Every believer has his needs and habits, and I see no reason why I or any other minister should interfere as long as we are convinced of his sincerity, but it is our duty to preserve the purity of the Bible, the hymnal, and the catechism, to safeguard public prayer and our sermons against falsification of the Word. God revealed Himself to man in the Word; the Word is holy, and to serve it is our priestly vocation. Undoubtedly, an unlearned believer, an artisan or peasant, can have profound thoughts and insights, more profound than a good many of our parsons, and no one should prevent him from interpreting the Holy Scriptures in accordance with his own lights and conscience. But if he feels called upon to address others, if he thinks of himself as a priest, he should, like every ordained priest, submit the words he uses to the judgment of the church and theology; that is, he should let his words be compared meticulously with the word of God. The moderation and circumspection of a good preacher derive from such responsible comparison. An ecstatic visionary may speak with more fire; his sermons may be more moving and more comforting, but unknowingly he is falsifying the pure doctrine in the minds both of himself and of his flock. It is not fitting for a priest—and this is one of the thousand imperfections of this world—to rely on his own feelings and enthusiasms, confident that God is speaking through his person, for between the word of God and the word of man there is an insuperable barrier, and the priest's vocation is to proclaim God's word, not his own."

On another occasion, when Knecht confessed to Bengel that he despaired of becoming a man like him, the teacher shook his head in disapproval. Then he set down a sheet of paper, marked a dot on it, and drew a circle around the dot. "There is one center," he said, "and that is God. But on the periphery there is room for countless millions of points; we human beings are these points. From every point on the periphery a straight line leads to the center; this straight line is what we must all seek, and each of us must seek his own, not his neighbor's, for that would take him the long way around. We should not have models, and we should not aspire to become models for others. Our model is Jesus; we need no other."

Reluctantly we shall refrain from saying any more about Bengel, that exemplary teacher, and from quoting more of his utterances. Two books about him appeared in the nineteenth century; though they have little to say of his life, they quote at length from his sayings, sermons, and letters. For many years he carried on a copious correspondence in Latin with certain of his friends.

Here we shall pass over the next phase of Knecht's education, the two years he spent as a seminarist at the Maulbronn cloister after leaving Denkendorf. At the end of his four years in the cloister schools, he was admitted to the well-known Tübingen Stift for students of theology, established two centuries before by Duke Ulrich.

At that time, Tübingen University was the scene of intense intellectual ferment; at least this was true of its theological and philosophical faculties. All the new systems grounded in mathematics and Aristotle that had sprung up largely under French and Dutch influence were discussed if not taught; the newest and most stimulating of these was that of Leibniz. The atmosphere was one of tension, rising from the conflicts on the one hand between philosophy and orthodox Lutheran theology, and on the other hand between Lutheran orthodoxy and the young pietist movement. Even more embattled was the religious and ecclesiastical life of the people, who in many places were merciless in their criticism of the Lutheran church. Everywhere separatist movements were afoot. Groups of pious laymen, the "Awakened Ones"—most conspicuous among them the "Inspired Ones," who had been awakened by the recent refugees from France—met to pray and read the Bible together. They distrusted scholars and ministers, and looked upon Christianity as an affair not of tradition, formulas, and erudition but of the heart and of human experience. They drew strength and popular appeal from the indubitable martyrdom of the French Camisards, the Moravian exiles, and other persecuted Protestants. The movement of the "Inspired Ones" created a great stir in the duchy and there, too, soon led to open conflict and martyrdom. Though their meetings were forbidden and dispersed by the police, though their itinerant preachers were spat upon, beaten, stoned, and driven out of towns and villages, there were doubtless a few official ministers who lovingly and courageously defended them; but for those sections of the population who were ripe for awakening and new forms of faith, the persecuted, spat-upon, imprisoned sectarians exerted a greater force of attraction in their martyrdom than the government-supported clergy in their gowns. However, the behavior of the "Inspired" was not without its unusual, not to say pathological, aspects, which aroused widespread suspicion and revulsion. When their inspiration came over them, they uttered penetrating prophecies, dire warnings, and golden words of Christian wisdom, but the states to which they owed their revelations were so repulsively violent, so much like epileptic fits, that even the favorably disposed were horrified. Friedrich Rock of Göppingen, the leader of the Württemberg "Inspired," had recently addressed a letter of admonition to the authorities, in which God castigated Württemberg and its church, saying, among other things: "I will exact blood retribution from the princes and potentates, the governors and judges who have sucked so much blood and sweat from the poor. O Württemberg, O Württemberg! O Stuttgart, O Stuttgart! What benefits I have conferred on you! But all my goodness has only made you more wanton, and each day you have fallen further away from me!"

This Friedrich Rock appeared one day in Tübingen, where, like Knecht, a nephew of his was studying at the Stift. Such were his boldness and determination that the Tübingen professors and clergy were obliged to listen to him; they treated him with respect and asked him to submit his writings, but adjured him not to hold any public meetings and to leave Tübingen with all possible dispatch. Nevertheless, the small group of "awakened" students went to see him at his lodgings, and the earnestness of his tone and bearing made a lasting impression on them.

Knecht was a zealous but quiet and diffident participant in all this. Like his comrades, he felt that this Rock who so courageously professed his faith and summoned the official church to repent bore a closer resemblance to an apostle than did the Tübingen cleric, who without confuting him had bidden him leave town as soon as possible. Knecht was in the same position as quite a few of his friends and coreligionaries: every experience and insight that reinforced them in their piety shook their confidence in their vocation. The more pious they became, the more they doubted the value of the priesthood to which they were destined. Some had special misgivings about the minister's responsibility in administering the Lord's Supper; others thought the present condition of the church utterly hopeless and secretly approved the separatists. A pious old burgher of Tübingen, the lessee of the powder mill, once said to Knecht and his friends, "You are students of theology, but they bind your eyes and mouth; you are forbidden to read those books which, after the Bible, are the best and most pious books in existence." Eagerly the students asked what books he was referring to. When he spoke of Jakob Böhme, they had no answer to make, for Böhme's books were indeed banned. These discussions made Knecht unhappy. From a purely intellectual pont of view, nothing could be nobler than to study theology, to improve one's knowledge of the Bible by at once harkening to one's inner voice and applying the methods of scholarship, to employ logic and metaphysics as means of creating and testing a *philosophia sacra*. But in practice the situation was very different; the teachings of the church were at odds with secular philosophy and with the religious needs of the people. It was necessary to make decisions, to choose between dogmas and formulations that even the professors quarreled over, and if the purpose and ultimate end of this study was to give the student certainty, to make him a useful and reliable servant of God and the church, the goal seemed to become more remote with each passing day.

But side by side with this confusing and often frightening study was something else that brought harmony and consolation. Knecht took organ and harpsichord lessons, sang in the church choir, practiced four-part songs with his friends, and spent many hours studying and copying organ and choral music. His teacher had once studied under the great Pachelbel and had been friends with J. G. C. Störl, the Stuttgart kappellmeister and organist who had published a hymnal entitled *King David's Harp Restrung,* and who had composed hymns which were widely sung at the time and several of which continued to be sung by Württemberg congregations for more than two hundred years. Whenever Knecht had half an hour to spare, he spent it practicing the organ. The difficulties and complications he encountered were never too much for him; here there was no discouragement, no self-doubt or sudden weariness. As far as music was concerned, Württemberg, apart from the court, was then a remote, insignificant province, but in those same years music, both religious and secular, flourished with such creative vigor that even in the poorer, less cultivated regions anyone born with a musical gift breathed a joyful, invigorating air, the freshness of which is hardly conceivable to us today. A century of song and melody had filled the world with music; though less exuberantly than in the past, folk songs still sprang from the heart of the people, and though certain branches of art music, choral polyphony, for example, were on the wane, a new era of awareness and creativity had dawned. Men seized upon their musical heritage with unprecedented enthusiasm, built more and more magnificent organs, and reorganized the orchestra; innumerable musicians were at work, composing cantatas, operas, oratorios, concerti, and in a few decades they built up the joyful, luminous edifice which today every worshipper of the most gracious of arts calls to mind when he utters one of the beloved names: Pachelbel, Buxtehude, Handel, Bach, Haydn, Gluck, Mozart. To Knecht in his student years, this vast treasure of achievement and perfection was still largely unknown; he had a vague notion of Pachelbel, some small knowledge of Buxtehude; it would be many years before he heard the names of Handel and Bach; but all unknowing, he was carried along by what we, with the melancholy knowledge of latecomers, recognize to have been a living stream.

Ever since his misgivings in Maulbronn, Knecht's love of music had repeatedly troubled his conscience, and not without reason, for it was music more than anything else that prevented him, despite his sincere quest for a true Christianity, from fully experiencing the conversion, the extinction of the natural man within oneself, which presupposes a hell of despair, a shattering of the ego. He had had more than his share of anguish and consciousness of sin, yet something within him stubbornly resisted the ultimate despair and contrition, and this something was closely connected with his love of music. Little by little his tormented conscience became reconciled with his love of music, and in this, from the outset of his Tübingen period, he found a staunch helper in Dr. Martin Luther, for it was then that he discovered Luther's 1538 preface in praise of music. He learned a number of passages, such as the following, by heart:

> Where natural music is sharpened and polished by art, we are filled with wonderment to see and recognize in part—for it cannot be wholly perceived or understood —God's great and perfect wisdom in His miraculous work of Musica. What is most rare and wonderful is that one man sings a simple air or tenor, while three or four

or five other voices play and leap around this simple air
or tenor as though in jubilation, marvelously gracing and
adorning it, and dancing as it were a heavenly round,
meeting one another fondly and seeming to caress and
embrace one another, so that those who understand this
a little and are moved by it cannot but be filled with wonder and convinced that there is nothing more precious in
the world than such song, adorned with many voices.
And he who takes no loving pleasure in it and who is not
moved by so gracious a miracle, must indeed be a gross
clod, unworthy to hear such gracious music, fit only for
the ass-like braying of Gregorian chants or the song and
music of dogs or swine.

The kind of music that had so delighted Luther was
also especially dear to the student Knecht: compositions
in which a principal voice carries the melody, and in
which around this *cantus firmus* a glass net of dancing,
jesting, lamenting, higher and lower voices is woven,
which circle round it in richly figured, richly mobile independent orbits, comparable to a network of lines tracing
the orbits of the planets and also recalling the network of
stone ribs from which one could read the structure of old
church vaults. Roos, Bengel, and sound training in languages and literature had prepared Knecht's mind for the
grammar and notation of music; he had long ago learned
to read figured basses, and now he applied himself with
joy to the secrets and artifices of the new signatures and
notations, until he was able to read and write the score of
a sacred concerto for organ, voices, and instruments.
When he had played his first passacaglia and his teacher
expressed his satisfaction, he enjoyed one of the happiest
moments of his student days, even though he could not
repress a bit of a sigh at the thought that for him theology
was by no means as easily mastered as music.

Still, Tübingen was on much more intimate terms with
the kingdom of God than with the world of music. Han-

del's operas and the existence of the cantor J. S. Bach
might be quite unknown, but Knecht and his friends were
all the more familiar with the events and personalities of
the pietist world. Except for Spener and Francke, the
fathers of pietism, Knecht had heard no name mentioned
as often in recent years as that of Count Zinzendorf, some
of whose hymns were widely known and about whom
numerous anecdotes were told. This Saxon count, the
child of pious parents, had been inspired from early childhood with a special love of the Saviour. As a young man,
so the story went, he saw a sculpture of Christ on the
cross, with the inscription

> *I did this for thee—*
> *What wilt thou do for me?*

and vowed in that moment to devote his whole life to the
Saviour. After studying with the venerated Francke at
Halle, he was said to have gone to the university at Wittenberg with a view to bringing about a reconciliation
between the pietistic Halle and the orthodox Lutheran
Wittenberg. Then, after the manner of aristocratic students, he was sent on travels; at the court in Paris he
professed his love of Jesus and won the friendship of the
famous Cardinal de Noailles, to whom he is said to have
written letters in later years urging him to be mindful of
the French Protestants in their hour of need.

But what aroused the interest and sympathy of Knecht
and his friends far more than these tales were the Moravian Brethren, exiles from Bohemia, who under the count's
aegis had established a church of their own at Herrnhut.
The names of Zinzendorf and Herrnhut were mentioned
more often and with greater interest than those of any
potentate or capital city of the day; the students spoke of
them lovingly yet critically, with enthusiasm but also with
a certain misgiving. For though no one doubted the
count's sincerity, his impassioned enthusiasm was a shade

too theatrical for the prudent, rather retiring Swabians. Some wondered whether the Herrnhut community should be regarded not as a separatist *ecclesia in ecclesia* but as a vainglorious, overweening sect. Others accused the count of the exact opposite, not of sectarianism, but of a nondescript syncretism, lacking any clear-cut creed and borrowing from every current that called itself Christian, not excluding pagan papism and loveless Calvinism. Some were repelled and others attracted by the fact that this controversial *novus homo* was a count, an aristocrat and big landowner who had frequented the courts of princes and hobnobbed with French cardinals; in either case, it contributed to making the man interesting.

Then one day this distant star took on a new reality. A new teacher appeared at the Stift; he came directly from Herrnhut, he had lived there and studied the community at firsthand; he had debated with the count, had been his guest and friend, and the count had made every effort to keep him in Herrnhut. The new instructor was a young man, still in his twenties, and his name was Oetinger. Even without his connections with the count and the Moravian Brethren, he would have appealed to the imagination of his students. It was bruited about that he had been a brilliant student and that if he had not experienced an awakening and conversion in the course of his schooling at Bebenhausen he would have become an outstanding jurist and statesman. Instead, he had studied theology, mathematics, and philosophy. He had read the works of the suspect mystic Jakob Böhme, had gained a thorough knowledge of Hebrew, and had gone on to other Oriental languages; he had read the Zohar and other cabalistic writings, as well as rabbinical literature, with Jewish scholars. And yet with all this vast erudition and all his pious zeal, conscientious scruples, notably in regard to the Lord's Supper, had deterred him from entering the Swabian ministry. For that reason he had left home with a view to attending the university at Jena, where the student body was in the grip of a truly apostolic awakening, and studying law at Halle; but first he had gone to see the learned cabalist Kappel Hecht at Frankfurt, had become his friend, and discussed the subtlest problems with him. Kappel Hecht had taught him many things, acquainting him for example with the cabalist theory that Plato had been a disciple of the prophet Jeremiah, from whom he had taken over his theory of ideas. The Jew had grown very fond of him, taken him to a celebration of the Feast of the Tabernacles, and given him much advice. For one thing, he had advised him to content himself with purely biblical studies and to give up hope of ever, as a Christian and a theologian, attaining the ultimate degrees of cabalistic wisdom. Actually, the Jew added with a smile, the Christians had a true sage who was very close to the Cabala and was indeed its Christian counterpart: his name was Jakob Böhme.

Thus Magister Oetinger had not only been at Frankfurt and Halle and had not only studied theology, mysticism, and the Cabala; he had also been at the celebrated Herrnhut, had shared and studied the life of the Moravian Brethren, had been distinguished by the count and invited to remain there for good, but had been unwilling to tie himself down. Instead, he had returned home, and for the present, since he still had misgivings about entering the ministry, was serving as an instructor at the Tübingen Stift. The students looked upon him with keen curiosity but also with a certain distrust. To the pious among them, Oetinger's many-sided erudition, his philosophy, his brilliant and complex intellect were suspect. Did a theologian, in order to find salvation and lead others to Jesus, require such an arsenal of philosophies, languages, and systems? The secular-minded students, on the other hand, were repelled by Oetinger's pietism, his habit of fraternizing, reading the Bible, and praying with unedu-

cated pietists, and his firm belief that all the conclusions
of secular philosophy must be tested by the words of the
Bible and rejected when not in agreement with them. In
this stubborn, uncompromising insistence on the words of
the Bible, he resembled Bengel. And indeed Bengel's admirers were the first to be won over by Oetinger, although
they almost unanimously disapproved of his admiration
for Böhme. He made no attempt to force Böhme on them,
but it grieved him that a theologian should be unwilling to
acquaint himself with every conceivable form and mani-
festation of the spirit, for he deplored all narrow-minded-
ness, and looked upon openness, curiosity, delight in
diversity as virtues worthy to be cultivated. He listened to
everyone and had the gift of taking in what he heard. He
reflected for a long while in silence before accepting or
rejecting another man's opinions. Chance has submerged
the memory of this great and pure mind; today his name is
known to few.

On taking up his post, Oetinger found a small community of earnest Christians among the students, the same
to which he himself had belonged in his student days
some years before. Under his influence it experienced a
new flowering. Knecht was among those who admired
and loved him most fervently. Apart from the rather
moderate Bengel and Rock, the zealot who had passed
through Tübingen like a flaming meteor and vanished,
Knecht had never before been close to a man who, as he
knew for certain in Oetinger's case, had traveled the road
of penance and grace to its end and had acquired a son-
ship that sublimated and hallowed his life. Undoubtedly,
Spener and Francke and the famous Count Zinzendorf
were such men, apostles directly moved and marked by
the spirit who prepared the way for God on earth. And
now there was Oetinger, as wise as Solomon and as
humble as a man who no longer lives in his self but has
become a child of God, a man full of spirit and tempera-

ment, yet a brother and servant to every poor sinner. He brought new inspiration and new methods to the little community's meetings for Bible reading and edification, and insisted with a friendly firmness peculiar to himself that these sessions should not be devoted to an impersonal, self-intoxicated worship that committed no one to anything, but that each worshipper should mercilessly examine himself and his fellows, that they should spur each other onward on the road to salvation. If one boasted of his inner experiences or another bemoaned his weaknesses, he admonished them, often taking a sarcastic tone, and he obliged them, first to give a scrupulous theological interpretation of a Bible passage, then to test and measure themselves, their opinions, experiences, struggles, and defeats against the words of Scripture. He himself submitted willingly to the examination, criticism, and admonition of others, never taking offense and giving serious consideration to every reproach or criticism before justifying himself or accepting the criticism as warranted. And time and again his bold and pious spirit compelled those present to enter into the Bible and into God's plan for humankind as into a sphere of pure light, to recognize that God as Creator and as Mind was incomparably superior to all human reason and all human virtue, to elucidate each passage in Scripture with the help of many other passages, and to see the Holy Scriptures as a single living whole. For him there were no contradictions in Scripture, no difference between important and unimportant, no ground for argument. The only possible attitude was one of unlimited confidence in a unity, which we human beings can see only in fragments colored by our inclinations and purposes, but which is in reality One, a pure and perfect light. He could be surprisingly tolerant about one-sided doctrines and judgments, not to say out-and-out heresies; he tested and tasted, took his time before rejecting and condemning, and in approaching a new idea, however farfetched or abstruse, always began by acquainting himself with it, by mastering its terminology, mythology, grammar, and logic. At the same time, he was without indulgence for either himself or others when it came to orderly thinking, which to him was a question of morality: he demanded lucidity and consistency and had no patience with "fine writing" or with philosophy embellished with poetry and sentiment. His own books, several of which have been preserved, are not beautifully written and not easy reading; it takes time, patience, and pains to penetrate to the sweet, living kernel. A ponderous, fussy speaker, he was a creative and original thinker. The era into which he was born scarcely understood him; he won no professorships and achieved little fame, but contented himself with humble obscurity. Yet the impact of his personality and teachings can be followed down to the generation of his great-grandchildren.

Perhaps the reader will forgive us this and various other digressions, since the intention of these pages is not so much narrative as reflective. A side glance at our "Glass Bead Game" may be in order. During the three centuries of its existence the Game has endeavored to select what was best and most highly developed, what was pure and classical, from among the cultural achievements of mankind, the myths and manifestations of the human spirit, and to translate them into hieroglyphics, the language of a game. We can express the outstanding artistic styles and works, the best known systems of mathematics and logic, the classical styles of music, philosophy, and literature allusively in our abbreviated, richly significant hieroglyphic language. In its most successful moments, our Game might be likened to a piano arrangement of an orchestral score. We delight in the possession of our Game, but we should bear in mind at all times that, though it suggests a cultural microcosm, it is much less than a microcosm, and that the extension and amplification of our Game language are subject to natural limitations. Theoretically, every cultural acquisition, every human achievement, every attitude of mind that has ever found its embodiment might be expressed in our Game—but then the rules would become so complicated that a human life span would not be time enough in which to learn them. Each one of us who has engaged for a while in historical studies has felt an almost irresistible craving to incorporate various insights and images into our Game language, to perpetuate through our Game the beliefs and conceptions of certain individuals. Here the Provincial Game Commissions and the secret Board of Overseers serve as a dam and a sieve. Only very rarely do they permit additions to the rules; yet, for all their precautions, there is no doubt that parts of our Game grammar have already ceased to be the self-evident possession of all players and have gradually become the private preserve of specialists so that they are in danger of being forgotten. If we were to indulge all such cravings, we could expand the Game language every day and quickly multiply it ten- or a hundredfold. The forms characteristic of every minor school of art or music, the dogmas and terminologies of every little sect, the peculiarities of every dialect could be captured; we could construct signs expressing the crude enthusiasm of Puritan community singing, the Swiss German of the eighteenth century, or any other out-of-the-way phenomenon; every such addition would present a certain charm and interest, but then our Game would become an archive, an Alexandrian library, too enormous for the mind to fathom, lifeless and static. Then we should possess a replica of all world history, fixed in Game symbols and shut up in archives.

While studying the movement known as pietism and acquainting himself with such figures as Bengel and Oetinger, the author of this narrative felt only too keenly

this very urge to capture a bit of history and perpetuate it
in signs. These men developed a new, sincere, and passionate form of devotion and piety, and we should be
quite justified in including them in our microcosm if the
whole movement had not, all in all, remained subterranean because of its inability to create an authentic language of its own. True, the pietists expressed themselves
in new ways, their thinking had a certain characteristic
tone, savor, and coloration, but since the movement culminated not in a unified church but in a plethora of small
sects, it produced not a language but many dialects. That
is why Bengel and Oetinger could be forgotten and why a
Voltaire, for example, is still remembered by historians.
We know, however, that though history gives us a blurred
picture of these "subterranean" movements, they are not
necessarily inferior in their effects to the most classical
and decorative of "superterranean" movements. Like
Böhme, his occult master, Oetinger remained subterranean, although he combined the entire intellectual arma-
ment of his time with an alert, creative mind. He was not
cut out to be a Voltaire or a Klopstock; his influence
remained almost anonymous, and no one knows how
many roots, whose flowers we admire, he helped without
their knowledge to nourish. We cannot hope to fit the
subterranean and superterranean movements into *one*
category; but we shall never cease to admire these manifestations of the spirit and to investigate them privately.
And some of us may harbor a heretical opinion in these
matters; that is, we may hold that the classical products
of the spirit should not be ranked higher than these subterranean and anonymous manifestations, but quite on
the contrary, that the classical thinkers and artists are not
creative givers of bounty but consumers of the spiritual
heritage, and that the unclassical and often anonymous
movements have been the true sources of energy, the true
preservers and augmenters of the heritage. All classical

thinkers and artists stand at the end of a process; they are heirs, consumers of the heritage. Even fine flowerings such as Mozart, along with their heartwarming radiance, always present a contrary aspect, a saddening intimation that in so perfect a flowering a slow, noble growth is not renewed but consumed and exhausted. On the other hand, there is always something profoundly gratifying about the study of those flowerless but quietly effective deeds and men, of seemingly minor figures such as Bengel and Oetinger; it gives strength and comfort, as if we had been granted a glance into the hidden, secret growth of nature and of peoples.

Enough digression! As for Oetinger, suffice it to add that after a second visit to Count Zinzendorf he made himself available to the authorities and entered the ministry despite his misgivings. Though often bitterly opposed, slandered, and impugned, he served successively as pastor, rector, and prelate, and died in 1782. In the course of his lifetime he studied many more books, wrote many, continued for years to polish and exercise his restless mind without concern for success or failure, and only toward the end, when he was a very old man, did he grant himself a rest. His last years were spent in serene silence, which some interpreted as senility, others as God-given wisdom. After his death, the poet Schubart wrote: "It is doubtful whether in recent times there has been another man whose mind took in so much, who possessed such all-embracing knowledge. To none of the sciences was he a stranger, and in many he was a master. I wanted to write the story of his life, but when I looked up at his greatness the pen fell from my hand."

For three terms Knecht studied under this man, who was only a few years older than himself. It was thanks to him that Knecht did not weary of theology and study. As his adviser in his studies and his reading, as guide and mainstay of the student conventicle of "awakened" Christians, Oetinger came into close contact with Knecht, and Knecht learned to love and to fear him. But the man whom Knecht occasionally feared was not so much the scholar and thinker as the Christian.

Knecht's piety was a strange thing. It seemed to him that from childhood on, or at least since his childhood experience with the rector, he had been destined and called to Christianity; his "awakening" in that hour had been a summons. Toward the end of his childhood, Bengel had given his piety new impetus; he had joined the small group of pupils who prayed and read the Bible together. Since then, however, his religious life had not been a steady progression but an ebb and flow of emotions and soul states; peace of mind had alternated with consciousness of guilt and spells of penitential asceticism and pious meditation. His conduct throughout was that of a good, modest, chaste young man, but when he considered some of his comrades, not to mention men like Bengel and Oetinger, he could not doubt that they were enormously different from him, and as Christians infinitely superior. All of them had had an inner experience, a conversion, a break with the old, an annihilation and resurrection. This Knecht was quite able to understand, the theory of it was familiar to him, but often as he had prayed for it, no such experience had come his way. He had been awakened but never truly converted. We use all these terms reluctantly and with caution: as we have said, Christian pietism never created and never possessed a universally valid, enduring language, just as it was the tragedy of all Protestant denominations to regard themselves for several centuries as the God-sent champions of the pure Word and the pure doctrine, yet never, even among themselves, to agree on the pure Word and the pure doctrine. Compared to the Vulgate, the Latin Creed and Mass, all Protestant formulations are feeble, and after Luther their language diminished steadily in vigor. After Luther, truly forceful language is found only in the poets who wrote hymns. Neither the Formula of Concord nor the many later adaptations of Luther's theological writings, neither Spener nor Zinzendorf, neither Bengel nor Oetinger created an enduring language; despite all their claims, the Word was not the forte of post-Luther Protestantism, and in some sects language degenerated to the point of caricature. It lived in Luther and after him in the hymn writers; yet even they were not independent creators of language for the most part but leaned heavily on music.

It may be—we do not know—that this had something to do with Knecht's inability to make as much progress in conversion as his friends. He revered the Word and the "pure doctrine," he held them sacred, but at bottom words meant less to him than his studies with Bengel had led him to suppose. He couldn't get very excited over distinctions between doctrines, let alone between words. He couldn't bring himself to feel that in formulating a thought one incurred the highest responsibility or that the misuse of a word was as shockingly irresponsible as a mistake in the scoring of a piece of music. In music, too, he was modest, a student who looked up with veneration to the masters, but here he was at home; here no one could persuade him of anything that he felt to be wrong; in music he was sure of his judgment, knowledge, and sense of rightness. In music his soul had a home, and not only a home but also an order, a cosmos, a way to harmony, to the integration and disintoxication of the self. And so, in the midst of pietist comrades whose emotional lives and paths of salvation often involved them in dramatic tensions, he remained a good-natured child, pleasing to the others by virtue of his friendly innocence, but also suspect for his lack of immediate religious experience.

Once again an intense experience was to fire Knecht's religious zeal. This happened in 1733, when the celebrated Count Zinzendorf visited Tübingen. He came with a definite purpose, hoping to obtain expert opinions on the charter of the Herrnhut community from the theological faculty. However, as in all of his journeys and undertakings, he did not let the business of the moment interfere with the main concern of his life, namely, to bear witness for Jesus and to promote the kingdom of God. Though he was ill when he arrived, though fever and pain obliged him to take to his bed, this extraordinary man did not hide his light. With no more heed for his health than for diplomacy, he immediately threw himself into his mission, received visitors—professors, his adherents, seekers after help and advice—in bed, preached, bore witness, sang his hymns, and engaged in disputations. When he had more or less recovered, he presided over meetings and hours of edification. No sooner was he up and about than he sought out every available Christian community, and one day appeared in the room at the Stift where the pietist students met. There Knecht saw him. From the very first moment he was enchanted and forgot whatever misgivings he may have had about the count's person and doctrine. The count was a tall, animated, but dignified man with a long, pale face and a high forehead; he had the easy, self-assured bearing of an aristocrat, a king among men, and an extraordinary gift of speech; but not only of speech: his eyes, bearing, gestures, voice, handshake, everything about him spoke, appealed, radiated; he was all life and fire, a conqueror of souls. Knecht gazed spellbound at the apostle, received his handshake and glance, a friendly, brotherly, yet majestic glance, which he blushingly and shyly evaded, only to seek it again in the next moment. The count greeted the students as brothers in Jesus, asked them their names, spoke briefly of his journey and of Herrnhut, professed his adherence to the universal Evangelical Church of the Augsburg Confession, and delivered a little sermon, taking the hymn "King, Whom We All Serve" as his text. All those present fell under the spell of his words, his eyes, his dedication to the Saviour. The hymn that Zinzendorf sang and that served as the text of his sermon was not out of the hymn book; he himself had composed it a year before. In retrospect, some of the listeners were none too pleased at the idea of a clergyman taking his own words as the text of a sermon, as though they were Gospel, and had their doubts about the hymn itself; but the man spoke so movingly, with such depth of feeling, that at the moment none of them had the slightest thought of criticism. Afterward, Martin Dober, who had come with the count, dictated the text of the hymn, and like all the others Knecht took it down. He too had his doubts about it later on; it no longer seemed as utterly beautiful as it had in his first enthusiasm, when he felt that it had been written especially for him, with a view to the present state of his soul. It ran in part:

> *Make us ask in fear and trembling*
> *Do our hearts beat candidly?*
> *Do our souls without dissembling*
> *Cleave in love and faith to Thee?*
>
> *Many hidden thoughts and deep*
> *Hath our tender inwardness,*
> *More than when we lay asleep*
> *Lost in sordid worldliness.*
>
> *Bridegroom, we belong to Thee,*
> *Hearts are Thy estate.*
> *Their reproach or purity*
> *Humbles Thee or makes Thee great.*

Later on, the students discussed various points among themselves, whether, for example, since all human hearts are sinful, it was right or permissible to say that the taint of a human heart brought disgrace on the Savior. But at the moment they were all overpowered by the speaker and his words. He seemed transfigured by the joy of his faith, almost as though he were no longer a man, no longer an erring sinner and seeker, but one redeemed and sanctified, suffused with light.

Zinzendorf remained at Tübingen for some two weeks, and Knecht missed no occasion to see him and listen to him. Though the linguistic conscience Bengel had instilled in him sometimes flared up in warning when the count spoke of Jesus in terms more appropriate to a poet in love, and rhapsodized about the cross and the wounds of the Lamb, Knecht's admiration and enthusiasm remained at their height and his spirit lived a festive revel throughout the count's stay. He felt forlorn and dejected when Zinzendorf left, and was bitterly offended when Oetinger said to him some days later, "I see you're still under the spell. That's not unusual; the count really is a great speaker and a good deal more, yes, undoubtedly, a good deal more. All the same, he's no model for a preacher, certainly not for us Swabians. From the Bible and the Christian faith he has taken only a small part; he's full of that part; he has given himself to it entirely, but the part is not the whole."

It might be mentioned in passing that the count himself did not take his enthusiastic reception in Swabia as a matter of course and that he was not unduly flattered by it. His admirers in Tübingen had thought him brilliant, inspired by God, but he was suspicious of such quick success and took it as a warning. A few days after his triumph in Tübingen, he wrote to his wife: "I cannot possibly forgo this occasion to kiss you affectionately and fervently in Jesus, although I have hardly a moment's free time. I have written so many letters that my head aches; dozens of people are waiting for me, and I am preparing to listen and speak to them. Great as are the shame and affliction in Lusatia, the exaltation of my person here in Württemberg frightens me a thousand times more and is a mortal torment to me."

Magister Knecht had passed his examination, paid visits to his professors and organists, packed a knapsack, and filled a chest with his books. Now he was pacing the floor in Oetinger's study; he had come to say goodbye. Summoning up his courage, he had confided his fear of entering the ministry. Oetinger took him by the shoulders, looked affectionately into his eyes, and said, "My dear Knecht, you are lying sick in the same hospital as I. I too have been unable to make up my mind to become a pastor, and I'm planning to travel again next term. Maybe I'll stop at some university, but I also want to go back to Herrnhut and see if I can work with them. Even there it won't be easy. If you're still undecided, I'm not the man to prod you. You know that our administration will grant you a leave if you wish to accept a position as tutor somewhere. Such work can be found, and I should be glad to help you. You would gain time and perhaps see something of the world. Would you like to become a tutor and do you feel you have the aptitude?"

"The aptitude? I don't think so, It would be hard for me; I'm shy, I don't know how to assert myself."

"That can be learned. But isn't there something you'd really like to do?"

"Yes, there is, but I mustn't think of it. Music—that's where my talent lies. But I'm not fit for secular music and besides, it's probably too late to begin a career as a harpsichordist or kapellmeister."

"Talk it over with your parents, Knecht. Tell them exactly how you feel. God has a use for each one of us; we need only be willing. Write to me or come and see me if there's anything I can do for you! A lot of men have had to go through this; with some it takes a long time before

God can really use them. We can only put the matter in God's hands, my friend; we have no other recourse."

Looking affectionately into the student's eyes, he knelt down and saw Knecht do the same. For a time, Oetinger's friendly but penetrating gaze held Knecht fast; then he began to pray. He prayed both for Knecht and for himself, entreating God to consider their weaknesses but also their desire to serve Him, to send them the joys and sorrows, the trials and encouragements they needed, and to use them as stones in His edifice wherever and however it pleased Him. In tears but comforted, Knecht took his leave.

The day was drawing to an end; clouds raced across the sky, now and then the small rain came down in showers, a murky yellow glow appeared in the west. Knecht had taken leave of all his friends. Early in the morning he would start for home on foot. Sadly he climbed up to the Schloss for the last time, then descended the Neckarhalde, took the Hirschauer Steg to the bridge, and crossed back over. Circling the town and returning by way of the Ammertal and Lange Gasse, he saw the towering Stiftskirche against the darkening sky. As he approached it, he heard the organ playing within. Slowly he crossed Holzmarkt, climbed the steps of the church, and stood for a long while by the balustrade, listening to the music, a Telemann toccata. Softly lighted windows shimmered in the houses below. There lay Tübingen; there lay a few years of his youth, years full of zeal and doubt, hard work and vague expectations. What was he taking away with him from this town, from these industrious, fearful, and hopeful years? A chest full of books, half of them copybooks filled with his own writing. A chest of books, a reference from his professors, and an anxious, uncertain heart. His heart was heavy, and not only with the sorrow of leave-taking; the future, it seemed to him, held out nothing but darkness and difficulty. When the toccata was ended, he crept away to spend his last night at the Stift.

Early in the morning, he made his way through the cool gray streets with his knapsack on his back. Leaving the town behind him, he headed for Bebenhausen and the Schönbuch hills. A goal had been attained; his family would be glad to see him and congratulate him. Still, the prospect gave him no joy. But when the sun broke through the clouds and the birds began to sing, his youthful spirits revived, and when he came to the forest he began to sing. The smell of the woods reminded him of his home, of his childhood, of his father, and of the songs they sang while resting beside the spring. He sang hymns and arias and folk songs, and as he thought of his father and the flute he had given him long ago, he realized for the first time how much he was looking forward to seeing him and Benigna, and that his dread of this journey and of the future was entirely on his mother's account. Only his mother would be really interested to learn that he was now a theologian, that he had passed his examination creditably and—to his horror—was supposedly on his way to becoming a pastor. And if he was troubled, it was only because of her. For she would never consent to his becoming anything else but a pastor. He would have to try it, to accept the first vicariate offered. At this thought he stopped singing and strode along grave and silent. He saw deer grazing in a clearing, he saw a hawk hovering in the fleecy sky, smelled ferns and mushrooms, heard an invisible brook flowing through blue clouds of forget-me-nots, stopped in a thicket to eat raspberries. Emerging from the woods into the open country, he passed through a village. At a farm he was given milk and black bread. In the late afternoon he approached Stuttgart, the capital, where he planned to spend the night and, the next day being Sunday, attend church services. Secretly he was hoping to hear some of the most recent music in this city famous for its love of the arts. And indeed, no sooner had he come to the inner city gate than he saw, on several street corners, a small printed notice announcing a recital by a harpsichord virtuoso. But the price of admission* was so high that he felt he couldn't afford it. Suddenly, as he plodded dejectedly down the cobbled street, he felt very tired and asked his way to Leonhardsplatz, where one of his fellow students had arranged for him to spend the night at the house of a cousin, one Frau Pfleiderer, the wife of the city registrar. Frau Pfleiderer was just leaving the house as Knecht prepared to pull the bell. She looked him over, asked if he was the Dr. Knecht she had been expecting, said she was sorry he had arrived so late, because she was on her way to the harpsichord recital and would be late if she didn't hurry. She added that she would gladly have asked him to go with her, but he must be tired and hungry from his journey.

Not at all. His tiredness was gone, he was bursting with joy. Hastening to thank her, he left his knapsack and walking stick on the steps. The concert hall was the ball-room of an inn. The audience sat on rough, backless wooden benches; the few armchairs up front were reserved for high patrons. Knecht listened with rapt attention. A French suite delighted him, and he was impressed by the virtuoso's skill. But the two sonatas, composed by the performer himself, left him indifferent, as did the virtuoso's improvisation on a theme. On the way home Frau Pfleiderer questioned him, and they struck up a lively conversation. She told him she had a harpsichord at home and that she was dying to hear what he would do with the virtuoso's theme. The registrar was reading in the living room when they arrived; he welcomed the

---

* Penciled note: Not yet customary in Stuttgart at that time to charge admission for concerts.

guest, they talked about the concert, and Frau Pfleiderer insisted that Knecht improvise on the theme. Despite his embarrassment, he soon complied; he sat down at the instrument, played the theme, introduced first a bass, then a treble voice, and developed the three voices in clear, vigorous counterpoint. His listeners applauded and served him bread and butter and a mug of cider. The three of them sat up for another hour.

"Tomorrow is Sunday," said the master of the house. "It hardly seems right for a theologian to spend the Sabbath traveling. Stay here with us. You're a free man, and you ought to see something of Stuttgart."

Knecht consented; they arose, the registrar lit two candles, gave one to his guest, picked up the other, and showed Knecht to his room. On Sunday, after their morning soup, Knecht's host took him for a walk through the town and the grounds of the Schloss. Then they called for Frau Pfleiderer and the three of them set out with their hymn books to attend services at the Stiftskirche. The sound of the organ was magnificent; Knecht knew at once that a master was playing. He listened to a choral prelude that rejoiced his whole being. The rector's sermon

Here the manuscript ends, although Hesse provided the following typewritten notes for its continuation.

Swabian Theology in the Eighteenth Century

Knecht becomes a theologian, studies at Tübingen under Oetinger, is torn between his piety and his love of music, is without ambition but longs for a fulfilled life, for harmony, a career in the service of perfection.

Hence increasingly dissatisfied with theology: too much conflict between doctrines, between churches, between parties, etc. Visits Zinzendorf and the "Inspired," is deeply moved by pietism, but finds all this too combative, too exalted, etc.

Becomes a pastor but finds no fulfillment.

Plays the organ, composes preludes, etc., hears of the legendary Seb. Bach. No longer young when at last he hears some of Bach's music: someone plays a few of B's choral preludes, etc., for him. Now he "knows" what he has been looking for all his life. A colleague has also heard the *St. John Passion,* tells him about it, and plays parts of it. Knecht acquires extracts from this work and sees that here, far from all doctrinal controversy, Christianity has once again found a magnificent new expression, has become radiance and harmony. He gives up his post, becomes a cantor, makes every effort to procure copies of Bach's music. Bach has just died. Knecht says, "There was a man who had everything I was searching for, and I knew nothing about him. Nevertheless, I am content; I have not lived in vain." He spends the rest of his days as an obscure organist, resigned to his lot.

The Fourth Life

Second Version

DURING the reign of one of the many obstinate, gifted, and for all their faults almost lovable dukes of Württemberg, who for several centuries fought perseveringly and victoriously, but also capriciously and childishly, with the Estates over money and rights, Knecht was born in the town of Beutelsperg, some ten or twelve years after the peace of Rijswijk freed the duchy from the devils who, at the instigation of Louis XIV, had long plundered, devastated, and despoiled it in a truly bestial manner. The peace, to be sure, was short-lived, but the able duke, in league with Prince Eugene of Savoy, then at the height of his fame, mustered his forces, inflicted several defeats on the French, and finally drove them out of the country, which for almost a hundred years had known more war than peace and more misery than happiness. The people were grateful to their enterprising prince, who, taking advantage of their gratitude, imposed a standing army on the country, so restoring the customary and normal state of hate-love between prince and people, which had been kept warm by endless friction and harassment.

Author's note: Knecht himself wrote the story of his life.

I, Joseph Knecht, sometime organist at Beitelsperg on the Koller, newly recovered from a severe attack of gout so that my hand is once again able to hold a pen, have resolved to set forth, for the benefit of my nephews and their descendants, a few recollections of my life, although it has not been a brilliant or significant life, but a poor and modest one. Nowadays we hear a good deal of discontented talk; we hear it said that the faith and morals of our fathers are dying out and that evil days are impending; some predict on the strength of the Apocalypse of St. John that the Antichrist will soon make his appearance. What to think of this I do not know, but with regard to my beloved Musica, I must own that although there have been many astonishing and inspiring innovations in our epoch, the purity, rigor, and nobility of the old masters have on the whole been lost, and that, though more modishly flattering to the ear, music has also become more frivolous and undisciplined. May the Lord hold all these things in His faithful hands and give us His peace, which is above all reason.

I was born here in Beitelsperg, in a house situated on the "Straight Road," which runs from Nonnengasse to the Spitalwald. The houses at the lower end of the lane are rather imposing, with polished doors and handsome half-timbered walls. Then comes the smithy, which fills the whole street with the shrill ring of its hammer strokes; in front there is a lean-to shed supported by two posts, which serves to shelter the horses that are brought to be shod from the rain and snow. After the smithy the road narrows abruptly and becomes very steep. The houses on this upper part are small and poor. One of these was my father's house. Its gable fronted on the street, and on that side the house looked very low and sunless. The back, however, rose high and bright over the ravine, through which a brook, the Täfelbach, flows down to the Middle Mill, where it empties into the river. Between the brook and the town wall lay our garden with its few fruit trees, among them two plum trees, which were my father's pride, for in those days such trees were a rarity in the region. Those few that existed had all been grown from a few slips or pits which the survivors of the celebrated Swabian regiment had brought back from distant Belgrade in 1688, thus earning the praise of the local fruit growers for many years to come. In the fall my father would say as he brought us the first plum to taste, "Children, when your father came into the world, there was not a single plum tree in the whole region. Then our duke sent a regiment of soldiers to Vienna to help the emperor; on the sixth day of September 1688, they stormed the bastion of Belgrade, and very few of them came home again. It was those few who brought the first plums to our country; we have had them since then, and we are very glad."

Our house was small and unassuming, but it was in the highest part of the town, high above the church, Rathaus, and market; from the upper rooms and the balcony there was a fine view up and down the wooded valley. The balcony was right above the ravine; after storms and during the spring thaw the brook came thundering down—black water and white foam—over the boulders and ferns. We children loved to watch it, but it gave my father no pleasure, for to him the floods brought only work and worry. He plied a none-too-profitable but uncommon and respected trade; he was a fountain master. He was responsible to the town council for keeping the fountains in the town and outskirts clean and supplied with water. True, there were, and still are, four springs in Beitelsperg that flow unaided; many a good housewife still carries her pitchers day after day to one of them, even if it is a long way off, and returns home with pure cold spring water. But all the other fountains and the watering troughs are supplied by distant springs, from grottoes and spring chambers in the woods, whence the water is conveyed into town by wooden pipes. These pipes are made from halved fir trunks with semicircular grooves, and hundreds of them are needed in the course of a year. To fashion them, to fasten them together so as to form conduits running sometimes above, sometimes below the ground, to locate damage and repair it—this was the work of the fountain master. In times of urgency, after floods, for example, he worked with several journeymen, who were supplied by the township. The town council was pleased with my father; he was a good, reliable worker, well versed in his trade, though perhaps somewhat taciturn and eccentric, as men tend to be who work by themselves and spend most of their time deep in the woods. The town children looked upon our good father as a strange and mysterious man, a friend of the water sprites, making his home in dark, remote spring chambers that no one could see into, that gave forth primeval gurglings, and were thought to be where babies came from. They were rather afraid of him, because he was a man of the woods and ruler over the water, and as a child I too, though I loved him with all my heart, stood greatly in awe of him. There was only one man in the town to whom I looked up with still greater awe and who seemed to me still nobler, more exalted, and awe-inspiring. This was the rector, the highest Evangelical dignitary in the town and district, with authority over all the parsons in the town and surrounding villages. He was an imposing figure of a man: tall, erect, invariably clothed and hatted in black, with a serene, bearded face and a high forehead. My extreme veneration for him was in part my mother's doing.

My mother had grown up in a parsonage, and though the family board had been meager and her brothers and sisters lived in poverty, she took great pride in her origins, spoke often of the parsonage, and held faithfully to her pious memories of her childhood home. She read the Bible to us, sang hymns with us, and raised us in a spirit of pious obedience to the Lutheran church and the pure doctrine that had been faithfully observed in the duchy since the days of Brenz and Andreä. We learned at an early age that the world and even our own country were rife with damnable heresies and false doctrines; in particular, we were taught to regard the devotees of the Roman Church as papists and servants of the devil, depraved idolators and hypocrites; but some Evangelical antipapist churches and doctrines were also lacking in purity and soundness and, when you came right down to it, little better than Roman paganism. A young cousin of mine was betrothed to a Swiss Calvinist. When she came to say goodbye, before going away to live abroad, my mother overwhelmed her with tears, prayers, and entreaties, as though she were going to live among enemies. Our father, who was a man of few words, kept silent throughout the scene; but when my mother was called away for a little while by a neighbor, he gently stroked the head of the bride-to-be and said in his deep, friendly voice, "Believe me, Bärbele, it's not nearly as bad as all that. The Calvinists are people just the same as we are, and God loves them as much as He loves us." In all matters connected with the household and the children, my mother's word and spirit ruled; there was a solemn, religious note in our home life, as though we were one step nearer to God than ordinary people. My father had great respect for my mother's piety, for he loved her dearly, but he did not share her strivings and at heart would have preferred a less priestly life. Consequently, he seldom opened his mouth at home. He went to church every Sunday and took communion several times a year. That was the extent of his religious needs; theological needs, such as his wife's, he had none. Even as small children, we knew that in certain respects they were very different from one another, and sometimes it seemed to us that each provoked the other by his contrary nature; that the less interest my father showed in religious matters, the more unyielding my mother became in her piety and the more she harped on her distinguished clerical origins.

But both in church and at home there was one habit and one need that the two of them had in common and that provided a pleasant yet powerful bond between them. This was music. When the congregation sang, both my parents enthusiastically lent their voices, and at home after the day's work was done, they almost always sang hymns or folk songs; then my father sang the second part skillfully, sometimes improvising, and when the two of us, my sister Babette and I, were still small children with as yet no thought of school, we too joined in with a will, and three- and four-part songs were neatly rendered. My father inclined more to folk songs, of which he seemed to have an inexhaustible store, but my mother preferred hymns, of which there were hardly fewer. When he was away from home, my more worldly-minded father indulged in other kinds of music; indeed, I believe that his whole life was accompanied by music. Most of all, it enriched the moments when he stopped to rest from his usually solitary toil in the woods and on the heath. Then he would sing or whistle his folk songs, marches, and dances, or pipe on some instrument that he himself had fashioned (his favorite was a thin little wooden flute without stops). In his younger years he had played the pipe or cornet at dances, but when he became engaged to the parson's daughter in the year 1695, she had made him promise never to do so again, and though by no means as deeply and passionately convinced as his wife that inns and dance floors were hotbeds of sin, he had kept his promise.

When I was still a very small boy, my father sometimes took me to his places of work outside the town. At that time I still had no inkling of the conflicts that often made the relations between my parents difficult or sad, much less of the conflicts that were later to burden my own life. All that was many years ago; my parents are lying in their graves and I myself am an old man. My parents' life struggles and my own are long past and almost forgotten. But even in hours of sorrow and turmoil, those days and hours in the dawn of my life that I spent with my beloved father in the woods, by the springs and brooks, in clearings among the white, peeled trunks of felled fir trees, have never been entirely forgotten. Indeed, the older I grow and the further they recede in time, the more brightly they rise up before me. Sometimes I dwell in them as in the present; and sometimes, when I think back, it seems to me that my happy childhood was an infinite gift, as though the whole of my manhood was only a brief interruption and distraction, only a moment between those happy days of childhood and my present old age, in which I never cease to savor them in memory.

In these memories I see my father at work in the woods, and I see myself, the little boy, sitting on the stones beside the brook, or picking flowers, or climbing about among the fragrant tree trunks and the high blowing ferns, entirely immersed and absorbed in the life around me, the smell of the wood and the plants, the deep droning of the bumblebees, the glitter of the beetles, the fluttering colors of the butterflies. Sometimes my father would creep up silently, or else he would warn me by waving from a distance, and then we would keep perfectly still and motionless for as long as we could, to watch a long snake glide through the grass and mysteriously disappear, or the deer stretching their beautiful necks as they stood among the trees, or a running hare, or a fish otter creeping down the bank and suddenly vanishing in the water, or a falcon halting in its glide and darting vertically downward like an arrow. Amid all these beautiful and frightening things, the trees, the brooks, the plants, the animals, I saw the venerable figure of my father striding like a sovereign, on familiar terms with all about him, the brother or master of all creatures, knowing their names and language, their voices, habits, and secrets. The town, our house, my mother—all that was far away and forgotten, powerless over these fragrant woods. Sometimes both of us would have preferred to live in the woods forever, like the to me uncanny charcoal burners, my father's friends, whom we sometimes visited outside their smoking kilns. The best of all was when, after my father's work was done and we had eaten our noonday or evening meal, he would sit down beside me on a stone or a tree trunk or stretch out on the grass; then he would bring out his little high-pitched wooden flute and play tune after tune. Neither his fingers nor his lungs ever seemed to grow tired. When he had finished a tune he would make me sing it, and little by little I learned to sing accompaniments to his airs. There was no folk song he did not know, and to many of them he knew variant words and tunes, some Swabian, some Upper or Lower Bavarian, and he could sing and play them all. I am certain that in the course of those days with my father I heard not a few old songs, dances, and sequences that no one today ever heard of, and that no one will ever hear again. Today, it seems to me, the spirit of the world has changed; it seems to me that in those days, sixty or more years ago, people put more art and care into their music; nowadays one seldom hears songs sung in more than two parts in the streets and fields, and in some regions even two-part songs are becoming rare. But perhaps all this is a dream and a delusion, for I am aware that old people have always tended to denigrate the younger generation. But throughout the life that God has allotted me, I have looked upon those childhood days as a paradise left behind, a paradise to which I have longed to return. But I can no longer find the way. The key is lost and the gate is locked; one day perhaps death will open it. The images of those early days, the image of my father showing me the secrets of the woods, or sitting in the ferns playing his hundreds and hundreds of tunes on his little homemade flute—for me these images are real and powerful, endowed with luminous colors such as one perceives only in certain dreams.

At home, however, my mother ruled; it was she who had charge of our upbringing. Especially after I started going to school, I came more and more under her influence and seemed to take after her. Through his marriage with an intelligent and pious woman belonging to an educated class, my father, if I may say so, had undergone a certain sublimation, which brought him much that was beautiful; in a sense, his life had been enriched and ennobled, transposed into a more spiritual key. He had found a wife who even knew a little Latin, but she had not come to him as a gratuitous gift; no, he had had to pay for her, and he kept on paying. For the sake first of his betrothed, then of his wife, he had had to forgo a good many habits of his younger days, in particular, drinking in taverns and playing at dances. But my mother had not wholly eradicated the old Adam in him. Unintentionally and unknowingly, he often showed a certain resistance to the spirit my mother had brought into the household. When he was alone with us children, there were no admonitions, prayers, Bible reading, or edifying conversations; and in my mother's absence, it was always his folk songs that we sang and never any of the hymns she delighted in. These were trifling matters, but between my father and my mother there was also a more serious secret, of which we children were not to learn until much later. Our dear father had a weakness that was a source of much grief to my mother and to himself as well. Though for months on end he scrupulously observed his duties as husband, father, burgher, fountain master, and member of the Christian community, and led an exemplary, unusually abstemious life, he occasionally, not more than once or twice a year, was led astray by an invincible urge: when this happened, he would drink and loll about in taverns for a whole day and sometimes for as much as two or three days, and then creep quietly home. Glances were exchanged between my parents over these unfortunate happenings, but for years no words were spoken. For despite my father's excesses, the discipline he imposed on himself was so strong that even in his hours of vice it never left him entirely free. When the urge to drink himself into a stupor came over him, he not only avoided our house and street but kept away from the town altogether, and even when he was so drunk that he seemed to have lost all willpower, he never set foot in his usual haunts, the scenes of his diurnal occupations, or laid himself bare before his fellow burghers, as a good number of others did only too frequently. No, he made his sacrifice to the night side of his nature in concealment, either taking his liquor out into the country with him or drinking it in obscure taverns on the outskirts, where there was no danger of meeting a burgher of his rank. And he never went home drunk but always sobered and repentant. Consequently, it was years before we children learned of the secret, and even then we long refused to believe it.

Thus I inherited my blood and nature from both parents; I am indebted and tied to both of them, and I cannot unravel the skein of my heritage. Often in the course of my life it has seemed to me that I was entirely my mother's son, resembling her in every way, even in ways that I should have preferred to disown and deny. But time and again, a contrary voice made itself heard, and in my whole being I recognized my father. In my younger years, when the question of my heritage often troubled me, I tried to clarify it in my mind; several times I even tried to draw up a chart of my personality with its qualities and defects; I would list all my passions, aptitudes, and incli-

nations in two columns, one of which I classified as paternal, the other as maternal. On the paternal side, I listed:
good nature, conflict between indolence and sense of
duty, good memory, love of nature, unworldliness, tendency to fall under the influence of others, etc. And on
the maternal side: piety, devotion to the Holy Scriptures
and the church, predisposition to theology, speculation,
etc. The love of music held an important place in the
makeup of both my parents, except that in my father it
was supreme, dominating or taking the place of all spiritual gifts and needs; while in my mother it was subject to
certain limitations. In pastimes of this kind, I tried to hold
up a mirror to myself, to know myself and sometimes to
improve my character or sit in judgment on it. But my
schema was always too rigid, and at the end of all these
endeavors I had achieved no greater understanding of my
nature but only made it seem more inexplicable and
puzzling, until with the years I abandoned this mode of
self-study as a futile game and consoled myself with the
thought that my father and mother were themselves not
self-contained units, but that they too were the products
of complex mixtures which had taken place over the
generations, and that perhaps they had both known the
same conflicts and doubts as their son.

It seems likely that I loved my father more than my
mother, at least in early childhood. My love for him was
boundless; I would have followed him through fire and
water. From him I learned to wander through the woods,
to spy out the secret life of the animals, to know the
flowers and herbs, to catch fish, to imitate bird calls; from
him I learned all sorts of skills and games. And above all I
learned to make music, to sing in pitch, and to keep time.
But in everything he taught me he remained the master
whom, to this day, I have never equaled; especially in the
use of his hands, he was a magician; with a pocket knife
and a piece of wood, a reed or a bit of tree bark, he could

make anything he wanted. He was always fashioning wind instruments of various kinds, some for the moment, to play a few pieces on and throw away, others for lasting use. And just as everything seemed to offer itself to his hands, to meet them halfway, and just as nothing in nature escaped his serene, often half-closed eyes, so the whole world of folk music seemed to belong to him. Just as he, the fountain master, knew all the springs and water courses and held them in his power, so his memory was a fountainhead in which all the springs, brooks and ground waters of melody lived and flowed. But all these riches only came to life outside the house, when he was alone or with one of us children. At home he was dwarfed and silent; often he seemed almost like a guest, and at such times my heart ached for him. Our house was not really his; it was my mother's.

If my father's home and world was nature, the forest with its fir trees and springs and its timeless groves of song, my mother lived in another, more spiritual and more rigorous world. Her life was governed by the laws of order, duty, and devotion, and behind these laws stood the solemn world of the church and religion. Her church, to be sure, was not the great ancient church that had once embraced all Christendom; it was only our little provincial church of Württemberg, but I couldn't know that at the time. To us it was holy, the only church on earth. In our town it was represented by Rector Bilfinger and in our home by my mother, the pious parson's daughter schooled in questions of faith. And so, as I grew older, I came to know, side by side with my father's natural world, another, which little by little estranged me from my father's world but gave me no less beautiful, no less holy and beloved images and memories: my mother and her beloved voice, the spirit of her Bible stories and hymns, our home devotions and the services in the beautiful town church, to which my parents began taking me when I was very young. I went gladly and I can still remember my childlike thoughts and dreams in church. Most clearly, I remember three things: the rector, tall and imposing in his black vestments, striding to the pulpit; the long-sustained waves of organ music flooding the sacred place; and the high vault over the nave, which I gazed at dreamily during the long, solemn, and largely incomprehensible sermons, fascinated by the strangely living ribwork, so old and stony and immobile, which, when I fixed my eyes on it, breathed life and magic and music, as though the organ music wove itself into those sharp, angular ribs and both together strove upward toward an infinite harmony.

When I was still a little boy, it struck me as quite self-evident that I should become what my father was, that I should learn his trade from him and become a fountain master, taking care of the springs, keeping the spring chambers clean, laying the wooden pipes, and, when I stopped in the woods to rest, playing tunes on flutes that I myself had made. Later on, I had other ideas; then it seemed to me that nothing could be more desirable in life than to stride through the town like the rector, clad in black dignity, a priest and servant of God, a father to his congregation. True, this implied talents and powers that it would have been presumptuous to impute to myself. And another calling which, though perhaps less noble and honorable, struck me as no less desirable, was that of a musician. Nothing would have pleased me more than to become a proficient organist and harpsichordist, but I saw no way of attaining that goal. Such were my childhood dreams; the earliest and most innocent of them—to become what my father was—waned with the waning of my childhood.

Now I must speak of my sister Babette. She was a few years younger than I, a beautiful, rather shy and self-willed child. In her singing and later in playing the lute, she showed unerring sureness, and she was equally de-

cided in her feelings, ways, and inclinations. All her life
she had a will of her own. From the very first, even before
she could walk, she was drawn more to her father than to
her mother, and as she grew older she took his part more
and more resolutely. She became his favorite and comrade, learned all his folk songs, even those that could not
be sung at home in her mother's presence, and was passionately attached to him. Here it should be said that we
were not our parents' only children; seven or eight were
born, and at times our little house was bursting with
children. But only Babette and I grew to maturity; the
others died young, and were mourned and forgotten.

Of all the experiences of my childhood, there is one in
particular that I feel impelled to record and once again
recall to my own mind. It was the experience of a moment, but it made a profound impression on me and
echoed in my heart for many years to come.

I had always known Rector B., but not really as a man
of flesh and blood; I knew him more as a heroic figure or
archangel, for the high priest seemed to live and stride in
a remote, inaccessible sphere. I knew him from church,
where with voice and gesture, standing either at the altar
or high up in the pulpit, he directed, admonished, counseled, comforted, and warned his Christian flock; or as an
intermediary and herald conveyed their pleas, their
thanks, and their cares to God's throne in prayer. There in
the church he seemed venerable and also heroic, not a
human individual but only a figure, representing and
embodying the priestly office, transmitting the divine
Word and administering the sacraments. I also knew him
from the street; there he was nearer, more accessible and
human, more a father than a priest. Greeted respectfully
by all who passed, the rector strode along, tall and imposing, stopped to chat with an old man, allowed a woman to
draw him into conversation, or bent down over a child.
Then his noble, spiritual countenance, no longer official

and unapproachable, radiated kindness and friendliness, while respect and trust came to him from every face, house, and street. The patriarch had spoken to me several times and I had felt his big hand around my little one or on my head, for the rector esteemed my mother both as a parson's daughter and as a zealously pious member of the congregation; he often spoke to her on the street and had several times, on occasions of illness, come to our house. Yet despite his friendliness I stood very much in awe of him. When I saw him officiating in his church, I feared him much less than on the street, where there was a possibility of his calling out to me or giving me his hand, and so I usually escaped from his path before he could recognize me. But during his sermon, or when on the street I was able to walk behind him unseen, I eagerly studied the man, who in my eyes was a lesser God, as mysterious as the church itself, with its vaults and stained glass, half to be feared and half to be loved. And the house where he lived also had something secret about it which attracted me. Situated above the marketplace and the church, the rectory was a handsome stone building, set slightly back from the street. A flight of wide stone steps led to a massive walnut door with heavy brass fittings. On the ground floor of this quiet, distinguished house there were no dwelling rooms but only a large empty vestibule with a stone floor and a low-vaulted assembly room. Here the rector received the parish elders and candidates for confirmation, and here too the district clergy gathered every few weeks for a few hours of ecclesiastical sociability interspersed with theological disputations. The rector's living quarters were on the second floor. Thus, also in his daily life he was nobly remote. I did not go to that street very often, but several times I had approached the stately, secretive house and looked at it with curiosity. I had crept up the cool stone steps, touched the shiny brass on the weather-darkened old door, examined the ornaments on it, and finding the door ajar had glanced into the silent, empty vestibule, at the back of which a flight of stairs could be seen. Only three people lived in that big tall house, and it revealed nothing of their lives. Other, ordinary houses were much more open and communicative. They allowed a glimpse at the life of their inhabitants; you could look through a window and see someone sitting inside; you might see the house owner or his hired man or maid at work, or children at play; you could hear voices. Here everything was hidden; the domestic life of the rector—a taciturn old relative kept house for him with the help of an equally elderly maid— was carried on in a silent, invisible higher sphere. The back garden with its fruit trees and berry bushes had high hedges around it, so that it too was well concealed; only the next door neighbor might occasionally see the rector strolling about on summer days.

Behind the rector's garden, high on the hillside, there were a few less imposing houses, and a maiden aunt of my mother's lived in two rooms on the top floor of one of them. One autumn day my mother took me to visit her, though I had no desire at all to go and tried my best to get out of it. So there we were. The ladies sat down together and embarked on a lively exchange of questions and tales, while I went to the window and looked out. At first I was rather bored and disgruntled, but then I discovered that it was the rector's garden I was looking down on. The trees were almost bare, losing leaf after faded leaf in the autumn wind. I could also see the rectory, but the windows of the living quarters were closed and behind the panes there was nothing to be seen. Up above, however, there was a loft that I was able to look into. I saw a pile of firewood and a clothesline with a few pieces of washing on it. Adjoining the loft was a rather bare attic room in which I could see a large box full of papers and, along the wall, a pile of cast-off household articles: a chest, an old cradle, and a ramshackle armchair with torn upholstery. With unthinking curiosity I stared into the cheerless room.

Then suddenly a tall figure appeared: the rector himself in a long black frock coat, his gray hair uncovered. Instantly my interest was aroused and I waited as tensely as a hunter to see what the venerable gentleman might have to do in this obscure corner of the house.

Several times Rector Bilfinger strode restlessly back and forth across the room. His face was careworn; clearly he was prey to grave and sorrowful thoughts. He stopped with his back to the window and slowly his head drooped. Thus he stood for a while; then suddenly he fell to his knees, folded his hands, pressed them together, raised and lowered them in prayer, then remained on his knees, bowing his head to the floor. I knew at once that he was praying. Shame and guilt weighed on my heart, but I could not tear myself away from the sight. Breathless and aghast, I stared at the kneeling man, saw the entreaty in his hands and the repeated bowing of his head. At length he stood up with some difficulty; again he was tall and erect. For a moment I could see his face. Though there were tears in his eyes, it shone with tranquil, pious happiness. It was so beautiful, so incredibly lovable that I, the little boy at the window, shuddered inwardly, and the tears came to my eyes.

I managed to hide my tears, my agitation, indeed my whole experience. It made a profound impression on me, which for many years affected my whole life. But in that first moment what I felt most keenly in my childlike soul was that I had a secret; that, all by myself, I had witnessed something ineffable and great, but secret. That gave me a sense of importance and also a task: to keep the secret. And so I hid my tears, the women were not aware that anything had happened. And all my life down to this hour I have kept my childhood secret; since I have never confided it to anyone, it has always preserved for me something of the holiness it had then. For many years I interpreted that moment as a call, God's first call to me, my first glimpse of the "kingdom of God." And now that I have spoken of it for the first time, I am almost inclined to believe that my most essential and secret reason for taking pen in hand was to utter "it" at last. "It" played an important part in my life, or at least in the years of my youth, too great a part as it seems to me now. For this reason, to record it is not enough; I must also try to explain it.

"It" meant that then, for the first time in my life, I saw a man really and truly prostrating himself before God in prayer. Anyone who regards this as little or insignificant will think my experience absurd. But to me it seemed great and enormously important. Why?

I believe I was seven years old at the time. As a child of Christian parents, I was thoroughly familiar with the custom of prayer; I myself prayed every night, and my mother said a prayer before every meal. It was a beautiful, solemn custom; I liked it, and I had some notion of what it meant: through prayer we tried to hallow our daily lives before God. To say a prayer before going to sleep or before meals was rather like talking in poetry rather than in ordinary words, or like taking not ordinary steps but march or dance steps to the accompaniment of music. Through prayer the heart was exalted, everyday things took on new meaning, one entered into a bond with higher powers. This mood was intensified at church services, enhanced by communion with many others, by the venerable edifice, by the choral singing, and most of all by the organ music. On several occasions this solemnity filled my heart with a strange emotion, compounded of joy and fear.

But now I had experienced something very different. I, as a child, had seen a big, grown man, an old man, pacing the floor, anguished and needful of help; I had seen him kneel down, had seen him pray and weep, humble himself and implore. Before my eyes he had become little, a child. And that man was not just anyone; he was the rector, the venerable and feared preacher, the man of God, the father of all his parishioners, to whom all bowed low, the embodiment of all human and priestly dignity. This was the man I had seen anguished and despondent, kneeling in the dust with the humility of a child, bowing down to One before whom he, so great and so revered, was no more than a child or a grain of dust.

My first thoughts were these: How truly pious the man was, and how great God must be, that such a man should kneel to Him in supplication! And more: his supplication had been heard; the tearful face of the supplicant had smiled, had glowed with release, appeasement, consolation, and sweet trust. Ah, it was more than my mind could fathom in weeks or months. From time to time, I had found pleasure in the dream of someday becoming a rector in a black coat and buckled shoes; now, for the first time, I gave serious thought to Him whose servant the rector was. What I had seen in the rector's attic room was a proof of the existence of God; no, it was a revelation that God lived.

And yet before God the rector was not only a servant, a minister; no, he was God's child; he appealed to God as a child appeals to his father, humbly but full of candor and trust. And in my eyes, since I had seen him on his knees, he was at once diminished and magnified; he had lost something of his proud dignity, but to make up for it he had grown in sanctity or inner nobility; removed from the common order of things, he had entered into an immediate bond with the heavenly Father. I myself had prayed hundreds of times; it was a good and noble ceremony, a respectful greeting to the distant God. But I had never known such affliction and such urgency, such devotion and such entreaty, nor had I ever seen a supplicant rise to his feet with such an aura of joy, reconciliation, and grace. This prayer had been like a battle or a storm! It showed me that behind the vestments and dignity of the clergyman, behind church, organ music, and hymns, there was concealed not only something mysterious and majestic but a power, a Lord, whom all this was made to serve and to glorify, namely, the God who is at once the commander over kings and the father of every man.

For a time I was possessed by my secret; it pursued me day and night. I had experienced something great, but I could not share my experience or rejoice in it with others, for I had witnessed an episode that shuns all witnesses, I had seen something that was not meant to be seen. From that time on, I felt greater love and veneration for the rector, but at the same time I feared him and felt ashamed in his presence as never before. My spirit was troubled. While my thoughts clung to my experience, reviving the memory of it over and over again and seeking to interpret it, a sense of shame turned me away from it; sometimes I tried to hold the unforgettable fast, and sometimes to forget it; try as I might to break away from it, I was drawn back to it time and time again. My secret weighed heavily on me.

Each year there was school from autumn to spring; apart from reading and writing, we learned Bible verses and hymns and the Short Catechism; it was often monotonous but never tiring. I learned to read music at an early age—without effort, from my parents. While still a child, I read and reread the few books my parents owned. The most important and inexhaustible was the Bible. My mother read a passage aloud every morning, after which a hymn was sung, usually in two or three parts. The texts of our hymns—there were a good many of them—were printed in a handsome little finely printed parchment-

bound book in 16° entitled *The Soul's Harp or Württemberg Hymn Book*. I was very fond of it, if only because it
was so small and beautiful. On the parchment cover was
stamped a narrow gold border, inside which was a delicately drawn and colored stamping of a potted plant with
five different flowers and three different leaves. Inside the
book, before the title page and the duke's patent, there
were two pages of copperplate engravings. On one, King
David was shown playing a gracefully carved harp, the
top of which was ornamented with an angel's head, surmounted by five Hebrew letters. On the second, the
Saviour sat by the side of a well, talking with a woman,
and the well was Jacob's well in the town of Sipar in
Samaria, and the woman was the Samaritan woman who
came to draw water at the sixth hour, when Jesus, weary
from his journey, was resting by the well. And Jesus said
to her, "Give me to drink," and she replied, "How is it that
thou, being a Jew, asketh drink of me, which am a
woman of Samaria?" (John 4:9). The bottom of this
page showed the ducal coat of arms with its three antlers,
the fishes of Montbéliard, and other emblems, and a tiny
engraving of the city of Tübingen. The book contained
more than three hundred hymns, written by Dr. Martin
Luther, Duke Wilhelm of Saxony, Clausnitzer, Rinkhardt, Rist, Heermann, Nicolai, Paulus Gerhard, Johann
Arnd, Goldevius, and many other poets, some of whom
had splendidly foreign-sounding names, such as Simphorianus Pollio. When I sang these hymns with my
parents, what really mattered to me was the harmony, the
interweaving of parts; I paid little attention to the words
or the poetry. It was only when I read the texts to myself
that I dwelt on the words; then I delighted in the joyful
expectation of the Advent hymns and the festive exuberance of the Christian carols, the bitter grief of the Passion
hymns, and the jubilation of the hymns of Resurrection,

the anguish of the penitential chorales, the rich imagery
of the Psalms, the freshness of the morning songs, and
the gentle sadness of the evening songs:

> All you who long for bed/Weary in bones and head,/
> Now go and lay you down./When your time has run/
> And your work is done,/You will be bedded in the ground.

Even before I could read the Bible, the words of these
hymns nourished and delighted my soul; to me they were
poetry and wisdom, entertainment and pleasure; through
them, the sufferings, death, and glory of Jesus became a
part of my intimate experience; they gave me my first
reading of the human heart with its fears and exaltations,
its courage and wickedness, its transience and striving for
eternity, my first knowledge of life in this world, where
evil so often triumphs, and of the kingdom of God, which
reaches into this world in exhortation and judgment:

> From wrath and envy keep thy soul,/In mildness never
> fail,/For though the godless get more gold,/Their wrath
> is no avail./My skin and bone/Will soon be mown/Like
> grass and meadow flower/For they and we/Are equally/
> In God's domain and power.

In this little book two hundred years of German Protestantism were preserved. Some of the pieces, like the Kyrie
eleison litany, rendered into German by Luther himself,
were even older and carried a note of still more venerable
and mysterious antiquity. Even before I knew the catechism, these hymns had made me familiar with the
Evangelical faith, which was still being persecuted and
bloodily repressed in France, Moravia, and elsewhere, and
had its heroes and martyrs.

It gave my mother pleasure to see me reading her little
book, and later on her Bible, and when I asked questions,
she answered patiently. She was glad that one of her
children should show religious leanings, and I believe that
long before any such thoughts occurred to me she had

secretly made up her mind that I was to become a theologian and preacher. A little later, she taught me the rudiments of Latin, and though she could not read the strange signs over the head of the harp-playing King David, she knew that they were Hebrew and that this ancient and venerable language was taught at theological schools. We often looked at the copperplate engraving of Tübingen together, and then she would speak in glowing terms of that city and its university.

It is not very often that a boy chooses a vocation that is capable not only of occupying his faculties but also of transforming the dream that lies dormant within him into reality, that will not only feed him and bring him honor but also magnify and fulfill him. Many conditions must be met before so fortunate a choice can be made and followed through. There is a tendency to draw from the careers of the so-called geniuses of the past the comforting conclusion that men endowed with true talent and strength of character have always found themselves in the end and won their proper place in the world. This is a cowardly consolation and a lie; in reality, many of these famous men, despite high achievement, were unable to fulfill their talents and vocation; in all periods of history, moreover, any number of gifted men have failed to achieve goals worthy of them, and many careers have been broken and ground into misery. Still, this should not lead us to deny that some men have not only borne up bravely under a botched, unhappy life but have even achieved nobility in their acceptance of it, their *amor fati*.

It seems likely that my parents accustomed themselves at an early date to the thought that I would not learn my father's trade. I was a gifted child, but I had little ambition; there is far more of the artist than of the scholar in my nature. What would have pleased me most and also struck me as most natural was to become a musician. If only I had grown up amid a higher musical culture, in a city blessed with theaters, concerts, and good church music, that profession would have been open to me. But such a possibility occurred neither to my parents nor to myself; as far as we were concerned, it did not exist. In our town there were no professional musicians; our organist was a schoolmaster by trade, and none of us had ever heard of a young man studying music and not only earning his daily bread but achieving prestige and fame as a musician. True, there were musicians in our town— the fiddlers and pipers who played at festivals and dances. But they were regarded as little better than vagabonds; they drifted from place to place in search of scant earnings, offered their services at every wedding, church fair, and Sunday dance. They were looked upon as drunken debauchees, and no self-respecting burgher would have dreamed of letting his son take up their trade. As a young man, my good father himself, though only for his own pleasure, had often played at dances, but on the day of his betrothal he had solemnly renounced his place among the fiddlers and pipers. I too had learned to play the flute when very young, and the lute some years later, but I should have shaken my head in disbelief if anyone had asked me if I was planning to become a strolling musician. But if I had known as a child that it was possible to study music with esteemed musicians and then to become an organist in one of the great churches, kapellmeister in an opera house, or even a chamber musician, it seems more than likely that I would never have nurtured any other dream for the future. As it was, music may have occupied the first place in my heart but not in my consciousness. I did not know that there were men who held music sacred and devoted their lives to it, just as others devoted their lives to the service of the duke, the church, or the town council. I knew three kinds of music: playing and singing at home with my family, which was glorious,

but only a pastime, something one did when there was no
work to do; then there was church music, consisting
solely of short organ preludes and postludes, it occupied a modest place in the church service and was condemned to fall silent the moment the preacher appeared;
and finally, the music of the fiddlers and pipers, the
threepenny music played at weddings and fairs, which,
for all the brilliance of an occasional performer, was not
to be taken seriously. Thus it never occurred to me to
become a musician. And since it was my mother's ambition to see me attain to a higher station than my father's,
it gradually came to be understood that I was to study
theology. My father hardly opened his mouth on the subject; I for my part was quite content.

And so—I believe I was nine or ten at the time—I was
taken out of school and entrusted to the aged Preceptor
Roos, who in the course of his career had taught a good
many boys Latin and prepared them for the higher
schools. In the weeks preceding this decision, my mother
called several times on Rector Bilfinger, who advised her
and encouraged her in her resolve. Then one day, just as
we were sitting down to our soup, he appeared at our
house. He had brought my parents the sum of ten florins
for my first year of Latin study. At the same time, he
informed us that the overseers of a certain foundation
had agreed to provide the same sum each year up to the
time of my admittance to theological school. My mother
was so overjoyed that she could eat no supper. In her
eyes, those ten florins transformed a bold and perhaps
somewhat presumptuous plan into a legitimate, God-
willed undertaking. If the respected Wool Weavers
Foundation sponsored her boy's studies and the rector
himself put the money down on the table, then clearly the
project had God's blessing. That day brought a festive air
into our house. I saw how happy my mother was, and
since the role that fell to me was so eminently important

and honorable, I too was glad and puffed myself up a little, although I was secretly terrified of the preceptor and would really have preferred to remain at the common school.

The last few summer weeks before the onset of my Latin studies, those last breaths of childhood freedom, have remained graven on my memory. Young as I was, a chapter in my life was ended. For a time I was the center of attention; consultations were held and plans made, with me as their object; I felt honored and important, and looked forward to my new life with curiosity, but also with dread. And now, before it began, I was entitled to be a child again, to while away the time and be on vacation. For a brief period I slipped quite naturally over to my father's side. I went out with him for half days or even whole days, watched him, and helped him; he let me carry his yardstick and made me a present of a new flute. My little sister Babette thought my brand-new deerskin trousers wonderfully becoming. Otherwise, she thought it disgusting that her brother was going to study and become a blackcoat; she had heard some talk of the plan, but had thought our father would not stand for it. Sometimes when the weather was good and my father took me out, she was allowed to come along. When we were tired out from walking, we would sit down to rest on the moss under the fir trees, and after we had eaten our bread and milk and berries we would sing the lovely old folk songs in two or three parts. In a clear, cold brook amid rocks and ferns, my father taught me to watch for trout, which he would catch in his hands. We would always bring home a bunch of flowers or some jars full of berries for our mother. All our neighbors knew I was to learn Latin and become a student; they would call out to me in the street, praise me, question me, congratulate me, give me a bun, a handful of quills, a piece of cherry cake. Some of them warned me jokingly about the preceptor's *baculus*.

The blacksmith, whose anvil sounds filled the street, called me into his high, sooty smithy with its blazing forge fire, held out his big, black, horny hand, laughed, and said, "So you're going to study Latin and be a minister? Look here, son, I don't give a hang for that, and neither does the Saviour; He didn't know any Latin Himself. When you're big enough to tie on your bands and climb up in the pulpit, don't forget that your father was an honest craftsman, which is as good or better than a scholar. Now don't fret, I don't mean any harm, but it's too bad. Well, that's that, and now wait a second." With that he walked out of the smithy. He was gone for quite some time and I was all by myself. His angry-friendly speech had shaken me. But finding myself all alone in the big, deathly silent smithy, I was overcome by curiosity: I picked up a small light hammer from the workbench and tapped lightly on the anvil, whose voice I knew so well. It gave off a wonderfully sweet, full tone; I listened until it had died away, then tapped again very softly and listened, and so on, several times until the blacksmith came back. He had something white in his dark hand, and when he opened it, there was a big goose egg, a present for me. I was quite bewildered when I arrived home with my egg. I gave it to my mother but said nothing of the blacksmith's speech, for I knew it would have hurt her feelings.

My short holiday was soon over. One day, in the cool of the morning, my mother brought me to Preceptor Roos. She took with her a basket full of peas and spinach as a gift. She left me in the preceptor's sitting room. As she went away, I followed her with my eyes, and from time to time she nodded back at me affectionately. Preceptor Roos was an old man; his hand trembled so that it took him quite some time to get a proper hold on his slate pencil or pen, but then, slowly and carefully, he wrote out row after row of beautiful, perfectly shaped letters and figures. He had once been famous and feared as a teacher; two of his pupils had become prelates and one a court astronomer; six had become rectors, and many had grown up to be town parsons, village parsons, or Latin teachers. In his old age, he was still a passionate and irascible teacher, but the atmosphere in his sitting room was calmer than in his old Latin school, where he sometimes devoted whole days to thrashing, scolding, and running furiously back and forth. All his pupils had feared the irascible man, some had hated him; many years ago one of them, in self-defense, had bitten him so hard on the left hand that the ugly scar was still to be seen. Though by the time I came to him he had given up the thrashings, or almost, he was still a strict, domineering, and jealous master, and I, his last and only pupil, was still subject to severe discipline. On the whole, however, he treated me well. This I owed to my mother, who had a way with the crotchety old man and to whom he responded with old-fashioned chivalry. And besides, luckily for me, he was not only a teacher but also a musician. For many years he had been the organist of his native town and had directed the chorus of the local Latin school. It was as a favor to my mother that he took me on as his pupil in his retirement. But he soon discovered that I was musical, and we began to sing and to play together. That made me very happy, and little by little, through music, I grew fond of my stern teacher. More and more often, my hours in the schoolroom, which were not always peaceful or pleasant, were followed by music lessons, in which scoldings were rare and moments of festive joy frequent.

At the start, Latin was my main subject. In addition to mastering the grammar, it would be necessary to learn, not only to translate correctly and fluently, but also to speak, write, and debate in Latin, and to compose Latin hexameters, distichs, and odes—a goal which in my first year seemed utterly beyond my reach. There was also a bit of arithmetic. As for Greek, I did not take it up until two years later. A whiff of scholarship carried over into our music lessons, as, for example, when we translated a number of German hymns into Latin and took to singing them in that language.

Every morning I spent five hours in the dark schoolroom alone with the aged preceptor, and in the afternoon two or three hours more, this quite apart from music. The preceptor owned a harpsichord. First I had to learn to tune it, and then on days of good humor he sometimes let me play it. He also borrowed a violin for me and taught me the fingering. I practiced at home until I was proficient enough to play suites and sonatas with my teacher. But for years I was unable to satisfy my most ardent desire, to learn the organ. The old man no longer had the strength for it, I was too little, and the day was not long enough.

The course of study imposed on me was cruelly exacting, and now that I think it over, I realize that something of my studies, and not only Latin, unfortunately, has stuck to me all my life. I soon became a little student and scholar, precocious and rather arrogant; my mind was no longer that of a child, and much of my childhood was lost. Yet, contradictory as it may seem, the childlike quality that stayed with me in my mature years is largely attributable to my schooling, and I have observed the same thing in others. For though my one-sided concentration on study banished me prematurely from the innocent joy and freedom of childhood, it also isolated me from many of the precocious experiences which ordinarily expand a child's knowledge of life and gradually teach him to confront the world as an adult. The world of learning was ageless and masculine, and those who entered into it excluded themselves from ordinary life. True scholars, it has often been observed, are often precocious in early childhood and youth, seeming older than they are; yet even in old age the same intellectually precocious men preserve an unworldliness that makes them seem like children. I did not entirely escape this fate, but I had an easier time of it than many others. I need only think of the prelate Oetinger, that pious, wise, and learned man who once told me that at the age of ten he had gone through hell and had been driven to despair and even to blasphemy by his teacher's brutal severity. I did not have it so hard, and I am convinced that my guardian angel was music. It not only had a magical effect on my stern teacher, whose heart it softened, but also helped to preserve my own soul. For music has a profound, healing power, and even more than other arts it can serve as a substitute for nature. It saved me from intellectual aridity, and it gave Preceptor Roos, who had drilled and thrashed so many generations of pupils, an inner gentleness.

My teacher, though a pedant, was not without originality. In the course of his long years as a teacher, he had devised various little distractions and games with which from time to time he interrupted the rigid school discipline, so giving his pupil a breathing spell when his attention threatened to flag. He would have had no use for the pedagogical systems that are now being heralded, and would have scoffed at such notions as combining work with play or adapting teaching methods to the individual. He was a sergeant of erudition; he knew and loved his duty, and would rather have driven himself and his pupil mad than deviate a hair's breadth from it. But he had imagination; in the course of a long, hard career he had found out that uninterrupted strain is likely to make a student dull and recalcitrant, and that children subjected to severe discipline are often astonishingly grateful for small rewards, such as the timely gift of a few minutes or a bit of variety. Early in my school career, I became acquainted with one of his little vagaries. I had been writing words with a goose-quill pen. When it seemed to me that my pen was blunted, I held it out to the preceptor and asked him to sharpen it.

With his somewhat rasping old man's voice, Roos said, "I will do it, *adulescentule,* but next year you will be eleven and in time you will be twelve and thirteen and fourteen, twenty and thirty and fifty. Now suppose that your pen is too worn to write with. By then, *O servus puer,* old Roos may well have got sick of sharpening pens and laid his bones to rest. Who will sharpen your pens for you then? Do you expect to have old Roos sitting beside you all your life? Oh no, my helpless child; one day, sooner or later, you will have to be your own handyman. So pay close attention: this once I will show you how a friend of letters sharpens his quill pen, his *penna anseris.* Watch me, *homuncule, novarum rerum cupidus,* and think in your tender mind: We shall have the knack in a twinkling. But we will not have the knack in a twinkling, or in a week or a month or a year. Like many generations that have gone before you, you will discover to your sorrow that cutting a goose quill is an art, and that *ars* is *longa.* And so, my boy, I shall show you. This once, I said, but to your shame there will be hundreds of times. You will often have occasion to struggle with this recalcitrant object, and then you will remember old Roos."

He took the quill, which was indeed in a sad state, and reached for his penknife—"Someday," he said, *"volente Deo,* you will also learn how to whet one of these knives." His hand trembled so, that for a long minute the undertaking seemed hopeless, but in the end he applied the sharp little knife to the quill, cut off the tip, and proceeded to show me how one went about making a new point. This was the beginning of a new, somewhat agonizing, sometimes delightful branch of knowledge—pen sharpening—which from time to time came as a welcome interruption to a lesson that was growing wearisome. I remember one such occasion. Under his eyes I had cut my quill, tried it, cut it again, tried it again, and cut once more. After chuckling over my efforts and my disappointment, the old man told me the story of Oknos, the rope plaiter, whose rope the she-ass kept gnawing away as fast as he could plait it.

To my regret, the preceptor strictly forbade his widowed daughter, who kept house for him, to send me on errands or to employ me for kitchen and garden chores; she was able to do so only occasionally and unofficially. But there were exceptions, and in these I took a festive pleasure. When there were special tasks that exceeded a woman's strength and intelligence, Roos himself took command and my services were welcome. And so it was that I helped to unload and pile up firewood, to put up fruit or sauerkraut, and to press pears for cider.

Religion played little part in my instruction. I merely had to learn the catechism and certain hymns by heart. The place of religious edification was taken by music. I soon discovered that my teacher possessed treasures. He himself had composed cantatas, and he had two chests full of manuscript scores, for the most part church music from Palestrina down to the contemporary organists Muffat and Pachelbel. With a certain awe, I observed that the older manuscripts, many of which the preceptor had copied with his own hand, were as brown and withered as antique books. There were some really old volumes which the old man occasionally leafed through and explained to me, liturgical songs with Latin texts and stiff, rhomboid notes inscribed in four rather than five lines.

When I had made some progress and gained his confidence, the whole treasure trove was put at my disposal. I would take a book or a few manuscript sheets home with me over Sunday and copy them carefully. I spent every groat I could lay hands on for paper. I myself would line it and then make copies of chorales, arias, motets, cantatas,

suites, etc., thus at an early age amassing a store of food
for the soul that would last me all my life.

At home my studies kept me busy well into the evening.
My place at the table was respected, and there I sat with
my Latin, translating my exercises, learning my vocabulary and conjugations. It seemed to me that I had almost
become a stranger to my loved ones, and often I yearned
forlornly to go back to my old life. For many hours each
day I was out of the house; then in the evening I deprived
the others of their table and their gayety; I was always
busy with things that were unknown to them, and that
made me feel that I was being untrue to my home, though
it was not my fault. True, nothing could have made my
mother happier than seeing me absorbed in my studies,
but my father, as I was only too well aware, withdrew into
a mournful silence. My sister Babette, on the other hand,
was far from silent. Since I had started going to the
preceptor's house, she felt neglected, deprived of her
brother. Often when I came home late and, instead of
playing with her, sat down at the table where my mother
would let no one disturb me, she clamored for her rights.
She hated the preceptor, she hated books and Latin, she
hated being left alone, she hated having to keep still and
wait for her distinguished brother to finish his work.
Seething with indignation, she would plot acts of ven-
geance; several times she hid my grammar, once she lit
the hearth fire with one of my copybooks, and once she
threw my inkwell from the balcony down into the ravine.
When I had finished my work and called her to come and
play, or to go out with me to meet our father, she was
either nowhere to be found or so hostile and full of spite
that it took no end of wheedling and pleading to bring her
around. She loved me and fought for my love. But more
and more she turned against her mother, whom she
regarded as her enemy. The more severely my mother
treated her, the more openly Babette took my father's

part. This child with the reddish-blond hair had a will of her own and often succeeded in getting her way. For example, she insisted that the family should go back to singing folk songs and secular arias along with the hymns. Time and again she would strike up a folk song, and when Mother protested that we all preferred hymns, she would say, "No, you're the only one who prefers hymns, you and no one else! I'm sure Father likes the other songs better, and Josef likes them too. If you won't let us sing them, I won't join in the hymns, not if you bite my nose off." Far from being gentle and yielding like Father, she had a strong, stubborn character. Like Mother, she had a will of her own, but not the same will as Mother's. The consequence was a battle, but fortunately, there again, music held the family together. The folk songs were reinstated, with the exception of those that were too worldly. There were still angry quarrels, but there was also singing, which I usually accompanied on my fiddle. I was always able to conciliate my sister with the help of music. I sang with her and brought her music; I taught her to read notes and to play a small flute.

Before I knew it, I was far enough advanced in my studies to be sent to a school of theology. I spoke Latin very nicely and read Cicero with ease. I had started Greek and even learned to cut pens quite tolerably. And then one day old Roos dismissed me. The learned old man had shared his study with me for several years and grown fond of me. He was so grieved at my going away that to hide his emotion he spoke more gruffly than usual in our last lesson. As we stood beside his desk, he delivered a parting sermon. Both of us so dreaded the leave-taking that we had lumps in our throats. "You've been doing tolerably well in Latin for the last year, I can't deny it, but what does a young flibbertigibbet know of the pains it has cost his teacher? And when it comes to Greek, you still have a long way to go. Preceptor Bengel will be amazed at some of those second aorists you invent. Oh well, it's too late to find fault now. So here you are, running away without a care in the world; you think the worst is over, but other teachers will have their work cut out for them before you're fit to be seen. You don't really deserve it, but I've got a farewell present for you. Here!" With this he picked up a book of old French chansons and slapped it down on the desk. When Knecht,* close to tears, tried to take his hand to thank him for the precious gift, he rebuffed him and started in again; "No need of thanks. What does an old man need all this music for? You can thank me by studying properly and making something of yourself that won't disgrace me. These chansons aren't bad. Those fellows knew something about part writing. And oh yes, so you won't be unfaithful to Musica, I've put aside two organ pieces for you, modern things by a man named Buxtehude; no one ever heard of him in these parts, but he knows how to write music and has ideas." Again he slapped a book down on the desk, and when he saw that young Knecht was getting ready to cry, he thumped him on the back and bellowed, "*Vade, festina, apage*, a big boy doesn't cry!" With that he pushed him out the door, which he slammed but immediately opened again and cried out, "It's not forever, you milksop. We'll be seeing each other again, child. In your vacation you'll come over and make music with me. You're not nearly as good at the harpsichord as you seem to think. Practice, child, practice!" And then he shut the door for good.

I was on vacation again, and again I was an important man, for I would soon be going away to the Denkendorf cloister school. Babette was very angry. She was quite a big girl by now and wore her hair in pigtails. We played a

---

* Here Hesse, in his manuscript, reverts to the third person, as in the first version.

good deal of music together. Once she stared at me, shook her head, and said sadly, "Maybe you're really going to be a blackcoat; I never believed it up to now."

I scolded her and told her to stop saying blackcoat; what, I asked her, had the parsons ever done to her that she should be so down on them? Hadn't our own grandfather been a parson?

She cried out, "Oh yes, and Mother is still proud of it and gives herself airs and thinks she's better than anybody else, but that doesn't stop her from eating the bread our father earns with his hard work."

Her blue-green eyes flashed angrily. I was aghast at the hatred with which she spoke of our mother.

"Good Lord," I cried out, "you mustn't talk like that!" She gave me a furious look, evidently on the point of putting it even more forcefully. But suddenly she turned away and started to taunt me by hopping around me on one foot, singing to the tune of a hymn:

> *"Blackcoat, blackcoat,*
> *You're a silly goat."*

And then she ran away.

I was on vacation again, and in many ways it was like the time before my Latin studies. Once again Schlatterer, the tailor, made me new clothes, but now, instead of deerskin breeches it was a seminarist's black suit. The first time I put it on, I disliked it; I also disliked the pleasure my mother took in it, and her saying, "The next time you get new clothes, maybe it will be for Tübingen."

It was hard for me to leave my home and parents for the first time. But at the Denkendorf cloister I found something more than the good friends, strict discipline, and excellent instruction I would have found at any other seminary. I found something very rare: a gifted and in every way extraordinary teacher. His name was Johann Albrecht Bengel, and he was not only the preceptor of the

school but also the Denkendorf preacher. When I became
his pupil, Bengel, though by no means an old man, was
already famous as a teacher. Though a great scholar, he
had managed with his self-effacing humility to avoid all
advancement. For almost thirty years he served as preceptor at Denkendorf; only then did he rise, quickly,
though with no pushing on his part, to the highest offices
and dignities. But even as an unassuming preceptor, he
exerted a quiet but profound influence for many years,
and not only on his own students, for many of whom he
remained throughout his lifetime a mentor, confessor,
and consoler. Indeed, his reputation as a great scholar
and incorruptible guardian of the word extended even to
foreign lands.

In his first conversation with me, he asked me: "What
is your father?" "A fountain master," I said. He looked at
me inquiringly and then said softly, choosing his words in
his deliberate way, "Become what your father is, a good
fountain master. In the spiritual sense; that is what I
myself try to be. The word of God and the Lutheran
doctrine are the fountainhead from which our people
draw the water of life. To keep this fountainhead pure is
obscure work; no one talks or thinks about it, but few
occupations are so holy and important." For years, in the
few hours that his two offices left free, Bengel had been
working faithfully and patiently on an edition of the original Greek text of the New Testament, carefully tracking
down the purest, oldest, most reliable sources, scrupulously weighing and testing every word. Not a few of his
pious friends thought it a sinful waste that an able minister and teacher should spend precious days and years on a
work of niggling and all in all superfluous scholarship,
but he never swerved from his purpose, and it was characteristic of the man that he should have appointed himself the task of "keeping the fountainhead pure." The
church to which Bengel belonged did not recognize canon-

ization, but Bengel stood high on the list of its secret saints.

When this teacher with the serene, bony face and kindly eyes came into the classroom bright and early for the morning prayer and his first lesson, he had spent several hours of the night over his Bible text and his wide-ranging, partly scholarly, partly pastoral correspondence, and had begun the new day with an examination of conscience and a prayer in which he entreated God to give him perseverance, patience, and wisdom. He brought with him not only a serene alertness and cool intelligence but also an aura of gentle devotion and inspiration to which few of his pupils were impervious. Like other Lutheran churches, the Swabian church had developed a rigid and rather pharisaic orthodoxy, and the clergy had taken on a certain upper-caste arrogance. Bengel was one of the first disciples and models of a new kind of Christianity known as pietism. Over the years, this vigorously spontaneous movement, like all other movements, was to slacken and degenerate. But then it was in its springtime, and there was something of its freshness and delicacy in the aura of this man, who by nature inclined far more to clarity, moderation, and order than to sentimentality and mysticism.

There was little or no difference between the teaching methods of Bengel and those of Preceptor Roos. With Bengel, however, study and erudition were no longer ends in themselves but wholly directed toward a supreme goal —divine worship. The ancient languages, to be sure, had their profane authors and humanistic charms; Bengel himself took pleasure in speaking Latin and Greek; but for this great philologist, all philology culminated in theology; it was an introduction to the word of God, a manner of teaching men to revere it and be faithful to it. When, as occasionally happened, a student did not seem to be getting ahead, the preceptor would admonish him not only to study harder but with equal urgency to pray, and when it seemed necessary, Bengel himself prayed with him. What with his earnestness, modesty, and utter lack of professorial arrogance, his attitude toward his pupils was that of an equal, and sometimes he almost humbled himself before them. In a talk with a former student, he once said that he looked up to each one of his pupils with respect, for in each of them he saw something better and nobler than himself, and that when he gazed at their young faces, he was often profoundly grieved at the thought of how pure and untainted these souls still were, while he himself had already squandered and bungled so much of his life.

In my two years at Denkendorf, I remained true to music. I continued to practice the violin, and with the help of an enthusiastic schoolmate organized a double vocal quartet. But more important than this or my studies was Bengel's influence on me. This venerable man, it seemed to me, was a true child of God; trust in God emanated from him like a gentle, joyful light.

Several of his pupils decided to take his path, to purify themselves in prayer and to make themselves into vessels of grace. I was one of them. We read Arnd's *True Christianity*, copied and discussed Bengel's Sunday sermons, confessed our trespasses to each other, and vowed to imitate Christ.

Here the manuscript ends.